ROYALLY TIED

A Crazy Royal Love Romantic Comedy, Book 3

MELANIE SUMMERS

Indigo Group

Cover by Victoria Cooper.

Edited by Kristi Yanta and Melissa Martin

Proofread by Nevia Brudnicki, Laura Albert, and Audrey Borst.

❀ Created with Vellum

Praise and Awards

- Two-time bronze medal winner at the Reader's Favorite Awards, Chick-lit category for *The Royal Treatment* and *Whisked Away.*
- Silver medalist at the Reader's Favorite Awards, Women's Fiction category for *The After Wife.*

"A fun, often humorous, escapist tale that will have readers blushing, laughing and rooting for its characters."

~ Kirkus Reviews

"A gorgeously funny, romantic and seductive modern fairy tale…"

~ MammieBabbie Book Club

"…perfect for someone that needs a break from this world and wants to delve into a modern-day fairy tale that will keep them laughing and rooting for the main characters throughout the story.

~ ChickLit Café

"I was totally gripped to this story. For the first time ever the Kindle came into the bath with me. This book is unputdownable. I absolutely loved it."

~ Philomena (Two Friends, Read Along with Us)

"Very rarely does a book make me literally hold my breath or has me feeling that actual ache in my heart for a character, but I did both."

~ Three Chicks Review for Net galley

Books by Melanie Summers

ROMANTIC COMEDIES
The Crown Jewels Series

The Royal Treatment

The Royal Wedding

The Royal Delivery

Paradise Bay Series

The Honeymooner

Whisked Away

The Suite Life

Resting Beach Face (Coming Soon)

Crazy Royal Love Series

Royally Crushed

Royally Wild

The Accidentally in Love Series
(With Whitney Dineen)

Text Me on Tuesday

The Text God

Text Wars

Text in Show (coming soon)

Mistle-Text (coming soon)

WOMEN'S FICTION

The After Wife

The Deep End (Coming Soon)

Dedication

For Emily, sister-in-law extraordinaire,

Who reminds me so much of Princess Arabella because she's young, beautiful, whip-smart, wears her heart on her sleeve, and will totally mess you up if it's warranted. Remember that guy on that plane that time?
Bet he never did that again.
Love you girl.
Fight like hell, sweetie,
mel

A Letter From The Author

Dear Lovely Reader,

So, this is it. The time has come to end this series and leave the world of Avonia once more, and I have to say, I've been stalling *big time* on getting to 'the end.' I love Gran, Arthur and Tessa, Arabella and Will, and the rest of the royals so much that I'm having trouble saying goodbye to them. This must be some sort of syndrome, no? A weird affliction only writers and readers share called…I don't know… Character Co-dependency or some such?

Anyway, whatever it is, I've got it bad and should probably join a support group. Wait—is that what book clubs are for?

Well, without further ado, I hope this final crazy royal love book will make you laugh, feel good, and that you'll fall in love all over again with the Langdons and the Banks family too.

Wishing you all the best in life—good food, great reads, laughter, and love. Always love.

xoxo,

mel

Chapter 1

MIRROR, MIRROR ON THE WALL

Arabella

"HAPPY BIRTHDAY, Your Highness! How does it feel to be thirty?" That question is brought to you by an eager reporter who has followed my car all the way from the palace to Lotus Flower Spa, where I am about to have a rare few hours with no obligations whatsoever.

I smile at him sweetly, while in my mind I'm telling him to *sod off.* "Wonderful. I believe the thirties are a time when a lot of women really start to come into their own, and I hope I'm no exception."

With that, I start toward the glass doors, but he clearly isn't done with his hard-hitting reporting just yet.

"Are you planning anything special for today?"

I stuff my hands into my pockets to get them out of the biting March wind. "Yes, I'm taking an afternoon to get a bit of pampering, then home for a quiet dinner with the family."

"Is Will going to be celebrating with you tonight?"

Bellford, my lead security guard, steps in between the reporter and me, holding up one hand to put an end to this impromptu interview. As welcome as his intervention is, if I don't answer the stupid question, the press'll have Will and I broken up by teatime. "He's still away filming, but he's the one who arranged for my spa visit and he sent me a lovely bouquet of roses this morning, so he's definitely part of today's festivities." I give him that smile and nod that says 'we're done here,' then spin around, this time picking up my pace as I walk away.

"So, he's a real romantic, then?" he asks, following me.

I stop and turn back, not wanting to miss the opportunity to publicly sing Will's praises. "Yes, he should write a book. It would be of great help to men everywhere."

He smiles at me in such an earnest way, I can't bear to blow him off. He looks to be about eighteen, although I know he must be older than that. Like, nineteen maybe?

"What's your name?" I ask him.

"Ian Parker with the Weekly Observer."

"Pleasure to meet you, Ian. I think Princess Tessa used to work there back in her reporting days. Lovely little paper."

"I think so too," he says. "Can you give me a hint as to when the wedding might be?"

I grin and shake a finger at him. "Nice try."

He blushes a little, then says, "Well, how about any hints about the wedding itself? The bookies are giving two-to-one odds that you'll hold the big event here in Valcourt, and ten-to-one that it'll be on Santa Valentina Island. Care to comment?"

"Yes, people should find better things to do with their money. Now, I really must run or I'll be late for my appointment," I say as the doors slide open and I step through them.

The warmth of the lobby, combined with the heavenly blend of lavender, orange, and peppermint, causes my shoulders to relax. I allow myself a long, deep inhale and forget all about the fact that I woke up in my thirties and I haven't seen my fiancé for close to six weeks. He's currently in Borneo filming a new season of his adventurous nature docu-series for the new Avonian Nature Network (a.k.a. ANN, or Ann, as people have taken to calling it). In short order, Will has become the face of ANN, as well as for Merrill hiking boots, Tru Earth laundry strips, and the Earth Wildlife Fund, for whom he stars in gorgeously adorable and heartbreaking commercials alongside some of the planet's sweetest orphaned baby animals. Seriously, the ads are like woman catnip — incredibly hot guy holding a tiny squirrel monkey and talking about how much she needs your help. Donations have tripled in the last month alone.

Will is also almost six months into a three-year deal with the network that sucks poopsicles because he spends more time away than he spends here with me. This has made planning our wedding rather a challenge since I insisted we don't go ahead without him and he's never here, so the date when we finally become Mr. and Mrs. is more of an abstract idea than a reality. His schedule is wildly unpredictable and even though I never complain to him about it, I do miss him every single hour of every day.

"Good morning, Princess Arabella," the woman behind the desk says. "The rest of your party is already in the change room."

She's referring to my sister-in-law, Tessa, and her bestie, Nikki, who have graciously brought me into their gang. A smile spreads across my face as I hurry down the hall to meet them. They're an absolute hoot. Nothing at all like the stuffy girls with whom I grew up. I can *really* be myself around them—or at least, I can be someone slightly more fun than normal. Who I am is yet to be determined, but I suppose that's the case with most people.

As soon as I open the door to the change room, I'm greeted by squeals of delight, big squeezy hugs, and birthday wishes.

"So? You okay?" Nikki asks, tugging on the sash of her white robe. "I went into a total funk when I turned thirty, but mind you, I wasn't about to marry a super hot celeb."

Nikki's a hairdresser on the prowl for a sugar daddy to make all her dreams come true. She's also the most wildly fun person I know and the only one who has ever-changing hair hues in all the colours of the rainbow. Today's is bright yellow with lime green tips.

I smile at her as I slide my coat off. "I'm great, really. Well, good, anyway. It's a bit of a shock maybe, which sounds stupid because I *knew* it was going to happen. I do know how to count, after all."

"But it's still the absolute shits, isn't it?" Tessa asks, dropping her handbag into her locker.

I nod. "Last night, I spotted a rather long frown line exactly one

3

third of the way between my eyebrows and my hairline." I point to it while Tessa and Nikki crane their necks and narrow their eyes.

"I don't see anything," Nikki says.

"Not a thing," Tessa adds. "It may be *in* your head, rather than on it."

"It's not carved in deeply yet," I say, feeling oddly defensive about a frown line that I don't want. "But it's just a matter of time. I was thinking maybe I should get a bit of…" Lowering my voice, I whisper, "Botox."

"Botox?!" Tessa yells. "Absolutely not!"

"Shhh!" I gesture for her to lower her voice.

"You don't want to start that shit now," Nikki says. "You'll be stuck going in for injections every three months for the rest of your life."

"Plus, you'll wind up looking like you should be on display at Madame Tussauds," Tessa says. "You're young and beautiful and screw anyone who tells you differently."

"Agreed. Screw 'em," Nikki says. "Besides, isn't aging gracefully more in line with your whole 'women are equal and should stop trying to please everyone' thing?"

I nod. "Excellent point." Although, now that I think about it, I feel a lot more comfortable about *other* women aging gracefully.

"Thank goodness you managed to squeak in an engagement already," Tessa says. "Can you imagine how badly the royal staff would be on your arse to find a husband by now?"

"It would have been dreadful," I say, plucking a folded robe off the shelf and walking into a changing cubicle. As I pull the heavy olive-green velvet curtain shut, I remember I'm supposed to be this super-strong, independent, kickass version of a princess. It's all so new for me and I find I keep forgetting. "For them," I add quickly. "Because if they tried it, they'd find out who's really in charge of this woman's life."

"Will?" Nikki asks.

Poking my head out of the cubicle, I give her a glare.

"Just teasing. You're incredibly terrifying," Nikki says.

"Thank you." I slide the curtain shut again and get back to undressing.

"That's what she wants us to think, right?" Nikki asks Tessa loudly enough to let me know she's having a go at me.

"I believe so," Tessa answers. "And you are, Arabella. You're utterly fierce."

"Shut up, both of you," I say.

There's a knock at the door, and a woman tells us it's time for our facials. "Let's go get our beauty on," Nikki says.

My phone buzzes and I glance down to see Will's gorgeous face on the screen. "I'll be right behind you, girls. Will is just calling via satellite phone." I love saying that. It sounds so…adventurous. My fiancé is in a place so remote, he can only call via satellite.

"Make it fast. We have loads of girl talk to catch up on," Tessa says.

"In other words, you don't have time for phone sex."

"Eww. I'd never do that here," I say, then quickly add, "I mean *at all*. I'd never do that at all. I'm a lady," I add, angling the phone just so, and swiping to answer.

"There's my birthday girl," Will says with that sexy, low voice, and that equally sexy grin of his. Behind him, I can see blue sky poking out behind a lot of trees.

"Hello, darling, do I look older? I feel so much older than I did last night when I went to bed." I give him a wry grin, pretending that I'm only kidding.

"Yes, I'd say instead of looking like you're seventeen, you appear almost old enough to have a drink at the pub now."

"I don't know whether to be flattered or horrified," I say.

"Flattered. Now, am I lucky enough to have caught you in nothing but a robe?" he asks, waggling his eyebrows.

"Yes, you have indeed," I say in a sultry tone.

"Come on, then. Undo the sash," he says. "Just the one time. For your birthday."

I let out a loud laugh. "That would be something for *your* birthday. Besides, I'm in public. Well, the dressing room at the spa. Thank you very much for arranging this, by the way."

"You're very welcome. Since I'm not there to pamper you myself, I thought it only fitting. Are Tessa and Nikki there already?"

"Yes, they just went to get started on their facials."

"I shouldn't keep you then," he says. "I just wanted to tell you I love you and to have a wonderful time."

"I will. But wait—I miss you terribly and I've been dying to know how things are going there." Also, I'm feeling horribly guilty for complicating his life with my stupid royalness. Since our engagement, poor Will is stuck dragging along a security team everywhere he goes, which, in this case, means having them slow him down in the jungle. They're now a week behind which has the network screaming about being over budget.

"Good," he says. He's lying and I can tell by his overly chipper tone. "We're shooting the promo reel today."

Yes! The promo reel day means they're done. "Really?!"

"Yup. One last day, then we hop on the plane."

"Did you talk to Enid about leaving your shirt on for once?"

Enid Nightingale is his new director. She's a no-nonsense woman with a ton of experience in reality television and documentary film-making. She also doesn't suffer fools, so Will and I are hoping this includes ANN's VP of Programming Dylan Sinclair, who insists on as many shirtless shots of him as possible.

Embarrassment crosses his face. "Not yet, but that's the first thing I'm going to do when I get off this call."

"Good luck, sweetheart." And I really mean it. As much as *I* enjoy seeing Will without a shirt, it doesn't exactly scream regal, which I'm reminded of by the senior advisers on a weekly basis. Not to mention that, in certain royal fan circles, they'd started calling him the Knight of the No Shirt (on account of the fact that my father will knight him the day before our wedding). Poor Will. That wouldn't be happening if he weren't stuck marrying me. He'd be free to go as shirtless as he wanted. Pantless too.

"Listen, what would you say to a quiet birthday celebration with your fiancé tomorrow night?"

Completely forgetting about how difficult I'm making his life, I grin at Will, my heart suddenly full at the thought of seeing him tomorrow. "I'd say what time."

He nods. "I should be back in town by nine at the latest."

"Perfect."

"Rest up," he says, glancing around to make sure no one can hear him. "I intend to help you start this next decade off with a bang."

I answer, "Best present ever."

"Better than the spa?"

"So much better," I say. "I can't even begin to describe how much I miss you."

"If it's even half as much as I miss you, it's absolute torture."

"It's at least double how much you miss me."

"Not possible," he says, trying very hard to look serious.

"Agree to disagree on the fact that I miss you more than you miss me."

I hear a voice in the background and I say, "You have to go," at the same time Will says, "I have to go."

"Love you so much," I tell him.

"Love you more."

Then he ends the call before I can argue. I sigh and smile, then start for the door while I text, *Love you most.*

Sorry, I know that was utterly sickening, but it can't be helped.

———

I walk into the facial room to find that Tessa and Nikki are already laying on two of the tables with masks on and cucumbers over their eyes. A third bed waits for me with a glass of champagne on a table next to it. A woman in a blue smock approaches. "Welcome, Your Highness. I'm Kate. Have you already chosen your facial today, or would you like to have a look at the menu?"

I actually *have* looked at the facial menu. In fact, last night, I spent a good hour poring over it, then googling all the included treatments along with 'Is this the best for wrinkle prevention?' In the end, I've decided to go with the After Glow Anti-aging and Tightening Service — for those clients with the earliest phases of sagging, drooping, and fine lines. Glancing at Tessa and Nikki, I lower my voice. "I'll take the After Glow."

Kate gives my face an intense inspection, her eyes locking on the line across my forehead. "Have you considered the Oxygen Goddess Treatment?"

Oh God. It's worse than I thought. The Oxygen Goddess is for those who are already experiencing fine lines, wrinkles, and sagging. It's a three-step process including a deep exfoliating glycolic acid peel, an antioxidant mask, then a hydrating vitamin C and peptide serum that is left on for twenty minutes.

I give her a slight nod and settle myself on the adjustable bed. Plucking the champagne off the table, I take two quick gulps to douse the flames of irritation flickering in my chest. New Age music is being piped in over the speakers but at the moment, instead of typical spa fare of flutes and rain sticks, it seems to be a blend of mating cats and cymbals being dropped down a set of stairs.

Kate exits the room to prepare my special old lady formula, leaving Tessa, Nikki, and me alone.

"So how was the phone sex?" Nikki asks.

"Our *conversation* was delightful," I answer. "Will is going to be back tomorrow night so he and I will celebrate then."

"Brilliant," Tessa says. "How long will he be in town this time?"

"Not sure," I answer. "I'm hoping long enough to get a good start on the wedding plans, but with Dylan running his life, it's doubtful we'll get past choosing invitations."

"I can't believe you're waiting for him to help choose everything," Tessa says. "I mean, it's taking forever and, at the end of the day, does he really even care that much?"

"Of course he cares," I say, feeling rather defensive. "This wedding is every bit as important to him as it is to me."

"Is it really?" Nikki asks, lifting both cucumber slices to give me a skeptical look. "Did *he* spend years cutting out pages from magazines and pasting together an album of his perfect future wedding?"

"I never should have shown you that," I say. "Stupid Margaritas and Man Bash Monday. There was a time, yes, when I would have obsessed over every detail, but not anymore. I'm older and wiser now."

"You mean since midnight?" Tessa teases.

"Hardy-har-har," I say, rolling my eyes. "No, since I started my work at the UN. My perspectives on what's truly important have changed drastically, and linen colour really doesn't make the cut."

"In that case, why don't you just hand your book over to a wedding planner and let them take it from there?" Tessa asks.

"God, no. Do you know how embarrassing that would be?" I say. "No one is *ever* going to see that book. In fact, I'm going to go home and burn it."

"Do *not* burn it," Tessa says. "It's like getting a glimpse into your lovely mind."

"The mind of a *teenager* who didn't know any better."

"I agree with Tessa. Use the book. Just pull out the page with your face superimposed on Posh Spice's body on her wedding day," Nikki says, leading to her and Tessa snickering.

"Or the brainstorming bit where you wonder if a white horse could be dyed pink and have a horn affixed to his head so he'll look like a unicorn," Tessa adds.

"Okay, thank you," I grind out. "Let's drop it. I'm not using any ideas from that stupid book. But maybe you're right about one thing —maybe Will and I should just hire someone, give them a quick overview of what we want, and let her do her thing. That way we can both get back to the important things in life."

"As nice as that sounds, that's not how royal weddings work," Tessa says. "It's a massive production that will eat up all your time and energy and drive you completely insane until you're a complete bridezilla by the time you're ready to walk down the aisle."

"The last thing I'm going to do is turn into a *bridezilla*," I answer, feeling quite put out. "I refuse to get upset about something so meaningless as flower arrangements or appetizers. I'm going to be a calm, breezy bride who keeps the entire event in perspective. The wedding is about the joining of two lives and two families. Period. That's what matters." I let out a long sigh. "I wish we could just keep it very small and very private like your wedding. Yours was lovely."

"It was only lovely because we buggered it all up by breaking off the engagement, then getting back together and insisting on having the wedding without enough time for the whole big royal fuss," Tessa says. "And I'm sorry to tell you, but because Arthur and I robbed the public of the very grand event they believe they're owed, it's going to fall to you to do that."

Dammit, she's right. There really is no way to escape it, is there? "Well, no matter. I can keep the big picture in mind, remain calm, and let any little issues that crop up pass me by."

Neither of them answer, and I look over to see they've both put their cucumbers back down again, presumably to avoid eye contact. "Seriously, I know you don't think it's possible, but I *am* going to be the world's most-Zen bride."

Kate walks back in the room with a tray bearing plates of cucumbers and a bowl with whatever anti-aging crap they've mixed together for me.

She sets the tray on the table next my glass of champagne, then walks over to a metal cabinet and opens it, taking out two hot towels. "Lie back, please."

I do as she asks, and a moment later feel a deliciously warm, moist towel covering the upper half of my face with my nostrils exposed. Then the second one is laid on the bottom half, covering my neck and décolletage.

"I'll be back in just a couple of minutes with your peel," she says.

I lie still, letting the warmth of the towels relax me for a moment. Ahhh…this is what I need—relaxation. But then my mind travels forward to me on my wedding day. Yes, not only am I going to be the most-Zen bride, I'm going to have youthful, baby-soft skin, and everyone is going to say, "Wow, look at how amazingly calm she is. She's positively glowing." Oh, and I'll also make sure Will's family feels utterly welcome and they'll love me right from the start. And Will is going to be blown away by his beautiful, graceful, and unbelievably serene bride. It's going to be perfect.

Kate returns and removes my towels. On a rolling tray next to me is a clear concoction in a glass bowl next to three aromatherapy bottles. She holds one up to me. "Please choose your favourite scent for your facial."

The first one is labeled *Rain Forest* and I give it a whiff. It smells absolutely nothing like the actual rain forest. I can tell you that from experience. The next one is called *Refresh* and claims to be a revitalizing, yet calming, oil. Smells like peppermint. I nod and hand the bottle to her.

"You know what else?" I say, turning to Nikki and Tessa. "I plan to use this opportunity as a way for Will's family to feel welcome at the palace and in our circles, and to let them know I'm not the type of person who believes that everything is all about me. I want to incorporate their family traditions and make sure that they are included."

"God, no," Tessa says, sitting up. "Do not do that. Have you forgotten my wedding shower?"

Tessa's wedding shower was an unmitigated disaster with her mother forcing the guests to play all sorts of tacky games. It ended with Tessa dressed from head to foot in toilet paper yelling at her mother in front of a hundred horrified women. I wince at the memory.

She gives me a meaningful nod. "Exactly. So, as nice as it is to *want* to include them, *don't*. My advice to you is this: have a long talk with Will. Find out what he wants to get out of the day—which will likely be something vague like getting married—then pick one thing each and realize that you'll be lucky to get that much. And make sure he understands that the wedding isn't for either of you, it's for the people of Avonia."

"Well, that's sort of a defeatist attitude, Tess," I say.

"Realistic, not defeatist. But fear not, because the *marriage* is for you two, and *that's* the really wonderful bit."

"Lie back and close your eyes," Kate says. "You may feel a slight tingling sensation, but that's a good thing. It means it's working."

I follow her orders, Tessa's words swirling in my mind while I tell myself to calm down and enjoy my level III anti-aging treatment. Really, I'm a tightly-wound bundle of nerves. I don't even have to talk to Will to know that he'd absolutely hate a big royal wedding. But it's not like we can sneak off to the jungle and have a private service. He'll probably tell me it doesn't matter to him, but at the end of the day, our wedding is the way that we're going to start our life together. It *does* matter, and the last thing I want is for him to be standing next to me, feeling utterly tortured the entire time. The truth is, the entire royal life is a lot to ask of any man, especially one like him. There's a tiny, nagging voice deep in my brain that tells me I need to be spectacular in order to be worth all the trouble. I can do that, can't I? Be fun and sexy and wonderful at all times? It won't be that hard. Yes, I can do it.

Slight tingling? It feels like someone has lit my pores on fire with tiny matchsticks. "Kate, it's a little more than a tingle."

"Some women experience it as more of a prickling feeling. Completely normal though, so not to worry."

Good God, it's getting worse. "No, not a prickle. It's more of a burning, almost as if you're taking a blow torch to my face."

"Hmm…" she says, and I can feel her breath on my cheek which means she must be leaning in to watch my skin melt. "It is a little more red than normal. Maybe you weren't ready for the Oxygen Goddess yet. It's supposed to stay on for another three minutes. Do you think you can stand it?"

The line across my forehead comes to mind. Beauty is pain, right? "Yes, I'm fine," I say, balling my fists up and sinking my nails into my palms to distract me from the fact that my face is currently being incinerated.

You can do this, Arabella. It's going to be worth it because you'll look ten years younger when you leave here.

But, bloody hell, that's excruciating. It's so very prickly. "How much longer?"

"One minute twenty."

Get it off, get it off, get it off!

That's what my brain is screaming at me. But I force my lips to stay firmly shut. In part because I'm terrified of getting whatever the hell is on my face in my mouth.

I hear the voice of another woman who I presume is one of the other estheticians. She whispers, "That doesn't look right."

"Do you think I should take it off?" Kate whispers back.

"I do, if that counts for anything," I answer.

"I'd get it off. She seems to be having some type of reaction," the woman says, a little louder.

Kate sets to work, rubbing my face with a wet cloth, which, honestly, doesn't feel all that nice, but I lay still, praying it'll bring me some relief. She and the other woman talk in low voices and I feel both of them working to quickly remove the acid. The other woman says, "So, Your Highness, do you have any important functions in the next couple of days? Like a ball or anything like that to attend?"

"Why?" I ask, feeling utterly panicked. "What does my face look like?"

I bolt up and look for a mirror, then see Tessa's eyes grow wider. "Oh dear, that's really red."

"Wow," Nikki says, covering her mouth with one hand. "You got a peel all right."

Brilliant.

––––––

Royal News –The Official Website for All Things Avonian Royal

Forum Thread: The Duchess of Bainbridge Celebrates her Birthday
(342 Currently Viewing, 12983 Total Views, 1744 Comments)

As of 2:04 a.m., Princess Arabella is officially thirty years old! Happy birthday to one of our royal family's most lovely members. Wishing you the best for this next decade.

Felix (Courtier): Wishing Her Royal Highness the best (but knowing it's likely to be a total disaster should she go through with the wedding to that ridiculous Knight of the No Shirt).

Stephen (Heir Presumptive): Agreed. I get the whole 'opposites attract' thing, but let's not take it too far. We need at least one blood line in the family to stay blue.

Cindy (Serene Highness): Happy Birthday, lovely Princess Arabella! Dump Will. There are dozens of eligible men much more suited to you than that embarrassment.

Chapter 2

OH NOTHING ... JUST GETTING RUBBED DOWN LIKE A LAMP WITH A GENIE IN IT ... YOU?

Will

"All right, people. Gather around," Enid says. She's a power-house with a low ponytail—a five-foot tall person with a seven-foot-tall presence. I've never worked with someone as professional or knowl-edgeable as her. And I've definitely never met someone who commands so much respect. She doesn't even have to raise her voice. People just listen to her. The entire crew hops to it, instantly going from leisurely preparing for the day ahead to double-timing it to form a large circle around her.

I hurry in her direction, glancing at my security team and throwing them a quick wave and a nod, grateful that they're keeping their distance for once. My head bodyguard—sorry, *security officer*—is Reynard Smit, a guy who looks like he should be puttering around in his garden rather than carrying a gun. Seriously, he's old. He's got to be sixty if he's a day. Enid's not a fan of my security detail, by the way. They've been a major hindrance the entire time we've been out here, insisting on going ahead of me to check for threats, which is ridiculous since this is a completely remote, uninhabited island, no one knows where we are, and no one wants to kidnap me in the first place. Every morning, they insist on doing 'sweeps' of the vicinity, only to lose two hours of daylight for them to determine it's 'all clear.' And it's not like any of them are equipped to deal with the real threats out here—poisonous plants and wild animals. Because of that, *I* have to go with them to keep them safe, only to have them determine *I'm* safe. A bit ridiculous, no?

Enid takes off her glasses and lets them hang from the chain around her neck. "Last day of filming. Just the promo reel stuff. I want to thank everyone for being professionals these past six weeks…with a couple of notable exceptions," she says, glancing at my friends, Tosh and Mac, who have been with me from the start. Tosh is a cameraman and Mac's a sound guy, and they're both what you'd call Type B to the max. Enid glares at them for a second, then adds, "The conditions have been challenging and we managed to get out of here with everyone alive and with all body parts intact, so mission accomplished. Now, let's get this over with so we can get the hell out of this jungle. I don't know about you, but I'd maim just about any of you for a cold beer and a hot shower."

The group breaks into a quick round of applause, but Enid waves it off. "No time. Let's do this."

I wait while people hustle off to get ready, then approach Enid. "So, promo reel day, hey?"

"Yup," she says, picking up her clipboard off a table and sliding her glasses on.

"I was hoping we could change things up a bit this time around," I say. "You know, to keep it fresh."

Glancing at me, she says, "I'm afraid the network *does* want the shirtless shots of you, if that's what you mean."

Damn. "What if we tell them we forgot?"

She stares at me from above the rims of her glasses. "Then I look like I forget things. Which I don't."

Lowering my voice, I say, "Listen, I don't want to be difficult or anything. It's just that the half-naked thing isn't exactly playing well with my fiancée's family."

"Too bad the audience at the palace is so much smaller than the one we're selling ads to," she says, walking away.

I follow her. "But, what if—"

"Sorry, Will. I know it makes you uncomfortable, but it's a must. Take it up with the executives when we get back to Valcourt. Maybe they'll change their minds. In the meantime, take off your shirt and go get oiled up. Trixie is ready for you."

"Come on, Enid," I say. "You can't want to do this, right? It's a little weird."

"Because I'm a lesbian?" she asks without looking up from her clipboard.

"Well…yeah. I mean, this must gross you out a bit and there's no way I'd want to contribute to a hostile workplace."

She gives me a deadpan expression and chews her gum at me in a way that feels somehow aggressive. "How thoughtful of you, but I assure you it's not a problem for me. I may not want to buy what you're selling, but that doesn't mean I don't like window shopping once in a while."

Okkkaaayyyy….

Trixie, one of the PA's, walks up with the bottle of baby oil and a huge grin. "Are you ready for me, Will?"

"Yup."

———

Letter from Gregory Jacobs, Senior Royal Advisor
  To: William Banks
  Subject: Protocol Tutelage and Various Updates

Dear Mr. Banks,

  In the enclosed envelope, you will find the Royal Protocol Handbook — it's the spiral bound book with the navy cover. Please utilize your travel time to familiarize yourself with its contents. You will find it most useful in the coming weeks, and the more prepared you are, the faster your protocol lessons will go.

  The red covered booklet contains a list of charities for your consideration as you will, of course, be expected to devote a great deal of time to charitable causes once you become the Duke of Bainbridge. Most working royals take on a minimum of twenty charities, however, with your career and current schedule, I'm not sure that that would be advisable. Upon your return, you'll meet with your advisory committee to discuss the matter, but it would be in your best interest to narrow down the list so as to ensure you have some say in the matter.

Your schedule for the week is attached. Please familiarize yourself with it, taking special note of the wedding preparations and plans meeting to take place upon your return. If the opportunity presents itself, might I suggest you discuss the matter with Princess Arabella privately before the meeting, as there will be many stakeholders at the table, and you'll want to ensure that you two are of one mind. Should you have any questions, concerns, or require any assistance, please contact me on my mobile phone. As always, I'm available to you twenty-four hours a day.

Safe journey,

Gregory

I set his letter down on the table in front of me and flip through the three heavy wire-bound booklets. This is going to be my life. This set of rules, protocols, and regulations I have to memorize by the time this plane lands. My heart drops and I scratch my chin, realizing I'm long overdue for a shave. I wonder what it says in the handbook about whiskers. I imagine there's a set length that is considered unacceptable. Hmm, I bet they'll have some assistant who will measure my facial hair daily and set up a strict shaving regimen for me.

Of course that won't happen. Snap out of it, idiot. Marrying Arabella is a privilege, not a burden, so you better bloody well keep reminding yourself how lucky you are.

I open the navy booklet and glance over the glossary. Bugger. There *is* a section on personal hygiene and grooming. I close the book, too tired from six weeks in the jungles of Borneo to start reading the fine print that comes with marrying a princess. I flag down the flight attendant and ask for a carafe of coffee, then stare out the window at the dark grey clouds. Maybe I should clear my email first. Get through all my work stuff so I can really focus on Arabella, the wedding, and er…my royal lessons when I get home. Opening my laptop, I sit back in the plush leather seat.

Email from Rosy Brown
    To: Will Banks
    Subject: Last Chance for Me to See One of My Babies Get Married

Dear Cuddle Bear,

    I hope your trip to Borneo is going well and that you are keeping yourself safe and healthy. We are all fine here but missing you, as always. I'm writing with a request that I don't think Harrison will make, even though I know for a fact he wants to. I'm wondering if you can talk to Arabella about possibly holding the wedding here at the resort. I know that it is not the traditional location for a royal wedding, but you are every bit a son of the Benavente Islands as you are of Avonia, and because our nation is one of the Commonwealth countries of Avonia, holding the wedding here would be a nice way for the royal family to honour citizens of the Commonwealth instead of just the kingdom itself. Obviously, it would be a huge boon for us and would set us up for many years to come. We have recently hired an event planner who could manage all the details for you.

    Please don't tell Harrison I've asked. He would never want to put this kind of pressure on you to help the family, whereas I'm not above tugging at your heart-strings if it's for the greater good.

    Stay safe and come home soon,

    Rosy (your mama bear)

———

Email from Dylan Sinclair, VP of Programming, Avonian Nature Network
    To: Will Banks
    cc: Victor Petty, Kira Taylor, Veronica Platt

Subject: Urgent Meeting

. . .

Hello William,

I am absolutely thrilled to learn that the shoot in Borneo has been completed and that, according to Enid, it has been a great success despite the security-related delays. Well done to you and the crew! I want to take this moment to acknowledge your commitment to ANN and recognize your contribution to our success. Over the past few months, we've seen a most welcome and sharp increase in our advertising income. We were not expecting to see these types of numbers until Q3 of next year, so give yourself a pat on the back.

I received your email regarding time off for your wedding, and although I'm not sure we'll be able to accommodate the entire two weeks you've requested, I know we can come to some sort of satisfactory agreement.

I'll need to see you in my office tomorrow afternoon at 1 p.m. so we can discuss a future project. It would be in your best interest to ask Princess Arabella to attend as well. I've got something epic in the works and there is no way I'd want you to miss this opportunity.

Regards,
Dylan

P.S. Were you surprised to see an eight-foot version of yourself on the side of the plane this morning?

I stare at her email for a full minute, then let out a long, irritated sigh. When Dylan says she's got something epic in the works, it usually involves me taking my clothes out of my suitcase, putting them directly through the wash, only to pack and leave again. Only now, I get to do it on a plane with a horrifyingly large image of me grinning and giving two giant thumbs up on both sides. When they said they were making me the face of the new network, this isn't what I had in mind. I forward the email to Arabella, knowing she's likely to say a big no to the meeting. She hates Dylan with a passion, and I can't blame her. Dylan did try to out her family's deepest, most painful secret for a ratings bump last year.

Arabella responds almost immediately via text. *Why on earth would she want me there?*

Me: *No clue. Probably a new show idea. It's fine, I'll tell her you can't make it.*

Her: *I think I should go. It'll give me a chance to put my diplomacy skills to work. See if we can't put a stop to the oiling up of my fiancé's upper body.*

"Don't tell me you're working," Mac says. He seats himself next to me. "Isn't this the part where the crew gets to celebrate on the flight home after weeks of filming?"

"I'm afraid I'll have to save my celebrating for another time. I need to get through these three booklets by the time we land."

The flight attendant appears with my coffee and some biscuits. She sets them on the table in front of me. "Will there be anything else, Mr. Banks?"

"No, thank you."

"Coffee?" Mac asks. "The rest of us have ordered whiskey sours."

"Well, have one for me," I say, returning my gaze to my laptop screen.

Mac picks up the Royal Protocol Handbook and starts flipping through it. *Here we go. I should not have left that out.*

He barks out a laugh, then says, "Proper bowing order?" He reads from the page, but not before switching from his Scottish accent to a very posh English one. "Upon entering the room, you must bow at the waist, first to King Winston, followed by Prince Arthur, followed by Princess Flora, Prince James…" He pauses and looks at me. "Aren't they the babies?"

I feel my skin heating up with embarrassment. "Preschoolers, yes. But they're third and fourth in line for the throne, so they outrank everyone else."

"And you're sure you're going to be happy having to bow to your wife every time you enter a room?"

"Obviously no one expects me to do this in everyday situations. It's only during formal occasions."

He flips another page and then busts out laughing again, getting Tosh's attention.

He walks up to us with a broad grin. "What's so funny?"

Mac's still chuckling while he says, "He has to study to become a royal husband. Get this—Will has to walk five paces behind his future wife for the rest of his life."

I grab the book out of his hands and place it underneath the other ones. "We're not going to follow that one."

"Then why'd they put it in the handbook?" Mac asks. He looks at Tosh, who's sporting a huge grin. "I don't think Will's going to be the one to wear the crown in his family."

"I don't think so either," Tosh says, making a clicking sound and wincing. "That's quite the life you're setting up for yourself."

"Yes, it is—an extraordinary one—so if you two tossers would excuse me, I owe it to my future wife to prepare."

"You sure you want to do this, mate?" Tosh asks. "You're not exactly the kind of guy who lets other people tell you what to do."

"What are you talking about?" Mac says to him. "He's spent the last six months letting Dylan Sinclair and Veronica Platt micromanage his every move. At least with Arabella, there are some lovely benefits that come with the package." Mac waggles his thick red eyebrows in a way that makes me want to pop him one.

"First of all, we are *not* going to talk about my benefits with Belle. *Ever.* Second, she's an incredible person and she's worth any amount of studying or whatever else I'd have to do because I'm lucky to get to spend the rest of my life with her." I narrow my eyes at Mac. "And third, Arabella and I are fully committed to making our decisions as a team—with both of us having equal say in everything."

He holds up his palms in surrender. "No need to get defensive. You clearly both are going to wear the crowns in your relationship," he says. "Hers'll just be a little bigger."

I sigh and roll my eyes, then it occurs to me that the more I show how irritating this conversation is, the longer it will last. "Okay, have your fun, but realize that when this plane lands, I'm going to spend the night with the love of my life and you're going home to your empty flats."

"Oooh, low blow," Tosh says.

"Yeah, that was offside, mate," Mac adds, looking hurt. "I was just having a bit of fun."

"Sorry, I'm just a bit…stressed."

I stare at him for a moment before realizing he couldn't care less about what I said and he's having another go. I chuckle and shake my head. "Sod off, the pair of you."

Chapter 3

THE TOO-AWFUL-TO-TURN-AWAY-FROM AIRPORT SCENE

Arabella

"Did you get the stuff?" I ask Nikki as soon as I slip inside the door to her flat.

She gives me a grave nod. "And plenty of it. I wanted to make sure you have a real variety so you can really wow him."

"You're a very good friend," I say. And it's true because Nikki is literally the only person I could ask for this type of favour. Last night after I got home from my day of anti-aging, then suffered through dinner with my family (who all thought it *hilarious* that I burnt my face in my attempt to hold on to my youth), I realized I've only got a very narrow window to be truly sexy. I hope I'm wrong, but what if I'm not? I mean, *eventually* I'm not going to want to wear tiny, lacey unmentionables, am I? My figure—like those of all women to go before me—shall endure changes brought on by time, gravity, and, with any luck, bearing children.

Yes, now is most certainly the time in which to really spice things up in the bedroom so I can provide Will with very sexy memories of his young bride to look back on when we're too old and tired to try things like the wheelbarrow position and I'm too wrinkled to strut around in a teddy.

To be honest, my newfound desire to be the sexiest princess I can does have a fair bit to do with an overwhelming sense of guilt about what Will is going to have to endure to marry me. I know for a fact he spent the entire flight studying the Royal Protocol Handbook, which is every bit as tedious and soul-sucking as you'd imagine. When he gets off that plane, he's going to have his head filled with the knowledge that his life once we are wed shall *never* be the same. Instead of being carefree and wild, there will be an unending list of obligations he'll return home to for the rest of his days. So, I texted Nikki and asked her for a favour I'll never be able to repay.

And no, I'm not trying to distract him with amazing sex so he won't notice how crap some aspects of this life are. I'm merely trying to balance the dread he'll have every time he returns to Valcourt with the thrill of knowing that, in between boring luncheons and ribbon-cutting ceremonies, he's going to have lots of very adventurous sex, starting with tonight's very naughty idea. See? I can be fabulous.

Nikki gives me a quick glance, then says, "Your face is recovering nicely. No skin flaking off yet, so that's a plus."

"Is it as red as yesterday? It's hard for me to tell."

She tilts her head from side to side, screwing up her mouth in a way that says, 'Yes, but I don't want to tell you the truth.' "Definitely better," she says finally before dumping the contents of a black plastic bag on her kitchen table.

"I didn't know what flavour he would like so I just got a bunch of things," she says as we both survey the coloured boxes strewn on the pine veneer table. "We've got your basic milk chocolate, chocolate mint, your garden-variety strawberry fruit roll-up, crotchless water-melon thong…"

My cheeks burn, adding to the waning heat from yesterday's deba-cle, as I stare at a white box labeled Sweet Eats Knickers. I'm far too embarrassed to even pick it up, so I'm not entirely sure how I'm going to manage to put the bloody things on. The next one comes in a black box. It's called Passionfruit and it claims to be so delicious you'll want to keep them in your purse just in case you're in the mood for a snack.

The third one is in a black box with a large picture of a watermelon on it. Big bubble letters scream out Yummy Gummy Crotchless Love Thong. I lean down to give it a closer look, unaware of my facial expression until Nikki says, "Yeah, that one's a bit out there. The woman at the store said they're really tasty, but it's kind of a DIY sort of contraption. If you want it to stay on, you'll probably need to add your own strings to fasten it to your nether regions."

I rub my eyebrows with one hand in an outward motion, feeling very hot under the collar. "Have you ever tried any of these yourself?"

"Oh, sure, loads of times," Nikki says casually. She picks up the gummy bra and thong set. "This one's kinda cute and reasonably durable. It's a little bit sticky, but it's not nearly as delicate as some of the other ones. The really papery thongs rip when you're putting them on, which isn't much use."

I give her a knowing nod, as though we're discussing the best type of sunscreen to use at the beach before I remember how utterly ridiculous this is. "Oh God. What if he thinks this is really weird and gross?"

Nikki shakes her head. "The guy eats larvae without batting an eyelash. I doubt this'll put him off."

"But, I'm not sure Will would even *like* any of these flavours. I mean, obviously chocolate," I say, nodding at the Strawberry Chocolate Brazen Bra and Naughty Knickers set that promises not to melt at room temperature.

"Yeah, I'd say chocolate is probably your safest bet," Nikki says, staring at the box.

I reach for it, then lift my hand away. "I don't know. Maybe this is a really bad idea," I say, chewing on my thumbnail.

"What's the worst that could happen? He doesn't like the flavour, you have a quick shower and a good laugh. He's definitely going to appreciate the effort," Nikki says with a firm nod.

"You're right. Of course he will. And you know what? Why *shouldn't* I do this? I mean, really. He and I are two young, healthy people in a committed relationship. And this really does say I'm still the daring and sexy girl he fell in love with in the jungle."

"Exactly. Just go for it, Arabella. He'll be *thrilled*."

"Righto. Definitely…" I say with a confident nod. Then worry creeps in again. "But, what if it's a bad idea to wear them to the airport? I could wear what I've got on to pick him up and then change when we get back to his flat."

Nikki purses her lips and gives me a slight glare. "Do *not* tell me you're going to chicken out. Not after I spent an hour and a half combing through the shelves of Sex Sex Sex, with a creepy old guy following me around the store, I might add."

"No, obviously I'm not going to back out. In fact, I'll probably try them *all* eventually. But you know, for now, I should just…" I'm about to say play it safe when internally I give myself a smack on the head. Playing it safe when you're with a guy like Will Banks is about the worst move you can make. I *must* be daring and ultra-sexy. "No, you're right, Nikki. I need to do this."

Without further reflection, I swipe the chocolate and strawberry bra and thong set off of the table.

I laugh a little, feeling a sense of excitement building in my chest. "Oh my God, this is seriously *ultra*-daring."

"It is. You *have* to do it," Nikki says. "Give him a preview of the fun life he's in for."

"Exactly," I say with a grin. "I'm going to blow his mind."

I hurry into her bathroom to get changed, my heart pounding in my chest. It's not even really *that* big of a risk when I think about it. I already know the exact minute his plane is going to land. And because he's coming in on a private jet, he doesn't have to go through the regular security queue. I'll have the limo pull right up in front of his terminal. The whole thing should only take a few minutes and we'll be on our way back to his place and onto a night of wild, adult fun.

Good God, that is sticky. And the bra is really cold. It's also clinging to my chest in a most unsettling way. It's like wearing two tiny squids on your knockers.

Okay, Arabella, never mind how it feels. This is fun and it's all in the name of love.

I carefully step into the thong, which has an extra-large chocolate heart over the front of my lady parts and the same sticky bright pink gummy strings to hold up the heart. I give myself a quick glance in the mirror and decide to pull my coat on before I lose my nerve. I rush to get all the buttons done up, then take a deep breath and open the door.

———

When I step out of the limo into the cold night air, a draft blows up my full-length camel hair coat and hits my chocha like a cold slap. Maybe this wasn't such a good idea. But it's too late now because I left everything I was wearing, other than my coat and heels, at Nikki's, and Will's plane is about to land.

I follow Bellford toward the building, spying a revolving door — my favourite type of door. It's like going on a mini-ride, only it's not scary and you don't have to queue up for it. Actually, revolving doors are strictly against royal protocol on account of the infinitesimal chance that someone might jam something in it, thus trapping you, but in this type of situation—a nearly empty airport late in the evening when no one knows I'm coming—I can totally get away with it.

Bellford glances at the door and gives me a nod. I grin excitedly as I step inside the wide moving entrance, smiling a little extra at what a naughty bird I've turned out to be. I definitely chose the right edible undies set. Will is going to be one very happy man in about five minutes when he walks out of the arrivals gate and I whisper to him what's for dinner.

I set a confident pace to match that of the doors, smiling to myself about what a badass I am when suddenly I hear a rather loud clanging sound. The doors stop moving, but I don't. Instead, I take another two strides, slamming my face against the glass with an embarrassing bang.

Bellford, who has just reached the inside of the airport through the boring sliding door, draws his pistol and does a quick three-sixty, looking for threats before realizing the sound came from in here. Well, that's the height of humiliation, isn't it? A few people in the terminal are now staring curiously.

Okay, door. Let's get going already.

Huh. It's not moving. That's odd. I'll just give it a little shove. That ought to do it. I place both hands on the glass door and push, but it doesn't budge, so I try again, harder this time.

Then I raise my voice and say, "Bellford! I'm stuck."

"Step away from the glass, Your Highness." He swiftly moves to the glass door on the far side and gives it a shove with one shoulder, but it doesn't move. Then he comes back toward me and tries pushing it backwards. Still nothing.

Shit. Now a few *more* people have stopped what they're doing and are slowly moving in my direction. Well, this is just craptastic because it's only a matter of time before one of them figures out who I am.

"Don't worry, Miss, I'll have you out of there in no time. Let me just get somebody from maintenance."

It's fine, it's just fine, Arabella, I tell myself, stuffing my hands in my pockets. This'll just be a couple minutes and then out I'll come, never to use a revolving door again.

Bellford waves down a security guard who comes rushing over. He then tries to force the door open by hand.

It won't work, numbskull.

The security guard's eyes narrow as he looks at me, then a look of recognition crosses his face. Through the glass, I hear his muffled voice. "That's Princess Arabella!"

A little louder, ninny.

Bellford nods at him and says something I can't hear but can only assume is a request to lower his voice.

Brilliant. A small crowd forms a few feet back from the door. And isn't that just the thing any girl dressed in only a coat and edible undies needs?

The security guard lifts his walkie-talkie out of his belt and starts speaking into it. "I'm going to need someone from maintenance immediately. Princess Arabella is trapped in the revolving door at gate C3. Who's available?"

I hear a crackling sound, followed by, "C3? Did somebody forget to put the sign up? That thing's been sticking all day."

They knew?! Bloody hell.

Okay, calm down, Arabella. The fact that they already know about the problem is a good thing. It presumably means it won't take long for them to get it fixed.

I tug at the collar of my coat, suddenly realizing I feel like I'm being toasted like a marshmallow. Glancing up, I see the ceiling is basically made of air vents blowing hot air on me.

Bellford and the security guard lower their voices and have a long conversation, then Bellford looks at me with an expression that no woman wearing edible undies wants to see. He moves his face close to the glass and says, "So, Your Highness, as it turns out, the gentleman who repairs these doors has gone home for the night. But they're already phoning him to get you out of there."

"Gone home for the night? You mean there's only one person in this entire bloody airport that knows how to fix the doors if something goes wrong? What if a baby got stuck in here? Or…or an old person who is having a heart attack?" Or a princess wearing nothing but a coat and food shaped like knickers?

The security guard leans in from behind Bellford. "You'll just have to hold tight, Your Highness. We'll have you out of there in a jiffy. Well, maybe not all that fast, to be honest. As it turns out, Roger's not home, he's at the pub and he took their only car so his wife's got to take a bus to go get him. She's just checking the schedule now."

Oh, is she? Fabo. I give him a tight smile and a nod. "Thank you."

It'll be fine. Arabella, it'll be just fine. The box guaranteed that these knickers won't melt at room temperature.

Does anybody actually know what temperature room temperature is? I mean, what do the people at the factory consider room temperature? Maybe, if I'm really lucky, they're made in some sort of factory in a very hot climate where room temperature could be, let's say, 40 degrees Celsius. Although technically I suppose that's called a sweatshop and I really shouldn't be wishing that I'm wearing edible undies that were made in a sweatshop. I mean, honestly, exploiting workers so I can get my jollies — despicable, Arabella. Not to mention what type of safety standards they have as far as the ingredients go. I mean, what if these edible undies are full of lead and I end up poisoning Will accidentally? Oh God, why did I think this was a good idea?

And why did I have to use the stupid revolving door? What am I

—a six-year-old? *Oh, it's like Disneyland.* There is no fucking way this is anything like any ride at Disneyland! It's not even as good as a ride at a sketchy travelling fair manned by parolees.

I dig around my jacket pockets to see if I've got any tissues or anything else that might be of use in case I have a literal meltdown, but the only thing I've got is my mobile phone which isn't exactly absorbent. I take it out and consider googling *edible undies emergencies*, but then realize that the likelihood of someone having come up with a solution for melting knickers while stuck in a glass box in a public place is probably slim to none.

I dial Nikki's number, hoping she'll have some wisdom to impart upon me in my hour of need. She is, after all, an edible undie expert. Her phone rings several times before she picks up and, by the time she does, I'm in a full panic in that way in which one gets when they're utterly desperate and reaching out for a lifeline.

"That was fast. Don't tell me you guys are done already?" she asks. "What'd you do, go for it in the loo or something?"

"No," I whisper yell. "I'm in a worst-case scenario situation and I need your help."

"Oh, are you allergic to one of the ingredients or something? Are your lady bits swelling up, burning, and/or itching?"

"No. That's a thing?"

"I've only heard of it once."

"You might've mentioned it."

"But then you probably wouldn't have done it and you just seemed so excited. Also, it's really good for you to step outside your box once in a while."

"Well, stepping outside this particular box landed me in another one," I say.

I turn away from Bellford and the helpful security guard, my face flush with shame. "I'm at the airport but the bloody revolving door broke and now I'm stuck with a crowd of people gathering while we wait for the maintenance guy. Only they can't find him because he's gone to the pub so his wife has gone searching for him, only she has to take the bus because he's got their car."

Nikki makes a strangled sound as though she's trying to choke back a laugh. "Did Will's flight land yet?"

"I think so, but he hasn't come out of the gate. Wait. How is that going to help me?"

"I don't know. I just have no idea what you should do. Oh, but definitely leave your coat on."

"Uh, yeah," I snap. "But there is another issue. They're piping a ton of heat into here. I'm starting to sweat like…like some animal that sweats profusely. I need you to look at the box to see if there are any numbers attached to the room temperature thing."

"Why?" she asks. "Is there a thermostat or something?"

"No, there's no thermostat," I bark. "I just want to know how hot you have to be before these bloody things melt."

"Okay," she says, even though clearly what I'm asking for is utterly insane and useless. "I'll check the box. Just a sec. I have to get out of the bath."

I wait, taking long, slow breaths to stop myself from panic crying, and finally, she starts to talk again. "Nothing. It just says room temperature. How hot does it feel in there? Like Starbucks or the facial room at Lotus Flower?"

"Hot. More like a sauna."

"Ooh," she says, making a clicking sound. "Does it feel more like an infrared sauna or an old timey one where you pour water on the rocks?"

"The first one."

"So, it's a *dry* heat. That's probably a good thing."

"Right. Better than if it was moist, I suppose."

"Exactly. So, it should buy you at least a few more minutes before the chocolate melts."

"What do I do?" I plead. "Nikki, please help me think of something fast."

"Oh God, I don't have the faintest. Let me patch Tessa in. She's good in an emergency."

"No!" I cry, but it's too late because she's clearly got the phone away from her ear.

In what feels like an eternity, I hear her again. "Okay, Arabella,

I'm back, I've got Tessa on the line, and I've given her the full debrief on your briefs."

"Hi, Tess," I say, feeling utterly defeated.

"Hey, you. So, this is a bit of a sticky situation," Tessa says before she and Nikki burst into laughter.

When I don't join them, Tessa says, "Too soon?"

"Obviously."

"Okay, the important thing is to not panic because the more you panic, the higher your body temperature is going to go and the faster those things are going to melt."

I gulp back a sob and say, "Don't panic. Okay."

"Have you got any tissues or did you maybe stuff your real undies in your pocket?" Tessa asks.

Then, much to my horror, I hear my brother's voice in the background. "Who are you talking to?"

"It's Arabella. She's trapped in the revolving door at the airport wearing nothing but a long coat and edible undies that are beginning to melt."

Oh, for fuck's sake.

"Seriously, Tess. You're telling my brother this?" I say at the same time that I hear Arthur say, "Seriously, Tess. You're telling *me* this?"

"Stop it, the pair of you. This is an all-hands-on-deck, brain trust emergency. I'm putting you on speaker, Arabella. Now, let's all get our thinking caps on so we can figure out a way to get her out of this before her knickers make an appearance around her ankles. Wait — is it chocolate or more of a strawberry gummy situation?" she asks.

"Both." I let out one sob, then look up, only to see the ABN news van pulling up. "Oh, bollocks, the mother fucking media is here."

I watch helplessly as the van screeches to a halt and two men rush out—a cameraman and a reporter. The cameraman lifts the equipment to his shoulder while the reporter readies himself to inform the world of this massively important bit of breaking news.

"Oh, yup, there you are," Nikki says. "I've got the telly on. They're going live. Try not to look suspicious."

"Oh, Christ," Arthur says. "What were you thinking?"

"This is hardly the time for that," Tessa says. "She already knows this was a terrible idea. A lecture is hardly going to help matters. Arabella, have you got anything to discreetly wipe with?"

"Nothing. Not even the tiniest shred of a tissue."

"Well, take them off, you ninny," Arthur says.

"How exactly am I supposed to do that? I am literally standing in a glass box surrounded on all sides by curious onlookers and reporters. There is no way I can get them off and into my pocket without someone seeing."

"Honestly, Arthur," Tessa says. "If you're not going to be of help, just go back to watching David Attenborough."

I glance up, only to see Will standing on the other side of the glass with an extremely concerned expression on his face. "Will's here," I say into the phone.

"Thank Christ," Arthur says. "Hang up and call him. Maybe Sir Knight of the No Shirt can rescue Princess No Knickers."

"He might be right about that," Tessa says. "After all, he is there and he's very resourceful."

"Okay, I'll do that," I say, hanging up, even though the last thing I want to do is tell Will what's really going on. This was supposed to be sexy, not tragically humiliating.

I dial his number then hold the phone up to my ear and watch as he answers. He puts one hand on the glass and I do the same like people in those shows where one of the characters is in prison in an orange jumpsuit and the other one is there to tell them to hang in there.

"Are you okay, sweetheart?"

"Yes, fine. I just feel a bit silly is all. How was your flight?" I ask as though I'm not trapped in a door.

"Fine," he says. "I got a lot of studying in so that's a positive." He gives me a thumbs up and does his best to look happy, even though I know he very likely is not. "But, more importantly, how do we get you out of there?"

"The maintenance guy is on his way. I've been told I'll be out in a jiffy." I smile graciously, even though I'm fighting back tears. Will is right there. After six weeks of being thousands of miles apart, I am literally a sheet of glass away from the man I love wearing edible undies that—let's face it because I can't deny it any longer—are melting.

"Darling, you look positively flushed," Will says. "Take your jacket off, sweetheart. You look like you're about to pass out from the heat."

"I'm fine," I say, giving him a confident smile. "Absolutely fine. I'm actually a little bit chilly."

"But your face is bright red and I can see beads of sweat on your forehead."

"Really?" I ask, dabbing at my face with my palms. "Must be a weird reflection because I'm as dry as a bone."

Oh God. Here it comes. Hot gooey liquid is running down the fronts of my thighs. Is it the strawberry or the chocolate running? Either way, this is going to look absolutely disgusting if it makes it all the way down past my coat. I'm either going to look like I shit myself or you know what.

I let out a sob. It's reached my knees.

Fuck.

Fucking hell.

Fuckity fuck fuck.

"Belle, what's wrong? Are you feeling faint?" Will asks. "Seriously, sweetheart, take your coat off. You'll feel so much better."

I shake my head and give him an urgent look. "I'm basically nude under my coat."

His eyes grow wide and his lips curve up in a very turned-on grin.

Clearing my throat, I add, "Also, I'm wearing edible knickers and they're melting down my legs."

"Fuck," he whispers before he lets his jaw drop.

"Yeah." I give him a tight nod.

He grins again, then shakes his head. "Sorry, we need to get you out of there."

"I'm afraid it's too late."

It's now also coming down the backs of my thighs. I try discreetly tucking my coat between my thighs and squeezing my legs against the fabric, praying my coat will absorb whatever the hell is leaking down there. *Please do not soak through. Dear God, do not soak through.*

Why the fuck did I go with the extra-large chocolate heart? For *sharesies*?

"It's happening, Will," I whisper, tears filling my eyes. The warm liquid is past my knees now.

He stares at me as I sink to my knees, letting the coat fan out around me. Looking up at the crowd, I raise my voice and say, "Let us use this time to reflect on our many blessings and pray for the less fortunate."

Chapter 4

THE DESPERATE GIRL'S GUIDE TO BEING TRAPPED IN A GLASS BOX...

Arabella

BREAKING NEWS from the ABN News Center with Giles Bigly

"Good evening, I'm Giles Bigly with the ABN news desk. We interrupt your regularly scheduled program to bring you a breaking story from the Valcourt International Airport where it appears as though Princess Arabella has somehow become trapped in a set of revolving doors. Our reporter, Zachary Jones, is live on the scene. Zachary, can you fill us in on what's happening at this moment?"

Zachary, a red-headed man in his late twenties, gives the camera a grave look. "Well, Giles, I'm standing outside of Valcourt International Airport at gate C3, where Princess Arabella is currently trapped in the revolving door you see behind me. It is my understanding that she was intending to make a brief appearance here to pick up her fiancé, Will Banks, who is returning from several weeks of filming his hit series *The Wild World*. As you can see, Princess Arabella is kneeling on the floor, where she is praying."

"Really? I had no idea she was so religious."

"Yes, this does appear to be a surprising development. The royal family attends St. Stephen's Church, but they generally are not known to be people of faith, or if they are, they are certainly private about it. But tonight, the princess has decided to use this time that she's got to give thanks for her many blessings and to pray for the less fortunate."

The camera zooms in on Arabella, then on the crowd of people. "Many of the people inside the airport have now joined her in prayer, in fact. The crowd has separated themselves into two groups — the one on the left is comprised of curious onlookers, while, on the right, we have a rather large group of people who are kneeling and praying alongside the princess. I managed to talk to one of them and she told me that she is praying for the princess's safe exit from the doors."

"Fascinating," Giles says. "And rather inspiring to see the princess use this time to think about others rather than, say, scrolling through her Instagram feed or panicking."

"Indeed," Zachary answers with a firm nod. "But, over the last year or so, the princess has certainly been a champion of those in need. She truly is a fine example of leadership and compassion, and, in fact, is quickly becoming Avonia's most popular royal."

"Quite so. Zachary, any word on how she got trapped? Some conspiracy theories are floating around on the Internet already that she has somehow been entrapped by a terrorist group or perhaps a jealous rival for Mr. Banks' affections."

Zachary chuckles and shakes his head. "While it is natural for people to speculate in unusual situations such as this, it seems as though it's simply a maintenance issue. Apparently, the door has been sticking all day and should have had an 'out of order' sign put up, but somehow that didn't happen."

"Any word on how long it may take for her to be rescued?"

"No word as of yet, Giles," Zachary says. "But rest assured, we'll be here all night if we have to until this story has a resolution."

"Thank you, Zachary. And of course, I'll be here at the anchor desk as the story unfolds."

The feed from the airport cuts and Giles's face fills the screen. "Stay tuned here on ABN for up-to-the-minute updates on the Emergency at the Airport. For now, we'll return you to your regularly scheduled program, *The Great Avonian Bake-Off*, already in progress."

———

That is the very last time I'm going to try to be sexy. Seriously. I know people make these sorts of declarations after suffering some type of humiliation, but in my case, I absolutely mean it. I'm striking sexy off the list of ways to be the perfect wife, and just doubling down on all the other stuff.

I am now in the bathtub at Will's apartment, where I've been for a solid forty-five minutes. First, I took a long shower and used the better part of a bar of soap scrubbing the disgusting sticky knickers off of my body, only to discover that the strawberry bra and thong strings have dyed my skin bright pink, leaving me looking like I have some sort of reverse sunburn, as though I wore a very weird cut-out full bodysuit with only my naughty bits showing.

Now I'm soaking in the small white tub, hoping against all hope that some of this awful red dye will come off my skin. A few minutes ago, Will came in to check on me and lit a few candles in the room and turned off the lights. "Thought you might need to relax a little," he said before slipping out of the room.

Isn't he dreamy? It almost makes me want to get out of the bath and…

But, when I think about him actually seeing me right now, I just can't. Not when I look so utterly insane. To be honest, all this heat hasn't been the best for my poor face, which is now piping hot after an evening trapped in a glass oven and now in a steamy bath. I'm sure I resemble a tomato at this point, which proves my point about not ever trying to be a total sex cat again because both my attempt at youthful skin and my attempt at edible naughtiness have ended in utter defeat.

Oh, and if you're wondering how I got out of there, here's how it unfolded: Will, Bellford, and Reynard (Will's bodyguard) devised a genius plan to have the airport staff put up tarps surrounding the entire revolving door under the guise of not wanting anyone to get injured in the case of broken glass. When Roger the maintenance guy finally showed up (half-cut, by the way) and got the door working, Will managed to sneak in a plastic bag and a container of baby wipes. He then helped me quickly clean my legs/heels so as to hide the true cause of my kneeling.

Now, as long as nobody says anything, I should be spared the public humiliation of the entire world knowing what a dirty idiot I am. Unfortunately, that still leaves the security staff, including Bellford, who is very much like a favourite uncle to me. He and I now have an unspoken agreement that we shall not make eye contact for quite some time. And then there's Will, who, although he's been absolutely marvelous about the entire thing, I'm not sure I can ever face again either. Not after he had to help wipe gooey chocolate off my ankles.

There's a knock on the door, then I hear it open.

"Hey, you," Will says in a gentle tone. "I'm not going to ask you to come out until you're ready, but I brought you a drink and I was hoping maybe I could just sit on this side of the curtain and we could talk. I just really miss you."

"Of course." I tuck my knees into my chest and wrap my arms around them, laying my cheek on my knees. "Sorry this evening has turned out to be such a disaster."

"I'm going to reach in and hand you your drink, but I promise not to peek." He slides his arm in and in his hand is my favourite drink — a gin and tonic with extra lemon.

I take it from him and press the cool glass to my forehead and cheeks before having a long sip. On the other side of the curtain, I hear him settling himself onto the floor next to the tub.

"Are you okay?" he asks for the twentieth time since my escape.

"I am. I just feel so stupid. I mean, what was I thinking? You must figure me for the biggest idiot in the world."

"Of course not. Honestly, meeting me at the airport in nothing but a coat and some undies? Very sexy."

"Or at least it would've been."

"It's still very sexy, Arabella. But honestly, to me, everything you do is a huge turn-on."

"Oh, please, I find that hard to believe. Out of the two of us, *you're* the sexy one. I'm the boring, proper one."

"Hey," he says in a slightly sharp tone. "You're talking about my fiancée and I won't have anyone slagging the woman I love—not even her."

I let out a small grin when normally I'd laugh at a comment like that.

"Is that why you did it?" Will asks. "Because you really believe you're boring?"

"Maybe," I say, my heart pounding a little bit quicker in my chest. I take another sip of my drink, feeling the icy cold liquid slide down my throat. "God. Here you had some sort of fun birthday celebration planned and I've gone and ruined the entire evening."

"Clearly, you also had different plans in mind — plans which I most certainly would've been on board for. And you didn't ruin anything. The dumbass at the airport who forgot to put the sign up is the one who ruined the evening."

"True," I say, closing my eyes as another flash of me kneeling on the floor in my own chocolatey mess assaults my senses.

"You know, the evening's not over yet…"

"Urgh, I'm a mess. The undies dyed my skin and, to be honest, my face wasn't so bright red because of the heat in there. I burned it yesterday at the spa, trying to get an advanced anti-aging treatment done."

"Anti-aging?" Will asks, sounding somewhere between confused and disappointed. "Why would you do that? You're so young and beautiful. Not that I'd ever want you to burn your skin. No matter how wrinkly it gets."

"God, it's all so stupid. It's like I turned thirty and I just got dumber than I ever have been."

"I hope I've never done anything to make you think you have to do crap like that to yourself," he says, his voice echoing around the room.

"Of course not," I say quickly. "You've never been anything but amazing to me. You do a remarkable job of making me feel beautiful."

"Yeah, well, I'm sure it doesn't help that I'm gone all the damn time."

"Oh, Will, we both know that the fact that you're gone a lot is my fault, so I hardly could blame you for it. Besides, all of this silliness is just me being in my own head." The curtain moves the tiniest bit beside me and I jump a little, then see it's just his hand. He's holding his palm out to me and I slide my wet fingers through his. He squeezes my hand gently, then pulls my arm onto his side of the curtain, and I feel his lips brush against my knuckles. His touch brings out my courage, so I suck back the rest of my drink, and set the glass down on the ledge of the tub. He deserves the whole truth.

"The thing is, since we got engaged, there's just this nagging little voice telling me I need to be absolutely perfect for you to stay…interested. I know it's not logical —"

"— or healthy."

"That too. But I just…I don't know… I think I was trying to find some way to make it up to you — the whole royal thing. I know what a pain in the arse the security team has been for you and I doubt you're going to enjoy even a second of our wedding and there's just always going to be things that you're going to have to show up for that I know you're going to hate."

"So you thought you needed to burn a layer of skin off?"

"I guess in some stupid way I thought that if I could be really exciting and really sexy, it would give you a reason to *want* to come home every time you leave."

Will presses his lips to the back of my hand for a long moment. When he speaks, his voice is full of emotion. "It breaks my heart to hear you say this. You're my reason to come home. Just you, exactly the way you are. You and your smile and your perfectly wonderful heart and your enormous sense of justice…"

I let out a small chuckle.

"Belle, I love my work, but I love you more. It used to be that nothing thrilled me like getting on a plane to my next adventure. Now, nothing thrills me like coming home to you. You really are sexy and beautiful and smart and you always will be, even when we're both old and grey. You'll always be it for me and you don't have to keep trying to impress me because I'm already yours."

My throat tightens as my eyes fill with tears. "Thank you. That's what I needed to hear."

"Remember it, okay? No matter what happens or how long I have to go away. Just know that the way I feel about you is *never* going to change. It couldn't. Not in a thousand years. Not even if I wanted it to."

I take a long gulp of air, hoping to stop myself from crying. On the other side of the curtain, Will rubs his thumb over my knuckles. "Are you okay?"

I nod, forgetting that he can't see me. "I keep worrying that you're going to hate this life so much that, at some point in the not-too-distant future, you're going to decide that I'm not worth all of it."

"Not worth—" he starts, his tone sounding angry.

"It's a lot, Will. I am asking *so much* of you."

"You're not."

"Come on, don't tell me you weren't filled with dread when you got the Royal Protocol Handbook."

He pauses for a second and the silence speaks for itself. "Okay, I'm not exactly excited about some of the stuff, sure, but every relationship has trade-offs, right?"

"But with me, the trade-offs are *massive*. Complicated, ridiculous, pompous, restrictive…"

"Somewhat, maybe," he says, "But those things are not going to define our marriage. To me, all that stuff is like your job. The *life* we're going to build is going to be our own. I can learn proper bowing order and memorize which spoon to use at which course. That's nothing, really. I don't really care about any of that because, at the end of the day, I'll be next to you at those stuffy, ridiculous, pompous events. If I can catch your eye and share a grin or whisper things to you that make you laugh, I'll enjoy every minute."

Tears fill my eyes and slide down my cheeks. Suddenly it hits me that this moment is the most intimate of my life. Even though he and I have been through so much together, this is the most honest I've been with him, or with myself, for that matter. But the truth isn't sending him running. It's drawing him closer. And I'm suddenly desperate to be in his arms.

"Belle?"

"Yes?" I whisper.

"Are you crying?"

"Yes."

"I'd really like to hold you right now. We don't have to do anything. I just want…to hold you. Can I do that?"

"Yes." I wipe the tears off my cheeks.

He lets go of my hand and slides the curtain back, his eyes shining with emotion as his gaze meets mine. He sees me. Not my burnt skin or the insane dyed-on bikini. He sees only me. It's like he's peering into my soul and he wants to dive in and stay. I swallow hard, trying to stop the tears as he reaches for my face with both hands, cupping my cheeks gently as he leans in to kiss me. His lips are soft and gentle on mine and I'm taken away from everything this world holds—all the fears and insecurities and nonsense. And it's only Will and me left.

I wrap my arms around his neck and lift my body closer to him, kissing him deeper now, letting him know what I want. His hands slide down my wet body and he dips his left hand into the water, cradling under my knees, while his right hand supports my back. He stands, lifting me out of the tub, not caring if he gets soaked.

He kisses me again, then presses his lips to my forehead and whispers, "You are perfect. Exactly the way you are, no matter what."

"I love you so much," I say, my voice almost not even there.

He pulls back and stares into my eyes, the warmth of his arms and the flickering glow of the candles cloaking me in a romantic haze. "This is forever. You know that, right?"

Nodding, I kiss him hard on the mouth, pressing myself against him, wanting to get as close as I can.

"I'm going to take you to bed now, okay? And when we get there, if you want to just hold each other, I'm okay with that."

I bite my lip and give him a mischievous look. "I'm not."

"No?" he asks, a wide grin spreading across his face.

"No, I want to do all the stuff."

"If you insist."

Chapter 5

SHOWING UP TO A MEETING UNPREPARED, NEGLECTING MAMA BEAR, AND OTHER BAD IDEAS...

Will

Royal Wedding Tentative Schedule

* PLEASE NOTE: *All line items are able to be shifted in accordance with the wishes of the bride and groom, however, the day has been carefully thought-out already, taking into account any and all variables. Any requested changes will likely cause a domino effect, making it difficult to manage the event. Please carefully review this schedule and put forth any requests in writing so as to avoid any miscommunication. We have a very narrow window in which to make changes, and once it closes, it shall not reopen.*

5 a.m.: Princess Arabella begins preparations for the day, starting with a light breakfast and a shower prior to the hair and makeup stylists' arrivals.

6:30 a.m.: Princess's hair to be styled.

8 a.m.: Makeup application.

9:12 a.m.: Refreshment break, including herbal tea, a selection of fresh fruits, and yogurt.

10:06 a.m.: Arrival of photographer and photos of dressing, as well as other family photographs. (Please see Appendix B for full details on traditional photos.)

10:40 a.m.: Bridal party (save bride and King Winston) departs for church.

10:52 a.m.: Princess Arabella departs in Rolls Royce with King Winston for St. Stephen's Church.

11:04 a.m.: Arrival at church.

11:05 a.m.: King Winston walks bride down the aisle to begin wedding ceremony. (Please see Appendix C for minute-by-minute ceremony itinerary.)

12:10 p.m.: Bride and groom exit church for photos on steps and traditional greeting of the crowd as a married couple.

12:32 p.m.: Couple departs church via horse-drawn carriage to return to palace for outdoor luncheon, weather permitting.

12:45 p.m.: Bride and groom will be given twelve minutes to freshen up and have a small snack to maintain energy levels during receiving line.

12:57 p.m.: Wedding party forms receiving line to greet guests.

2:03 p.m.: Luncheon, including speeches and performances by various musical/dance artists (line up to be determined).

4:06 p.m.: Bride and groom retire to Princess Arabella's apartment for rest and to change into eveningwear for second meal and reception including dancing.

7:06 p.m.: Bride and groom leave apartment and walk to grand dining hall for intimate dinner of two hundred guests.

9:12 p.m.: Bride and groom exit grand dining hall and make their way to the ballroom for reception where they will greet guests.

10:18 p.m.: First dance as married couple, followed by father-daughter dance, wedding party, then dance floor will be open to all guests.

10:55 p.m.: Cutting of the cake and ceremonial offering of slices to honoured guests, including reigning monarchs, prime ministers, presidents, as well as Oprah and Stedman.

12:42 a.m.: Bride and groom retire to apartment.

"Urgh, this must sound positively awful to you," Arabella says, looking up from the wedding handbook with a worried expression.

Giving her an easy smile, I say, "I don't know, it's nice that they have a very well-laid-out itinerary for us. Keep everything on track and all that."

"Be honest," she says, raising one eyebrow. "That is your version of wedding hell."

"At one time in my life, yes, but I'm much more mature now, and, to be honest, I've come to enjoy wearing a monkey suit."

Arabella sighs, her face screwing up with worry. "We really should have spent the better part of the morning discussing all of this instead of… well, you know."

My lips quirk up into a smile. "I regret nothing."

Actually, that's not entirely true because, at the moment, we are ever so slightly screwed. We're on our way to the palace to face Arabella's family and the team of senior royal advisors to start the wedding plans. Then, we're zipping over to the Avonian Nature Network studios where we're to have a meeting with Dylan Sinclair to find out what insane (yet epic) idea she's got cooking these days, at which point, we're going to drop the hammer on the network falling in line with royal protocol in order to secure a future with me after my contract is up (i.e., No more shirtless anything).

As fun as this morning was, in hindsight, it may have been better for us to have actually had a lengthy conversation about what it is we each want out of our wedding day. I haven't even had a chance to tell her that my family is hoping we'll hold the event at the resort. I'm not even sure if I should bother mentioning it, since there's absolutely no way it's going to happen. "Okay, we've got exactly four minutes to learn everything we need to about each other as far as weddings go we can present a united front. Difficult, but not impossible."

Arabella gives me one firm nod. "Okay, what's your dream wedding?"

"I don't have one. I'm a guy."

"Excellent point. Let's attack this from a different angle then. What's your nightmare wedding?"

The one on the itinerary we're staring at. "Again, guy."

"Fine, in that case, what would be absolute deal-breakers for you?"

"Honestly, there's really nothing."

"Nothing." She purses her lips and stares at me for a second. "Not one thing would be a deal-breaker for you as far as your wedding goes."

"Okay, there is one thing," I say. "I didn't want to mention it at first because I didn't want you to think I'm being picky, but there is something that would cause me not to go through with it." I pause for dramatic effect, then say, "If they replaced you with some other bride."

Arabella chuckles reluctantly, then swats me lightly on the chest. "Idiot."

"That's why I didn't want to say anything," I answer with a little grin. "Okay now, as far as this itinerary goes, it's fine with me if it's fine with you."

"Yes, it's okay. Honestly, my biggest concern is making sure that your family feels completely welcome and as important as my side of the family. I'd hate it if they were standing in the church or at the reception feeling out of place."

"That is why I picked the right woman to propose to," I say, leaning over and giving her a kiss on the lips.

The car pulls up in front of the palace and comes to a stop.

"I'm so glad they were available for the meeting," Arabella says casually before both our doors are opened, letting in a chilly blast of air. She climbs out, leaving me with my jaw at my chest for a solid ten seconds.

I hurry up the steps to catch her. "Umm, my family's invited?"

"Yes, of course," Arabella says with a bright smile.

"Who exactly?" *Don't say Rosy. Don't say Rosy.*

"Harrison and Libby, Emma and Pierce—Pierce can't make it though— and of course, Rosy."

Shit. Rosy. My heart sinks as I recall the email she wrote that I have yet to respond to.

Arabella stops and stares at me. "What's wrong? You don't look happy."

"No, it's a very, very kind gesture. The only thing is, there's a possibility that they may push to have the wedding at the resort—specifically Rosy."

"At the resort? In the Caribbean?" Arabella asks, blinking a few times.

"It's nothing you need to worry about. I got an email from her a couple of days ago and I haven't had a chance to reply, but honestly, I doubt anyone else in my family is going to be expecting anything."

"Oh dear," she says. "We've never even discussed it. I just assumed it would be here, but really, why not have it there? I mean, we should at least consider it, right?"

"Should we?" I ask. "I really don't think it's realistic. The sheer amount of people who would have to fly there, and add all the security considerations… Wouldn't it be much more sensible to have it here?"

"I suppose, yes," Arabella answers, looking a lot less relaxed than she did a few minutes ago.

Two pages open the massive wooden doors and we walk in, only to see Gregory, my assistant, and Mrs. Chapman, Arabella's assistant, waiting for us. Gregory is a stout, short, middle-aged man with a back so straight, it seems as though he's hoping good posture will actually cause him to grow. He bows while Mrs. Chapman curtsies, and we exchange hellos before Arabella gets back to the topic at hand—my family. "The last thing I want is to have your family feel like they don't have any say."

"Honestly, it shouldn't be a problem, but I really should've gotten back to Rosy," I say. "Maybe I could call her right now and sort it out before the meeting."

"It starts in less than a minute and it takes nearly three minutes to get to the boardroom from here," Mrs. Chapman says, turning and leading us toward the meeting room, her heels clicking away on the marble floor.

Gregory turns to me. "Is there anything I can help you with, Mr. Banks?"

"No, thank you, Gregory." I smile at him even though inside I'm more than a little concerned about what's about to happen.

When we arrive in the boardroom, all but four chairs at the long, wooden table are filled. King Winston, the Princess Dowager, Prince Arthur, and Princess Tessa, as well as all of their senior advisers, are already sitting with cups of tea and small plates of scones and fruit in front of them. On the large screen mounted to the wall, I see my family already patched in via Zoom. Arabella and I make our apologies for being late, then take our seats next to each other at the end of the table.

Phillip Crawford stands and clears his throat. "Good morning. I'm Phillip Crawford, head advisor to King Winston. I'd like to welcome you all today as we embark on the exciting journey of matrimony for Princess Arabella and Mr. Banks." He pauses for a split second to give me a slightly disappointed once-over, then continues. "If everyone could please open the royal wedding hand-book, we'll get started discussing the events surrounding the big day, as well as the wedding itinerary. I trust each of you has had a chance to read this over in full and familiarize yourself with expecta-tions as well as the flow of the order of events. Before we get started, does anyone have any questions about the contents of the package?"

"I do," Rosy says, causing my heart to drop down to my bottom.

Phillip looks at the screen from above the top rims of his glasses. "And you would be?"

"Rosy Brown. I've known William since he was seven years old. I love him and his siblings like I would my own children. Now, I noticed that everything seems to have been determined already, including the location. What we would like to propose is that, for once, the royal family holds a wedding somewhere other than Avonia — in one of your other Commonwealth countries, as a way to bridge the royal family's presence in the outer realm." She gives a satisfied smile to the camera, but next to her, Harrison is covering his face with one hand.

Phillip folds his arms. "I'm assuming you intend to hold the event at the Paradise Bay Resort so that your family can profit off of the nuptials?"

"No, that's okay," Harrison interjects, holding up one hand. "Thanks to Rosy here for always thinking of our family, but honestly, we have absolutely no desire to profit off of my brother's wedding."

Rosy mutters something that sounds a lot like 'Yes, we do,' to him. "Why should *they* be the only ones to profit?"

Damn. My entire head feels hot with shame and I stumble over my words. "It's fine, it's totally fine. Let's just not worry about holding the wedding at the resort. Obviously, it needs to be held here in

Valcourt for logistical reasons, and nobody is going to profit off anything, so let's just move on to the first item, okay?"

Rosy's head snaps back. "But Cuddle Bear, think of how beautiful it would be? A beach wedding followed by the two of you sailing off on Matilda into the sunset?"

Phillip answers for me. "Yes, as romantic as that sounds, we have strict protocols to follow and there is no way we could even handle security for that many dignitaries in a foreign country. So, the resort is off the table and we really must forge on. His Majesty has an extremely full schedule today and therefore we will need to wrap this up in short order."

"So, you're not even going to consider it, King Winston?" Rosy asks.

The king sits right up and looks at the screen. "Umm...I think... our advisory team is more able to discuss logistics."

"Who exactly makes the decisions around there? Because it seems as though that tall, skinny guy is the one in charge."

Oh no, no, no, no, no. Do not question the king! My entire body is hot with shame and I feel sweat pool above my top lip.

"Err..." King Winston starts, but I cut him off (which is a risky move, believe me).

"Rosy," I plead. "I should have discussed this with you earlier. The logistics of having a thousand or so guests fly to the Benavente Islands seem rather difficult. Besides, the media would skewer us for the unnecessary expenses, not to mention the carbon emissions for hosting the wedding in such a remote location."

Arabella leans forward. "But, Rosy, I promise we'll find some way to honour your homeland and promote the resort."

"Out of the question. Royals don't promote hotels," Phillip quips. "Just like they shouldn't be selling shoes or laundry soap. Now, we really must move on to the guest list."

Arabella glares at him, then smiles at the screen. "Rosy, Will and I are going to call you later so we can work something out, okay? As to the date, we definitely need to avoid the busy season in the Caribbean."

"Thank you, Arabella," Harrison says with a smile. "Truthfully, it will be quite challenging to leave here anytime between November and the end of March."

"Which is why *they* should come *here*," Rosy mutters.

"As difficult as I'm sure running a resort is, running a kingdom is also a rather large undertaking," Phillip sneers. "But since November through April are not times that are conducive to drawing a crowd, we can agree to strike them from the options. Anyone else? Prince Arthur? Princess Tessa?"

Tessa speaks up. "I honestly have no preference whatsoever other than a gentle request to give me enough time to lose the baby weight again."

Arthur gives her a sideways glance and I can tell by the look on his face he's about to say it isn't pregnancy weight this time, but the glare she gives him causes him to think better of it. Good choice, buddy.

Arthur turns to Phillip and says, "You've got my schedule. There's nothing I need to add, but back to this Cuddle Bear thing…there's a story there I absolutely must hear."

My face flames again but I give him a nod and a grin that says 'good one' to show I can take a ribbing. I take a look at the agenda and see we're still on item one of thirty-nine. Arabella leans into my ear and whispers, "I say we elope."

I stifle a laugh, then grin at her, even though I wish she meant it. "Deal."

Chapter 6

SOMETIMES WATER UNDER THE BRIDGE JUST SITS THERE ALL STAGNANT AND STINKY...

Will

"THERE THEY ARE!" Dylan says, rushing across her large corner office in our direction. "My favourite young couple."

She gives me two quick air kisses, then does the same for Arabella. When she finishes, she stares at Arabella for a moment. "You had a chemical peel, didn't you?"

Arabella starts to say something, but Dylan cuts her off. "You don't have to tell me. I did exactly the same thing when I turned thirty—took four layers of skin off and had to hide in my flat for three weeks. But trust me when I tell you this — thirty is *so much younger* than you actually think, and you look amazing, by the way," Dylan says, raising her voice and sing-yelling, "Truly, truly, GORGEOUS!"

She leans in and focuses in on Arabella's forehead. "There is just the one tiny line there, but no one else is going to notice, I promise you. I'm only saying it because *my job* is to notice these things. Now, you two have a seat and let's talk because I have the *most exciting* opportunity for you, you are going to be jumping for joy in a few minutes."

Whatever she's about to offer, there is no way in hell we'll be jumping for joy. Dylan is pretty much the worst person I've ever met

—calculated, cold, and conniving. Her decisions are made purely based on what's going to make the biggest splash and the most cash with no thought (and I mean *none*) to consequences for the human beings involved in her schemes. We're going to say a hard no to everything she offers. I take Arabella's hand as we cross the room to the round meeting table in the far corner. We settle ourselves in side-by-side chairs and wait while Dylan makes her customary stop at her minibar for a can of Red Bull. "Can I get either of you one?"

When we answer in the negative (See? Our first no!), Dylan sweeps across the room, cracking the can open and taking a long swig of her drink before sitting down. "Okay, now I think we all know that the contract Will signed—although a heroic thing for him to do at the time—has not exactly been easy on either of you. I've been working our number one man here incredibly hard these last six months as we launch the network and things have been incredible. *Beyond* incredible, really. But I also know that there is one thing we could do that would boost our ratings and give us the international visibility that would take ten years to establish. And it will most definitely be the answer to your problems as well. Can either of you answer me this question: Other than the Olympics and the World Cup, what do you think the most-watched television event has been in the last twenty years?"

"Prince William and Kate's wedding," we both say at the same time in deadpan voices.

Dylan looks taken aback. "Well, that's no fun. I didn't think you'd get it. But anyway, yes. Royal weddings are the *absolute best way* to get people around the world in front of their tellies. Now, a little bird told me that the rights to the wedding—including the lead-up events—are still available, and it is the opinion of the executives here at ANN that ours is the perfect place to share your joy with the world while also increasing our viewership. Our early numbers indicate a possibility of a 1200% increase in regular viewers should we secure exclusive worldwide rights to the big event."

She takes a quick swig of her drink, then continues. "Veronica, Victor, Kira, and I are *so* excited about this idea that we would like to offer you something that may be more valuable to you than cold hard cash—an offer that the Godfather himself would call 'too good to refuse.' What would you say to having your wedding *paid for and produced by* your network family here at ANN?"

"No," we both say at the same time.

She sits back and gives us a skeptical grin. "What? Did you two decide to say no to anything I offered before you came in?"

"Well, if we did, you can hardly blame us," I say. "After what you tried to do to Arabella's family…"

"Water under the bridge," Dylan says. "The princess and I had a lovely conversation at the wrap-up show and we decided all is forgiven. Didn't we, Your Highness?"

"Forgiven, yes, forgotten, no."

"Fair point, but picture this: the cost for the entire wedding covered by the network, pleasing taxpayers all over the kingdom. We bring on the world's best event planners to take *all the pressure* off the two of you so that you can continue doing the important work you do while the big wedding machine is running in the background. And the most enticing bit of my offer—don't shake your head. No. Do *not*. You haven't heard the best part. The moment the wedding is over, we tear up Will's contract and he's a free man." She pauses dramatically and gives us an open-mouthed smile. "Yes, a FREE!! MAN! Think about *that*. You two can finally start your life together with Will calling the shots on his career instead of yours truly."

Well, this sucks arse. It's like scratching a winning lotto ticket for a million bucks on Christmas morning, only to find it's one of those novelty ones your jackass uncle got you as a joke. She's offering me what I want most—to tear up the crap contract I signed with ANN. It means I won't have to work for peanuts anymore. No more shirtless photo shoots with baby animals or shirtless videos of me scuba diving, parasailing, and rock-climbing (even more painful than it sounds). No more of this schedule that is so jam-packed I'm lucky to see Arabella once every month. It means I could leverage my new-found fame and pole-vault myself to the next level—getting paid what I'm worth, calling my own shots, and saying *no* to any and all 'opportunities' that make me a laughingstock among Arabella's upper crust frenemies.

And I have to decline.

I'm definitely going to need Arabella to be the one to say no to this because I honestly don't know if I have the strength to make my mouth form that word. Here I am being offered everything I've been wanting for the past six months, but the offer is *literally* coming from one of the worst people on the planet. *Come on, Arabella. Say no. Say no and we'll fight for the time off and fully-dressed promotional material, then we leave and forget that this opportunity ever presented itself.*

But Arabella doesn't say no. Her mouth opens, then shuts, giving Dylan the chance to keep going.

"Now, we very much wish to continue working with Will, which should be made obvious by the recent wrap on the ANN corporate jet. Do you love it? I bet you love it."

"Not a bit," I say.

"That's because, in addition to being so handsome, he's modest," Dylan tells Arabella. "Of course he secretly loves the wrap. *Everyone* loves the wrap. Did you see it?"

"No."

"Oh, you *have* to see it. It's epic. What could be more masculine than a giant Will on a jet?" She gives a happy sigh that makes me feel slightly violated, then says. "First thoughts on this incredible, once-in-a-lifetime offer?"

I have no thoughts other than the 'hell yes' my brain is screaming at me. No, forget it. There is no way Arabella will—or even should—say yes to this. It's a hard no.

Arabella crosses her arms and sits back. "Why should we trust you?"

Huh, that's not a no, is it?

"Simple. Because we both want the same thing—for you to have an incredible wedding and to be able to start your life together." She tips back the can, finishes her drink, then tosses it into the bin near her desk. "The truth is, I've been feeling the teensiest bit guilty about how much money we're making off of Will, given how low his salary is. Now, I know you've made a small fortune from Merrill and the other companies you're promoting, but still, somehow it just doesn't feel quite right. This would be a very fair trade-off. I give you a gorgeous wedding, free of charge—an absolute fairy-tale that will have people talking for years to come. I get *massive* amounts of exposure for the network, which will allow us to land some very lucrative global streaming contracts that I have on my radar. And after you've had your honeymoon, I'll come back to you with a new contract that gives you everything you deserve from whatever network you partner with—buckets of cash, more flexibility, and control over production decisions."

"No more shirtless videos?" Arabella asks, seeming to suddenly remember what our goal was in the first place.

"If that's what Will wants," Dylan says with a shrug. "It may not be the savviest business choice, but it'll be up to him."

My heart pounds in my chest and I have to grip the armrest of my chair to stop myself from saying yes and asking where to sign.

"What's the catch?" Arabella asks, narrowing her eyes.

"Why does there have to be a catch?" Dylan asks innocently.

Arabella meets her question with a raised eyebrow.

"Okay, okay," Dylan says. "I can see why you wouldn't find it exactly *easy* to trust me, which is why I've had the contract written up for you and I want you to take it to your own legal team."

She stands up and walks over to her desk, returning with a manila folder. "It's all outlined here. We'll donate a million dollars to a charity of your choosing. We'll also cover the costs of the wedding, including receptions, up to ten million. I also want to film a primetime special to air on the Sunday before the wedding. It'll include an at-home look at life in the palace, and a growing up in Paradise Bay thing. That'll really give people a sense of who each of you are, which will whip them up into a frenzy for the big event. We'll be showing reruns of *Princess in the Wild* the entire week as well so the audience gets a chance to watch you fall in love all over again. And I'd never cross you again, not when Will is so key to the network. I need him to *want* to come back to ANN under his own terms, and he certainly will never do that if I mess this up."

Is it me, or is Dylan making a lot of sense? I open the folder and Arabella leans in so we can both read it.

"Tell you what," Dylan says. "I'm all out of energy drinks, so why don't I pop down to the cafeteria and grab myself one and give you two a moment to look this over and talk."

We sit silently waiting until the door closes. The second it does, Arabella turns to me. "Okay, we have to take this deal, Will. Can you imagine? You could be free of her *permanently*, never having to go back again, and we gain more than two years of our life back."

I shake my head, terrified that this is going to all go sour very soon. "I don't know. If there's anything we've learned from Dylan, it's that she cannot be trusted."

"The legal team can tie up any loose ends. We'll have a clause put in that if *anything* happens that is to our dissatisfaction, we can rip up the entire contract," Arabella says, her eyes wild with excitement. "This is it, Will. This is what we've been waiting for. We can finally buy a house or…or two houses. Maybe one here and one on Santa Valentina Island. We can start our life together. We can actually wake up in the same bed every morning and fall asleep in each other's arms each night. Oh! And have breakfast and suppers together, and well…all the other meals on weekends. We can binge watch Bridgerton and do all sorts of things that *normal* couples do. We won't have to go months at a time settling for our sad little phone calls. And what if we film the pre-wedding special at the resort? Your family will get a ton of free publicity! They'll be thrilled."

"But, are you sure *your family* is going to be okay with this? I mean, they probably have some sort of long-standing agreement with another network or something."

Shaking her head, Arabella says, "At the end of the day, my family just wants me to be happy. They know how difficult the last six months have been for us, and they'll be glad to not have to foot the bill for the whole thing. It'll be super helpful as far as taxpayer perception goes. As far as I'm concerned, this is a no-lose situation." Arabella grins, looking more excited than I've seen her in a long time.

"Okay," I say, relief filling my veins. "When she comes back, we give her a maybe, based on your family's legal team's advice."

As if on cue, Dylan walks back into the room. Instead of sitting down, she walks over to her minibar, opens the door, and starts emptying her suit jacket pockets, in which she has somehow managed to cram four cans of Red Bull. When she finishes loading them into the fridge, she shuts the door, and turns to us with an expectant look. "Well? Are you ready to make the best deal of your lives?"

"Maybe," Arabella says, lifting her chin at Dylan. "We're willing to take it to our lawyers."

Dylan claps her hands together. "Yes! This is going to be the beginning of an *epic* partnership. I am going to elevate you to the status of the most popular royal couple on the planet and you are going to elevate ANN to the most-watched nature channel in all of Europe, the UK, and North America, excluding Michigan — they're pretty big on OLN over there." She walks around behind us and puts one hand on each of our shoulders.

"Well, we certainly have no desire to be the most popular royal couple," I say. "But the rest of what you've offered sounds mildly interesting." I do my best to sound slightly disinterested.

Dylan ignores my comment and yells, "Here we are! The dream team. Together, we are going to do epic shit." Clapping her hands so loud that Arabella and I both wince, she says, "Okay, I have much to do. If we're going to pull off the wedding of the century, I'm going to take your maybe as a yes and move ahead with the plans until I hear otherwise, so I need to get straight to work."

With that, she spins on her heel and walks toward her desk, effectively dismissing us.

A few minutes later, Arabella and I are settled into the back of her limo, enveloped in a sense of excitement. "Could this really be legit?" I ask.

"I think so," Arabella says.

"I *want* to get really excited about this, only I'm a little concerned this could crash and burn."

"Get excited, Will," Arabella says, leaning her head back against the seat and grinning at me. "It's in her best interest to make sure everything goes smoothly because this time, *you and I* will have the upper hand. Trust me, I'm going to see to it that nothing can possibly go wrong."

Chapter 7

YOU CAN'T MAKE AN OMELETTE WITHOUT CRACKING SOME EGGS...

Arabella

WELL, that was easy. It took me all of about ten minutes to convince my family and the advisors that having ANN produce the wedding was a sound idea. Literally as soon as the phrase 'fully paid for' came out of my mouth, Phillip Crawford was on the phone with legal. I'm sure he was dreading the usual questions about taxpayers having to foot the bill on yet another royal event (which they don't, but they think they do), so being able to announce that a private entity is accepting responsibility for this one? Huge win for him. He's going to be the smuggest royal advisor ever at that press conference.

Four days later, we have a contract, complete with us having ultimate control over major production decisions. The only thing left to do is set the date, fill it in on the contract, and sign.

And this is where things are going to get tricky because it occurred to me that the longer the preparations drag on, the better end of the deal Dylan is getting. And if there's anything I'd love to know as I'm walking down the aisle, it's that I managed to screw Dylan out of every minute possible that she owns Will. Er, I mean, other than the knowledge that I'm about to marry my best friend and we'll be together forever.

If we move at lightning speed, I'll—I mean, *Will* is going to best Dylan at her own game. Hurrah for him! (And me.) Luckily, I have a plan. It's rather devious and somewhat risky, but I'm going for it anyway. It was my big mouth that got Will into this whole mess in the first place and I'm going to bloody well be the one to get him out as fast as possible. So, last night at Margaritas and Man Bash Monday, I hatched a plan with my brain trust — Tessa and Nikki. They were totally onboard. Well, that's not strictly true. Tessa said something about it having 'about a ten percent chance of working and a one hundred percent chance of forever ruining my working relationship with Phillip Crawford, which will likely come back to bite me in the arse later.' But Nikki said I should go for it. Mind you, she was deep into her fourth drink at the time and I may have been on my third. It's all a bit fuzzy actually.

And even though I'm sober as a judge (with a slight hangover), I'm going through with it. I'm going to need a surprise attack, so by the time Phillip knows, it'll be too late. My heart pounds in my chest as I walk toward Arthur's office, dressed in my navy power suit with a pencil skirt. The closer I get, the more I straighten my back and lift my head high. I catch a glimpse of myself in an antique French gilt mirror as I walk the hall and surprise myself with how formidable I appear. I open the door to Arthur's outer office and nod at his two secretaries as I breeze past them. Once I pass them, I come face-to-face with Vincent Hendriks, Arthur's senior assistant (who smells strongly of blue cheese at all times). I lean in as close as possible without getting a whiff of cheese and ask if I can see my brother.

"Good morning, Your Highness," Vincent says with a warm smile. Then he whispers, "He's in a bit of a mood today so you may want to come back. Apparently, Prince James couldn't sleep last night so he was up with him until the sun came up."

Normally I'd take Vincent's solid advice. He's the best. In fact, I often wish he and Mrs. Chapman (my rather nasty assistant) would just switch jobs. But then I'd have to put up with the cheese smell.

Also, Arthur would never allow it. Vincent's his right-hand man. "I'm afraid it really can't wait."

Nodding, he says, "Of course," then picks up the phone and informs my brother I'm outside. After a pause, he says, "She didn't say but apparently it is quite urgent." There's another pause, then Vincent gives me an apologetic look. "How long will this take, Miss?"

Raising my voice, I say, "Tell him to stop being a wanker and let me in."

Vincent's mouth drops, then he hangs up. "Go right in."

Arthur's office is like an homage to dark academia with dark wooden bookshelves lining the walls and a massive mahogany desk at the far side of the room. He sits back in his chair and stares at me for a moment without speaking, then finally says, "Really? A wanker?"

"Sorry, but you often are."

"At least I didn't get trapped in a glass box in public with my knickers melting down to my shoes," he mutters.

"Do you often wear knickers, Arthur?" I ask.

He narrows his eyes. "What do you want?"

"I want you to help me screw over Dylan Sinclair."

Raising one eyebrow, a grin spreads across his face. "How can I be of service?"

———

Two minutes later, I'm on the way back to my office. I pull my phone out of my pocket and send a group text to Tessa and Nikki. *I actually did it. Arthur tweeted the announcement. I'm getting married on June 3rd, ladies!*

Nikki: *June 3rd?! Yay! This seems so real now.*

Me: *Doesn't it?*

Tessa: *You didn't tell Arthur I knew, did you?*

Me: *Of course not. But honestly, he's totally onboard for sticking it to Dylan Sinclair once and for all.*

———

It's Really Happening…and my Heart is Broken

Will's Wild Fangirls Blog Post 287

Hello fellow fangirls,

Prince Arthur tweeted this morning that he's thrilled to announce the wedding date of his sister (the very dull Princess Pukeface) to the King of Our Hearts, Will Banks.

June 3rd. As in less than eighty short days from now.

To say I'm devastated would be an understatement. My world has been shaken to the core like an 8.0 earthquake has struck. It took me nearly three hours to drag myself out of bed and over to my laptop to let you all know what has happened.

In addition, the palace media department just released a statement that the royal family has entered into a contract with ANN (Will's home network), not just for the television rights to the nuptials but also to pay for the damn thing! Like seriously? The royals can't afford to pay for it themselves?

Also, word on the street is Princess Pukeface bullied the royal staff AND the execs at ANN to push the wedding date to an impossible timeframe. That is SO her. Run, Will, run!!!

Anyway, I'm not giving up on my beloved. As hurt as I am that he wants to marry someone else, I know he's going to come to his senses soon because I am his destiny. NOT some dull as dishwater, prim and proper, probably can't hold her liquor, pampered princess.

I don't know how, but I will find a way to stop this insanity before they get to the I Do's.

Peace Out Bitches,
The Future Mrs. Will Banks (AKA Hannah Goble)

COMMENTS:

WillGirl25: I heard she went into King Winston's office and screamed until he agreed to it. Apparently, it was so loud, one of the staffers had to go home with a migraine.

Reply: FutureMrsBanks: Wouldn't surprise me. She's an awful person. All that charity work is just for show.

RealHouseWivesRock: I have a friend over at ABN who said that someone at ANN told her they didn't even know about the date until after the announcement. Now, they're all screwed, scrambling to get everything set up in time.

Reply: FutureMrsBanks: Wow. I'm totally checking my sources over there. We've got to get the word out on this story. Will needs to know who she really is before it's too late.

Chapter 8

FOUR-YEAR-OLD HEARTBREAKERS, FRUIT FORKS, AND HOT TO TROT DANCE INSTRUCTORS...

Will

"WOULD you like to take a break, sir?" Gregory asks with an overly-bright smile to hide what I'm sure is a significant level of disappointment.

I started my royal protocol lessons early this morning, and so far, I doubt anyone would call me a quick study. We're in the Petite Ballroom at the palace where various stations have been set up for me to practice bowing, eating various meals from a simple tea to state dinners, and ballroom dancing. I cannot think of a time I've enjoyed less than this one—and I'm including the night I spent in a ravine in the jungle with my ankle so badly broken, my right foot was aiming back at me. So, it's been a bad, bad day.

"Thanks, Gregory. I could use a break," I say before walking over to the refreshment cart and pouring myself a tall glass of water. I hope I'm drinking it properly, although somehow, I doubt it. After a few long gulps, I turn toward the round table with eight different place settings for me to memorize. I stroll over and start with number one, which is the six-course state dinner setup. I stare at the unusual cutlery, wishing they could just use sporks and knives, which is really all you need to eat any meal. I glance over at Gregory, who is sitting on a chair at the far end of the ballroom with his eyes closed, clearly worn out from the amount of patience I require.

Honestly, I can't remember a time when I felt this stupid. Reynard, my bodyguard, has been standing near the main entrance with a hopeful smile the entire time. Every once in a while, he gives me the thumbs-up. I know he's trying to be encouraging, but the truth is, having a witness as I repeatedly fail isn't exactly making me feel better.

I dig into the inside pocket of my suit jacket (attire which I was told was mandatory in the Petite Ballroom) and pull out the small flipchart Gregory made me. I spend the next couple of minutes on the cutlery identification page trying to memorize the difference between a fish fork and a fruit fork. It's subtle, believe me. My phone buzzes and I take it out and see a message from Emma: *Hey wanker, don't forget to call Clara. It's her birthday today.*

Nuts. I totally would have forgotten. Thank goodness for Emma. As much as we irritate each other, she's a good egg. I tell Gregory I need to make a quick call and make my way out into the hallway. I smile as I hit send on the video chat, excited to see the familiar faces of my family. After a moment, Harrison's face lights up the screen. He grins and says, "Hey, you remembered!"

"Of course I did," I lie.

"So it's just a coincidence that Emma sent you a text about it a few seconds ago."

Emma's face appears on the screen. "Haha! You're so busted!"

"Brilliant," I say. Did I say Emma was a good egg? I meant good and rotten.

Harrison shakes his head at me, but he's smiling so I'm sure he's not bothered by his forgetful brother. "Let me put the birthday girl on."

A moment later, my adorable redheaded niece grins at me. My heart squeezes at her chubby little face. I can't believe she's four already. She looks so much older than the last time I saw her. Guilt rips through me, but I tell myself not to worry. I'll see my family soon enough. Besides, she and I have such a strong bond, nothing could break it. I'm definitely her favourite uncle. "Happy birthday, Clara!" I say, waving into my phone screen.

Clara narrows her eyes and says, "Who's him?"

Who's him? She doesn't know me? That can't be. They're outside, so the screen is probably too dark to see me.

Harrison comes into view now, looking flustered. "You know Uncle Will, sweetheart. Daddy's little brother?"

She stares up at him and shakes her head. Oh wow. This hurts. My only niece doesn't know me?

I hear the sound of my sister-in-law, Libby, letting out an uncomfortable laugh, then she comes into view. "He and Auntie Arabella are the ones who sent you your giant teddy bear—Mr. Snuggles."

Clara looks back at me and says, "Thank you for the bear, Mr. Will." Then she takes off across the yard, leaving her parents with identical shocked expressions.

"Sorry, Will," Libby says. "Of course she knows who you are. She's just so excited about her party."

"Totally," Harrison adds, nodding vigorously. "She's also…in a bit of a mood today. Overstimulated."

Libby nods at Harrison. "It's true. She barely slept last night."

In the background, I can hear Clara holler, "Uncle Pierce is here! YAY!!!!!"

Libby winces and Harrison shuts his eyes for a second before telling Libby he's going to take the call inside where it's quiet.

I wait patiently for him to walk into their house and shut the sliding doors that lead to their kitchen. "Okay, now I'll be able to hear you better. How are you?"

Devastated. "Good, yeah. Busy getting ready for my trip to Bolivia and trying to prepare for the wedding."

"I bet. About the wedding, I'm really sorry about Rosy," he says. "I had no idea she was going to pull that at the meeting."

"Oh, don't worry about it. My fault entirely. She emailed me ahead of time and I didn't get back to her."

His smile fades. "Seriously?"

"Yeah, well, I didn't know you guys would be at the planning meeting. Arabella invited you, so…" Now that I'm saying this out loud, I can see how bad it is.

He blinks a couple of times, then says, "I see."

"Oh, man, I just meant I didn't invite *anyone* to the meeting. The thing is, I haven't been all that involved in the whole wedding so far. I'm never here so Arabella's had to shoulder all of it herself. But if I had been around, I definitely would have thought to include you guys."

"Right, sure," Harrison says with a tight smile.

I sigh. "I'm making a real mess of everything, aren't I?"

"A little bit, yeah," he tells me, looking disappointed, which is the worst thing he can do to me.

Disappointing a brother like Harrison, who pretty much gave up his entire youth for my sister and me, is like punching a little old lady. You can't do it and still pretend to be a good person. "I…I'm going to call Rosy and make it up to her."

"Yeah, you should definitely do that. I'm sure it really hurt her feelings that you couldn't be bothered to get back to her."

"I'm sorry. Half the time, I don't know if I'm coming or going. Not that it's an excuse, but…it's just been really nuts," I tell him. "I've been traveling almost constantly and now I'm also studying these manuals about royal protocol and etiquette. Today, I'm spending the entire day doing lessons—how to eat, how to bow, how to dance, unacceptable words to use in the presence of the family."

"Yeah, we got that booklet too."

My head snaps back. "What?"

Harrison nods. "It came in the mail yesterday. Ten copies for us to memorize and pass around."

I let out a long puff of air. "Oh, wow. I had no idea. I'm sure Arabella didn't either. She would have gone through the roof if she knew the advisors were going to make you guys feel uncomfortable."

"She actually included a handwritten note to us," Harrison says.

My chest feels tight all of a sudden. "Really? What did it say?"

"That she's so excited to have us join her family and to be joining ours, and that the handbook might help us feel more at ease at the wedding."

I open my mouth, then close it, not having the first clue how to respond.

"Don't worry about it," Harrison says. "It's no big deal. Besides, she's not wrong. Emma marrying Pierce was one thing, but you marrying a princess? Whole other level of terror. Having a study guide is probably not a bad thing."

Rubbing the back of my neck, I say, "It's not exactly a good one either. Was anyone offended?"

One of the pages walks by and I hope he isn't listening to the conversation. God, I hate having zero privacy.

"Rosy and Darnell were a little put out, to be honest, but Libby's on board. She got straight to work making flash cards for everyone. Pierce already knows all of it, and Emma's had more than a few laughs at your expense."

The sliding door opens, and Clara comes running into the kitchen. "Dad! I need a juice box!"

"That's not how you ask, Peanut," he says.

"PULLEEEEAAAASSSEEE!" she yells.

"All right, one second," he tells her, then he brings me along for the walk to the fridge. "Anyway, it's all good. We'll be ready to arrive without embarrassing you."

"You guys could never embarrass me. Well, maybe if Rosy brought Starsky and Hutch..." Those are her humpy Jack Russell terriers.

Harrison offers me a hint of a smile, instead of a laugh like he normally would, then hands the juice box to Clara. Damn, he is upset. "Listen, I'm glad you called because I have some news that Libby and I have been wanting to share with you, but we never seem to get a chance."

"Oh yeah?" *They're having another baby.*

"We're having another baby," he says with a grin.

Act super-surprised. "Really? That's wonderful, man! When?"

"Middle of July."

"Whoa! That's coming right up. How's Libby feeling?"

"Pukey, starving, emotional, exhausted...the usual at this stage of the game."

"That's great. Well, not how she's feeling—that sounds awful—but about the baby," I say. Feeling slightly put out, I add, "I can't believe you didn't tell me."

"We were going to tell you last month when you were supposed to be here, but you never made it."

"Right," I tell him. "Of course. Well, never mind that. Congratulations to you both! I'm thrilled for you."

"Thanks," he says. "We're pretty thrilled ourselves."

He stares at me for a second, then says, "Can I ask you something?"

Can I say no? "Sure."

"Did you pick out that big bear yourself or did someone do it for you?" he asks.

I briefly wish the connection would fail so I wouldn't have to answer that question. "I...um...well, they have people who do that sort of thing. People who are much better at it than me. Why? Does she not like the bear?"

Harrison's eyes harden at the truth and my heart sinks to my stomach. "She loves the bear. It's a little...over the top though. Takes up half her bedroom."

Shit. "Sorry about that. I'll do my own shopping from now on. I just asked my assistant to take care of it because I was in Borneo longer than I expected and I wanted to make sure it got to her on time."

Shrugging, Harrison says, "No, it's no big deal. I just wanted to know."

"Are we okay?" I ask him.

"Sure, yeah. Relationships change, right?" Harrison says. "Your life has taken you in a new direction and that's a good thing. As long as you're happy, I'm happy."

"You don't seem happy," I tell him.

"I'll be fine. I just need to know what to expect going forward. Things are going to be different. And that's okay. Anyway, I gotta go. I have a birthday party to run here, then I should probably memorize the new rules of being your brother." He smiles to soften the blow of his words, but it really doesn't work.

I swallow hard, feeling like I'm not much above stagnant pond scum in the order of things. "Harrison, I'm really sorry about all of this. I know I promised to make you guys a priority and I haven't lived up to my word."

"Yeah, you're kind of doing a shit job of it, to be honest."

"You're right, I am," I tell him. "Listen, I'm going to get out of the contract with ANN as soon as the wedding is over. We gave them exclusive rights to everything in exchange for ripping up my contract. I promise that once that's done, I'll be around more."

Harrison stares at me, then says, "I hope so."

"Seriously, I will."

"Don't write cheques you can't cash."

Shit.

"I gotta go. Stay safe in Bolivia." With that, he hangs up. I end the call and tap my phone on my forehead a few times as penance. I am the world's worst brother. My own niece doesn't even know me.

I start dialing Rosy's number so I can apologize and beg her forgiveness, but Gregory clears his throat. I turn, hoping he didn't hear any of that. "We really should resume our lessons, sir."

"Of course," I tell him, pocketing my phone and following him into the ballroom.

I put on a grin and pretend everything is fine, even though I've hurt everyone who matters to me in the world, other than my fiancée. Speaking of her, I can't help but feel irritation clawing at my insides when I think of my future bride. She really should have told me she was sending the handbooks so I could tell her not to. Also, she didn't tell me my family would be at the meeting. And, possibly worst of all, I am starting to second-guess whether my future is going to be anywhere close to what I want it to be, because so far, things are *very much* the opposite.

Gregory and I make our way over to the table to go over the settings again. After I go through each piece of cutlery, getting them all wrong of course, he says, "Try not to get discouraged, sir. I'm throwing a lot at you at once, but we don't have to learn it all in one day. We've got several months to practice. You'll have this all down pat in plenty of time."

I nod and offer him a grateful smile, even though inside I'm calculating the actual number of weeks that I'll be here over the next six months, and it only adds up to about four. But, truth be told, four weeks is probably all I can stand of this. Four well-spaced-out weeks. I glance at my watch. Oh, bollocks, it's only noon. I was hoping it was almost four in the afternoon so we could be done already.

"Perhaps now would be a good time to practice with actual food," Gregory says. "I've taken the liberty of ordering a four-course lunch. I thought maybe if you saw the tools in action, it might stick a little better. While we're waiting, why don't we take a break from meals and move on to proper bowing order at the second station?"

I glance over at the grouping of chairs with pieces of paper taped to the backs of them, each with the names of my future in-laws on it. I stand and make my way over. "Okay, let's do this."

Two hours later, I have bowed until I can feel it in my hamstrings and consumed a heavy lunch including Peking Duck Consommé, Escargots with Shallot Mousse and Parsley Coulis, Beef Wellington with a side of French beans, and a strawberry tart on a Breton short-bread-style base with *Crème à la Verveine* (whatever that is) for dessert. And now that I'm about to slip into a food coma, my ballroom dance instructor has shown up—an extremely tall, thin, middle-aged woman dressed in a flowy light blue gown, along with a short woman who looks like she's in her eighties.

Gregory rushes over to meet them. "Madame Truffaut, Mrs. Murphy. Lovely to see you again."

After they give each other quick air kisses, Gregory turns and introduces me and tells me Mme. Truffaut is one of the best dance instructors in the kingdom and Mrs. Murphy is her pianist. Mrs. Murphy gives me a bored nod, then makes a beeline for the grand piano in the corner while Mme. Truffaut hurries toward me as though she knows there's no time to lose. "Mr. Banks, look at you!" She says in a thick French accent.

Oh, this is weird. She's squeezing my biceps. And now she's pressing both hands to my chest as she looks me up and down. I feel totally violated. I don't think I want to learn to dance after all.

Finally, her eyes come back to mine and she removes her hands from my body. "Yes, we've got a lot to work with here. Have you had any formal dance training?"

Yes, yes, I have. A lot actually. In fact, this should be the easiest part of my day. "My family's resort offers salsa lessons, so I used to stand in for guests without a partner from time to time. I can do a mean salsa," I tell her with a broad smile.

Her expression morphs from overly excited to utter disdain. "No, salsa is no good. What about the waltz? Surely you must know this?"

I shake my head.

"Tango? Foxtrot? Quickstep?"

As she lists them off on her fingers, I continue to shake my head.

"Never mind," she says, glancing at my pecs again. *Eyes up here, lady.* "I'm sure you're going to be a quick study. Let us waltz like lovers."

Oh no. Let us not.

———

Okay, so according to the clock it's only been an hour, but it feels like at least six years since this 'dance lesson' started. If you could call it that. It's more like me being repeatedly groped by a horny French woman under the guise of teaching me to waltz. Oh, and to make matters worse, she alternates between groping and yelling at me when I mess up. I've stepped on her toes at least a dozen times now and each time it happens, she mutters, "Ouch! *Merde*," or my favourite, "*Toi idiot!*" which causes me to get more flustered, which means I inevitably do it again, only sooner this time. You know what else has me flustered? Her hand on my left buttock. I should really have some sort of signal for Reynard when I'm being sexually violated.

Like, right now.

Seriously, no one else sees this? She's kneading my cheek. *Kneading!*

I let go of her and jump back, yelling, "I'm getting married!"

Mrs. Murphy stops playing, and the room goes dead silent.

"Yes, I know this. It is why we are doing these lessons," Mme. Truffaut tells me, shaking her head.

Lowering my voice, I say, "Is *that* really necessary?"

"What?" she asks, looking completely confused, even though I know damn well she knows what she was doing.

"You were kneading my butt cheek. I don't see how that is going to help me learn to waltz."

"Kneading? What is this word?" she asks loudly.

I mime the action of kneading. "You know? Like what you do to bread dough? Squeezing? Kneading."

She stares at me for a second, looking like I just slapped her in the face. "You think I'm...how you say...hitting on you?"

"A little bit, yeah," I say. "Isn't your right hand supposed to be on my shoulder, not my rear end?"

"But, of course it would be if we were *dancing*, but I do this to try to get you to relax so you can feel the flow of the music," she says, then she bursts out laughing. "You think I want to make sex with you?"

My face heats up with humiliation because she basically yelled that, and I can practically feel the wind from Gregory's jaw dropping. "No, I didn't—"

"You silly Avonians. So uptight when it comes to the body. It is not working when I touch your bottom?"

'No. In fact, it's having the opposite effect."

The doors to the ballroom open, and in walks Arabella. There's a part of me that wants to rush over to her and tell on Mme. Handsy. She'd put a stop to it. No, wait. I'm an adult and I'm already doing that.

Arabella grins at me, then spots Mme. Truffaut and her eyes light up. They hurry toward each other with their arms out for a long embrace. Then they start speaking in French while I listen carefully for my name in case my dance instructor is telling Arabella to call the whole thing off. *He is a complete buffoon. He thinks I want to make sex with him. Also, he is a terrible dancer. Do not marry him, cheri.*

And now Arabella is probably saying, *"Yes, I know, but I already said yes so I can't get out of it now."*

They link arms and walk in my direction, still chatting excitedly. When they reach me, Arabella says, "Darling, you are *so lucky* to have

Mme. Truffaut. She taught me ballet and ballroom for what?" she asks, turning to Mme. Truffaut. "Twelve years?"

Twelve years? Poor Arabella's bottom.

"At least. The princess is a pleasure to work with—such a quick study," she tells me. "If she were not already a royal with important humanitarian work to do, she most certainly could have danced for the Avonian National Ballet."

"She's being very kind, I assure you," Arabella says. "So? How are the lessons coming? I'm sure Will is sailing through at record pace since he's one of the most coordinated people I've met."

Mme. Truffaut lets her eyes land on my torso again and says something in French, but I distinctly hear a word that sounds timid.

"No," Arabella answers. "Not at all inhibited." She looks up at me. "Are you all right, darling? Mme. Truffaut thinks you are not enjoying your lesson? Is something making you nervous?"

Uh, yeah. Mme. Gropey over here is making me pretty damn nervous. "There was one little thing, but I think Mme. Truffaut and I were just about to sort that out actually."

"Brilliant!" Arabella says. "Can I watch?"

Are you kidding me? Please, floor, open up and swallow me whole. I have to get out of here.

"*Certainement*," Mme. Truffaut says, snapping her fingers at poor Mrs. Murphy. The music starts up again and we take our positions. This time, Mme. Truffaut puts her hands where they should go.

Things start out well enough, with her counting out the steps. I'm keeping up and starting to feel like I might have it. Then, she squeezes my upper arm and makes a little moaning sound which causes me to jerk back while letting out a high-pitched yipping sound like a little girl.

The music stops mid-bar and Arabella, who is standing only a few feet away, says, "Oh dear. I see what you mean, Mme. He is extremely tense."

Mme. Gropy nods. "Perhaps we should end for today and try again when he is not so afraid of waltzing."

Afraid? I'm not afraid of waltzing. I've jumped off the Cascata del Salto in Switzerland, for God's sake.

74

Before I can set the record straight, she pats me on the arm. "Not everyone can have the heart of a dancer, but if we work together twice a week for the next year, you should be almost passable."

Arabella's face drops. "I'm afraid we won't have that much time. The date has been set as June third and Will is going to be away a lot between now and the wedding."

The older woman bursts out laughing, then glances at Arabella and stops short. "You're serious."

"Yes."

"June third?" I ask, my brain just now catching up with the news. "When did that happen?"

"A few minutes ago." She gives me a wink and drops her voice. "I'll explain later."

"This is not possible," Mme. Truffaut says. "You will end up swaying in a circle like a couple of...how you say...nitwits."

Nitwits? She knows that word, but not the word knead? *Come on.*

"I must go now," Mme. Truffaut says. "Gregory, please email me with every hour that Mr. Banks is available between now and the wedding." With that, she snaps at Mrs. Murphy, then floats out of the room, leaving me with a strong desire to have a long shower. But, first things first. I need to deal with the fact that, as of a few minutes ago, I'll have to learn everything there is to know about being a royal husband in an impossibly short amount of time.

———

"How did this happen?" I ask Arabella as soon as we're alone in her apartment. I'm mad. Like, steaming mad, to be honest. First, she sends those stupid handbooks to my family without asking, then she sets the date without talking to me first. What's next? I'm almost scared to find out. I'm going to stay calm though. No sense in overreacting, right?

"Well, last night I was having dinner with Tessa and Nikki —"

"Right, Manbash Mondays, I know," I say, a sense of impatience taking over.

"I'll change the name of that now that we're together. You know, we would never bash you, right?" She reaches out and pats me on the hand in an extremely condescending way that tells me she most certainly has bashed me at one point or another—hopefully only when we broke up. But from the look on her face…

"Anyway," she says, sliding her hand away from me. "I was telling them about Dylan and the offer, and it occurred to me that the longer we drag out the pre-wedding phase, the longer you're stuck working for her. Which means that each day between us signing the contract and the wedding is a day that she wins. And we can't let her win, Will. Not this time. I—I mean, *you* need to win this time around."

I stare at her for a moment, slightly shocked at what I'm hearing. My lovely, generous, ultra-compassionate princess has a crazed look in her eyes as she talks about winning. "But… how did you even get anyone to agree to it?"

"Simple, really. I realized if we announce the date publicly, the network won't be able to do anything about it. So, I got Arthur to tweet it." She stands and starts walking over to the kitchen, calling over her shoulder, "Would you like some tea? I'm going to make myself a cup."

"No, thank you. I'm actually still full from lunch," I say, following her. I actually would like some tea, but I'm too angry to admit it.

She busies herself with the kettle and I can't help but get the feeling she's trying to avoid eye contact with me. "Just think—this next trip of yours will be *the last one* on her terms. After this, you can go anywhere, work for anyone, or no one. You could be your own boss if you want. And we can start house hunting, start planning our future…" She grins over her shoulder at me, then her smile fades. "What's wrong? You don't look happy. I thought you would be happy."

"You really should have asked me. From my end of things, this is all pretty overwhelming." I rub the back of my neck with one hand to release the tension. "There is *so much* to learn and, to be honest, I'm not really good at any of it. Like none of it. Not even the damn spoons. I mean, does *anyone* really know the difference between a bouillon spoon and a cream soup spoon?"

"Oh, that's easy. The bouillon spoon has the more shallow bowl because it's for—"

I hold up one hand, stopping her mid-sentence. "It's *not* easy for me."

"Well, I'm happy to tutor you, darling. My nanny had a fun little rhyme about spoons. Let me see if I can remember it."

Sighing, I say, "It's not about the spoons. It's about us deciding things together *and* me not wanting to make a fool of myself at our wedding in front of the entire planet!" I'm almost yelling now. I need to rein it in. "Is there any way we can move it back a few months?"

"No! We can't. It's too late. It's already been announced." She starts blinking quickly, then the kettle whistles and she turns away from me.

Oh great, she's upset.

But you know who else is upset? *ME!*

I've had to put up with *a lot* so far, and there's more coming. I take a deep breath and summon all the patience I possess (and it's not much at the moment). "Try to see it from my side. I'm doing my best to get ready so I won't humiliate you, but you could help me out here by at least giving me time to prepare."

She turns to me and says, "You could never embarrass me."

"I don't think that's true," I tell her. "I'm already Sir Knight of the No Shirt, which is going over like a lead balloon among your crowd."

"And that's precisely why we need to get you away from Dylan as swiftly as possible." Opening the cupboard, she takes out a box of chocolate digestive biscuits. "Are you sure you wouldn't at least like a digestive?"

"No thanks," I say, my gut churning with the knowledge that there's no possible way I'll be ready in time.

"Look, I completely understand that you're worried, but honestly, you'll be fine. Fake it 'til you make it, right?"

"That only works if a billion people aren't watching you fake it," I grumble.

Arabella plants one hand on her hip. "Why do I get the feeling there's more bothering you than a tight timeline?"

Shoving my hands in the front pockets of my dress pants, I say,

"That's because there *are* a few things that are bothering me. Big ones, starting with the fact that I feel like a pawn in a game between you and Dylan."

Arabella's head snaps back. "A pawn?! What are you talking about?"

"You said it by accident when we first started talking—you want to beat Dylan at her own game. This is about you and Dylan."

Scoffing, she says, "Can you blame me for wanting to get back at that awful woman after what she tried to do to my family?"

"No, but—"

"But what? Are you telling me you actually *want* to continue working under those terrible conditions?"

"You're making it sound like I'm in a coal mine all day," I say with a shrug. "I host a nature show."

"You know what I meant," Arabella answers. "I can't believe you're actually upset about this. If I didn't know any better, I'd think you are having second thoughts about the wedding."

"Do not try to turn this around on me. You're the one that decided to stoop to Dylan's level. Not to mention, you did it without bothering to consult me about it."

"Only because I thought you would be thrilled."

"Do you know how mad you would be at me if I pulled something like this without talking to you first? We actually broke up over it."

A sheepish look crosses her face. "Okay, you may have a point there."

"Yeah, I have a point."

"I'm sorry. I should've talk to you about it first."

"Yes, you should have," I say, raising my voice slightly.

She walks over to me, taking hold of both my hands and rubbing the backs of them with her thumbs. I mentally prepare myself to accept her apology and hear some sweet sentiments about how much I mean to her. But then, she speaks... "Come on. Isn't there just the tiniest bit of you that is happy to screw her over? I mean, just the teensiest bit? Here she thought that we would jump at this contract without even realizing how long she could keep you," she says, with a wide grin that looks like a cross between a smile and a wild animal baring its teeth. "For her, it was a no-brainer—she probably assumed it would take a good eighteen months, or two years even, at which point your contract would be almost done. And the whole time, she'd be getting exactly what she wants—she'd have you under her thumb *and* she'd have the rights to our wedding. And I took that from her today. In under three short months, you will be free from her forever. Just think of that. Will the staff be pissed?" She nods. "But they'll get over it. And at the end of the day, you and I win for once. Don't you want to win, Will?"

"What I want is to be on the same team as you."

"The same *winning* team, right?" she asks with a hopeful smile. When I don't smile back, she lets her shoulders drop. "Okay, fair enough. I messed up and I can admit it. And I promise I will never do anything like this again without speaking to you first," she says, reaching up on her tiptoes to give me a kiss on the cheek. "I'm really sorry. But I did do this with you in mind too. Are we okay?" she asks, looking concerned.

"Not really," I tell her.

She takes a step back. "What do you mean?"

"I spoke with Harrison today. He told me you sent my family the etiquette handbooks."

Her face fills with confusion. "Won't that be helpful for them?"

"It's a little insulting, to be honest," I say. "I mean, it's like saying 'Here are the rules to being acceptable for us.'"

Gasping, Arabella says, "That's not how I meant it and you know it! I only thought it would help them feel more comfortable. I even wrote a note to that effect."

"He told me, but *again*, this is something you should have checked with me about before you did it."

Ignoring my last comment, Arabella says, "Are they hurt? The last thing I wanted to do was to hurt their feelings."

"They're fine. Rosy was a bit put out, but Harrison and Libby are already studying, and Emma just finds it hilarious. In fact, I'll never hear the end of it, I'm sure."

"Damn. I am so sorry," Arabella says. "How can I fix it?"

"Just don't do it again."

"Well, I have to do something to make it up to them," she says, and from the look on her face, I can see her mind is spinning again.

"Just please, whatever you come up with, run it by me first."

"Of course," Arabella answers. Letting out a long sigh, she says, "I really am sorry. About everything."

I nod, starting to feel less angry. "This wedding is going to be stressful for both of us, so it's absolutely key that we stick together here."

"Absolutely. I promise, from now on, everything goes through you." She reaches up and gives me a soft kiss on the lips. "And don't worry about all the silly royal protocol stuff. I'll be with you the entire day. Most of it you can fake by just following my lead."

"And if I can't?"

"Then I'll whisper the answers to you."

Chapter 9

TEN-POUND PREEMIES

Arabella

EMAIL FROM DYLAN SINCLAIR to Princess Arabella and Will Banks
   Subject: Wedding Contract

Dear Arabella and Will,
   Thank you for returning the signed contract so quickly. I'm more than a little miffed about you jumping the gun on the announcement—especially the date. I'm afraid we won't be able to whip up the world's most glorious wedding in under three months. How about June 22nd of next year?
   Warmest regards,
   Dylan

Email from Princess Arabella
   To: Dylan Sinclair
   cc: Will Banks
   Subject: RE: Wedding Contract

Dear Dylan,

The date is non-negotiable, but I know it won't be a problem for you, being the miracle worker that you are. You'll put together the best team and get the job done with plenty of time to spare.

Alternatively, we can just rip up the contract. It'll take my staff all of one phone call to find a more agreeable network.

All the best,
Princess Arabella

————

Email from Dylan Sinclair
To: Princess Arabella, Will Banks
Subject: RE: RE: Wedding Contract

Dear Princess Arabella,
Hard ball, is it? Fine. We'll go ahead and rush it if that's really what you want (even though it may very well be a total disaster), BUT I'm going to need a lot more airtime from you. I'll want cameras with you both most of the time leading up to the big day—dress fittings, family gatherings, cake tasting…EVERY-THING. We'll stream live and have a weekly round-up on the network every Thursday. If this is a no, then we tear up the contract.

Regards,
Dylan

————

Email from Princess Arabella
To: Dylan Sinclair

cc: Will Banks
Subject: RE: RE: RE: Wedding Contract

Dear Dylan,

After lengthy discussions with Will and some of the senior advisors, we are willing to accept your new terms with the following caveat: You may have access to wedding-related events only and will not be allowed to film whilst either of us are working on charitable causes, regular royal duties, or other non-wedding-related business.

I shall have our attorneys work that into a new version of the contract and will send it to you shortly.

Regards,
Arabella

———

Email from Dylan Sinclair
To: Princess Arabella, Will Banks
Subject: RE: RE: RE: RE: Wedding Contract

Dear William and Princess Arabella,

Agreed. I'll have the planning and execution team ready to roll by tomorrow morning so we can immerse ourselves in creating the greatest speed wedding of all time. I've already got one of the best in the biz at the ready (after a hefty retainer).

Know that I intend to get every minute I can out of Will's existing contract.

Regards,
Dylan

———

ABN Evening News with Giles Bigly

"Good evening, I'm Giles Bigly, and this is your ABN Evening News. Our top story tonight—an explosive announcement from Valcourt palace today as the royal family sets a date and shares some surprising wedding plans." Giles stares intently at the camera as the screen splits and Zachary Jones appears, standing in front of the palace gates which are lit up from below against the night sky. "Zachary Jones is live at Valcourt Palace to give us more details. Zachary, what exactly is going on?"

"Yes, hello, Giles. Can you hear me?"

"I can hear you Zachary. Please go ahead," Giles says, looking slightly agitated.

"Oh, good. Shocking news today from the royal family as Princess Arabella's wedding date is set for June third, less than twelve weeks from today. "According to the statement from the palace, and I quote: 'Mr. Banks' extremely tight filming schedule, as well as Princess Arabella's many charitable obligations—specifically her work for the United Nations Equal Everywhere Campaign – were the driving forces behind the selection of such a quickly-approaching date.'"

"Zachary, this is quite unusual for a royal wedding, is it not?" Giles asks, needling his eyebrows together in a most intelligent way.

"Yes, the average time frame is approximately eighteen months in the planning and execution of a royal wedding. When Prince Arthur and Princess Tessa were married, they insisted on a six-month turn-around and it appears as though Princess Arabella has decided to push the royal staff even harder."

"What a difficult task, indeed. As we all know, there are dozens of moving parts when it comes to an affair of this magnitude. It's surprising that this senior royal, who is normally so gracious, is possibly turning into a real bridezilla."

Zachary chuckles, then says, "Indeed. The Internet is abuzz with this news as royal watchers take to the message boards to discuss this monumental decision."

Giles nods. "And what seems to be the verdict online?"

Zachary glances at his notepad, then says, "A real mishmash of opinions, to be honest. Obviously, there are a number of people who believe a royal accident is the true cause. In fact, this particular theory seems to have taken hold among the bookies who are now paying 2 to 5 odds on an heir appearing within six months of now."

"Perhaps a ten-pound preemie will be on the way," Giles chuckles.

Zachary laughs along, then says, "No doubt. Other people online are suggesting that Arabella is actually a royal nightmare who bullied everyone into making this happen on *her* preferred timeline."

Shaking his head, Giles says, "Shocking, really. She has this snow-white reputation, but maybe she's a bit of a wolf in a sheep's skin."

"Could be."

"Is anyone siding with Princess Arabella on this?"

"No. It appears as though the Internet has decided she's just this side of being canceled."

"Wow," Giles says. "Zachary, there is more to this story that has come as quite a surprise to the kingdom. Can you fill us in on that?"

Zachary narrows his eyes. "Which bit exactly?"

"The *network* bit," Giles says through gritted teeth.

"Oh, right, yes. It seems as though, rather than going with the traditional network, us here at ABN, Princess Arabella and William Banks have sold the exclusive right to their wedding-airing production to our sister network, ANN, or the Avonian Nature Network for those who are not familiar, for an undisclosed amount."

"That seems a rather odd choice for a wedding, does it not?" Giles asks, stroking his chin thoughtfully.

"Indeed, but perhaps less so when you think about the fact that William Banks is their most popular personality. We're not sure exactly how this deal came about, but there are those who suspect that William is the driving force behind this. Perhaps because he's got a definite familiarity with the executives and staff at ANN."

"Interesting," Giles says. "If that is, in fact, how this happened, it would seem that this is one groom who definitely wants to be a driving force behind his wedding, rather than someone who merely shows up in time for the nuptials."

"One blogger suggested that ANN is the perfect network due to their experience in large-scale live productions such as their *World's Best Survivor Challenge*. They certainly do have several crews who are adept at pulling things together on location without the luxury of having a lot of time to set up. They call it guerrilla filming and possibly it could work for a wedding, I suppose."

"A guerilla royal wedding? How odd, indeed."

"Quite right. Well, we'll certainly find out soon enough if they can pull it off, won't we?"

"Indeed, we will. It'll be sink or swim for ANN because an estimated 1.5 billion people will be watching," Zachary adds.

Giles smiles confidently. "Exciting news. Keep it here on ABN News as we count down to the big day and keep you abreast of every detail as this story unfolds."

"I, for one, am going to be very curious to see whether or not the bridezilla assumption comes to fruition."

"As are most people," Giles answers. "We did see her fiery side when she shoved Dylan Sinclair, the now-vice president of programming at ANN, to the ground. So it's not entirely impossible to imagine that this normally-docile young woman may have a real fiery side when it comes to the most important day in any woman's life."

Footage of Arabella reaching up and shoving Dylan in the face starts to roll, ending with Dylan sliding backwards in the mud. When the clip ends, the split screen with the two newsmen appears again.

Giles shakes his head and laughs. "I'll never get sick of that clip. Is it bad of me to admit that?"

"Probably, but I must confess I share your opinion," Zachary answers.

"Okay, thanks, Zachary," Giles says as his face fills the screen. "That was Zachary Jones live on location at Valcourt Palace. Up next, a fundraiser for the Valcourt Kite Flyers Association ends in tangled kites and a giant brawl. We'll have that and tomorrow's weather forecast after these messages."

———

"Bloody bastards," I say under my breath even though I'm alone. I dig around the covers on my bed to find the remote and shut off the TV, then toss the remote to the foot of the bed. I imitate Giles. "I'll never get sick of the clip. Hardy-har-har, what very funny men."

Why did I watch that? I had to know that the media was going to find a way to make me look terrible, and of course they did. Sighing, I lift my lap desk up and set it to the side, then climb off the bed and go in search of some ice cream.

I'm supposed to be preparing for my first meeting with the production team and our wedding planning team tomorrow. Dylan must have gotten over how 'miffed' she was at me for making the announcement because she had both teams set up within a couple of hours. I didn't mean it when I wrote it, but she really is a bit of a miracle worker.

The woman in charge of the wedding, a seasoned event planner named Imogen Arbuckle, emailed a lengthy list of questions for Will and me to answer before we meet. Will is at the ABN Studios tonight as a guest judge on *Avonia's Got Talent*, so I imagine he'll be up very late tonight filling in this inane questionnaire. We're not supposed to share answers with each other because Imogen says it's her job to take both of our dreams and make them a blended reality — whatever the hell that means.

To be honest, I'm a little out of sorts after our argument the other day. We managed to leave things on a good note, but I still can't help but feel like I'm messing everything up. The last thing I wanted to do was upset anyone. Well, Dylan, I suppose. I definitely don't mind her being the injured party for once. But that's it. Instead, I have put Will into a total panic to be ready in time, *and* I offended his family with the stupid handbooks. What was I thinking? Argh!

I grab a spoon out of the drawer, slam it shut, then take a pint of Chunky Choco Monkey out of the freezer, rip the lid off, toss it in the sink, then take the entire carton back to bed with me. When I climb into bed, the stupid newscast—if you can call that trash the news— pops into my mind again. "Bridezilla?! How about a fiercely protective fiancée looking out for her man? How about that for a news story?"

I settle myself back on my bed and have another big mouthful of ice cream. After a moment, the creamy treat calms my senses enough to get back to work. I pick up the forms and get started.

Question One: Provide three adjectives that describe your perfect wedding.

Picking up my pen, I write: *elegant, simple, unfussy.*

Is unfussy a word? Whatever, I'm leaving it.

I shovel a large spoonful into my mouth, daring brain freeze to kick in as the indulgent chocolatey goodness slides over my tongue. Flipping through the pages, I see I have only one answer down and sixty-two more to go. I'm tempted to just write, "Anything's fine because I'm the least-picky bride of all time," but then I think better of it. I mean, after all, what if this Imogen person has terrible taste and I end up with a laughingstock of a wedding? We can't have that now, can we? There's no way Will would like that.

Question Two: Provide examples of weddings you've attended that fit your concept of ideal and what were the exact elements of those weddings that you especially like?

Groaning, I sit back on my pillows and have another bite of ice cream. Well, that's hardly fair, it's a two-parter.

Meghan Markle and Prince Harry - Understated elegance.

Arthur and Tessa — Intimate North Country setting, casual feel to it.

An hour later, I'm filled with regret and ice cream and I'm only on question thirty which, as I glance over the next ten questions, I see is the start to a deep dive into what she terms my 'bridal psyche.'

Question Thirty-Two: Think back to age fourteen. What type of wedding did you imagine at that age?

"How the hell am I expected to remember that? Hire a hypnotist?" I mutter.

Snapping my fingers, I realize I *do* in fact have a way to find that out. I get out of bed and hurry down the hall to my den, open the closet, and start searching through the marked boxes of childhood memorabilia. My wedding dream album sits neatly on the top of the box marked 'Teenage Arabella,' exactly where I left it after I made the mistake of showing it to Tessa and Nikki. I pluck it out of the box, then hurry out of the room, shutting the light off and making my way back to bed.

Flipping through it, I open the first page and roll my eyes at what

I've written. In big loopy letters with all the I's dotted with hearts, it says:

This book is dedicated to my future husband.
Even though we haven't met, I already love you.
You are my heart. You are my everything.

Oh brother. Fourteen-year-old me was a sappy moron.

I flip through it as quickly as possible, hoping for some type of answer that won't make me sound like a complete idiot. Pink unicorn—no. Puffy peach bridesmaid dresses—absolutely not. How was that ever a thing? Random picture of Disney's Sleeping Beauty in the blue gown. Still love that damn dress.

Photo of Patrick Dempsey in tuxedo. I flip to the next page, then stop. "Well, actually, that is rather nice."

It's a photograph of an old stone church filled with wisteria vines that drop down from the ceiling. The next several pages are all similar in nature in that they include pictures of various tree- and flower-filled churches, twinkly lights and candles everywhere. There's even an outdoor wedding set in a forest with an enormous wooden arbor covered in vines and a happy couple standing with their hands joined underneath it. I wonder how they're doing now. I hope they're still so in love.

I slow my pace and look at each page, carefully eying the pictures and imagining Will and I smiling at each other in each setting. After a few minutes, I hear myself let out a wistful sigh and realize that *this* is what I want—something completely romantic with greenery and warm lights and butterflies flitting about and even a couple of birds sitting atop the rafters singing sweetly. Although, I suppose one of them might let a poo go, which wouldn't be all that pleasant, especially if it lands on one of the guests.

Okay, so not that, but I do know I don't want to stand in a stark, stone church with a few tall flowerpots set out here and there. I want the fairy-tale. I want the dream.

Bugger. That's not convenient at all, really. Not if I'm going to avoid the bridezilla reputation that is already teetering on the edge of becoming public perception. I *do* want to give very exact instructions for every last detail of the day. But I can't really do that if I'm pretending — I mean if I'm *going* to be a very Zen bride who has a mature outlook on life and is to be respected wherever she goes. And let's face it, I had to fight way too hard to get anyone to respect me. I'm not going to lose an inch of ground I've gained over a wedding. No way.

Closing the book, I give a firm nod (to whom, I don't know. Me, maybe?), then I stare at it, my heart aching just the tiniest bit and calling "Have the fairy-tale, Arabella."

Hmm…I suppose what happens behind the scenes doesn't necessarily have to become public knowledge, does it?

Unless it does….and it *always* does.

Dammit.

On the form, I jot down *natural elements at the wedding and reception*, and in brackets, I add *to honour Will's beloved career.*

There, that ought to move things in the proper direction without making it seem like I have any needs whatsoever. I flip the page to the wisteria-filled church again and my heart fills with longing. I'm suddenly desperate to have that. Why not, right? Why can't I care about the world *and* my wedding? The two aren't mutually exclusive, are they?

I glance up at the telly and see those reporters' sneering faces again in my mind. Double damn. They are not compatible. I must choose. I either need to be a very sensible, practical bride, which would prove that I'm mature and have my priorities straight. Or I can be a very silly, whimsical bride, which says the exact opposite. And I choose my reputation over the fairy-tale. After all, my wedding is one day, my reputation is forever.

Closing the book, I lean back on my pillow for a second, tapping my fingers on my lap desk. I can let go of the dream. I'm *thirty*, for goodness' sake. I stand and scoop up the album, my carton of shame, and the spoon, and walk back to the kitchen, tossing the spoon in the sink and depositing the album and the carton in the trash. "I choose sensible."

The teenager in me wants to grab the album back out and clean it off, then clutch it to my chest forever. Well, not forever. That would be ridiculous. But at least put it back in the box. But no. I won't.

Although, if I'm going to let go of the dream, I bloody well am going to get credit for it. Spinning on my heel, I hurry back to my room and swipe my cell phone off my night table. Then, I text Dylan: *Just wanted to make sure you'll have a camera crew at our planning session tomorrow.*

In under a minute, I get a response back from Dylan: *I'll have a crew at EVERYTHING over the next eleven weeks. EVERY. THING.*

My heart stills as I stare at her words. I have a bad feeling I've started a war with a most capable opponent. One who never sleeps either, so she's got twenty-four hours a day to scheme.

Shit.

Chapter 10

HUMANKIND'S HIGHEST CALLING

Will

"THERE'S OUR HANDSOME GROOM!" Dylan says, spreading her arms out wide in my direction.

She's standing at the head of the table in the king's boardroom where at least thirty people are sitting, two and three-deep in some spots. The wedding planning session started at nine a.m. sharp and, due to being stuck at the studio last night until well after one a.m. and trying to fill in this beast of a questionnaire until after three, I overslept.

It is now 9:07 as I make my apologies to everyone and search for Arabella, finding her squeezed into a spot between Mrs. Chapman and Gregory, who gets up and gestures for me to take his chair.

As I rush to the opposite end of the table from Dylan, I am treated to a little jab courtesy of her. "I hope you'll make it to the wedding on time."

I can feel my ears burning with embarrassment as I sit down. "Yes, of course I'll be very early."

I take Arabella's hand and give it a squeeze, whispering, "Sorry."

She offers me a soft smile and whispers, "Don't worry about it."

"To bring you up to speed, William," Dylan says in her character-istic speed talking. "You already know the people to your left, the ANN crew in charge of production, and on your right is the wedding planning team led by the esteemed Imogen Arbuckle—event planner to the stars. She's the mastermind behind such great weddings as Lady Brooke Beddingfield's wedding to movie star Blake Cunningham, and Barrett Richfield's wedding to Helena Jones. We're extremely lucky to get her on such short notice."

I glance at the woman who Dylan is pointing at and she reaches her arm out to me. She's got short, spikey salt-and-pepper hair and turquoise glasses. In order to shake her hand, I have to do a weird half-standing/stretching thing across the table that feels extremely awkward and manages to squish my boys in a most unpleasant way. "Lovely to meet you," I say, doing my best not to wince. "And thank you for taking us on."

She gives me a broad smile, then says, "With what they're paying me, it's totally worth it. Now, I was just explaining to all of your advi-sors and ANN executives that my process is called strategic intuitive event creation. I'll be using your answers from the extensive question-naires and blending them with current trends as well as my own intu-ition through a process of deep meditation and reflection. It may sound a little airy-fairy to you, but it works. I have successfully executed over four-hundred large-scale events in my twenty-five years in the industry and am widely known as a trendsetter."

"Brilliant," I say with a nod.

I glance around the room, only to notice a film crew spread out throughout the room, including Mac and Tosh.

"William, if you could pass your questionnaire to Cassandra over here, she'll start inputting your answers into our system."

I slide the folder toward the young woman, then say, "I filled it in as best I can, but I'm really quite flexible about the entire event. For me, I'll be happy with whatever makes Arabella happy."

People around the table start to chuckle and I glance at Arabella, feeling rather confused until she leans over and says, "That's precisely what I was just saying right before you came in."

"That I'll be happy with whatever makes you happy?" I ask with a grin.

"No, that *I'll* be happy with whatever makes *you* happy." Arabella offers an odd smile around the room that looks…almost…phony. "I was just explaining that we're not in need of a lavish, over-the-top event, but rather would prefer something simple and elegant and understated." She gives a quick smile in the direction of the camera, then continues, "Especially given the current economic situation of people around the world." Turning to me, she says, "Right, darling?"

"Right," I say with a nod. "Definitely."

We all sit in an awkward silence for several minutes while Cassandra taps away on her laptop. When she finishes, she turns to Imogen. "Done and analyzing."

She sits back and stares at the screen for a moment, then leans forward and says, "Huh, well, that's never happened before."

Imogen stands and walks over to her, leaning over the screen. "This is the first time my software hasn't worked. It's saying inconclusive."

She picks up the paper versions of the questionnaires and starts flipping through them then gives us both a hard look. "Have neither of you given any thought whatsoever to your wedding?"

"Umm…" I start, but trail off, not wanting to answer in the affirmative.

Imogen shifts her focus to Arabella. "It's normal to have a *groom* who hasn't put any thought into this, but for a bride, your answers are unusually vague."

Arabella nods. "To be honest, other than a few small requests, I feel quite comfortable trusting your team to make decisions. Will and I are both far more concerned with our humanitarian efforts than fussing over our wedding. I did write down that I would like to carry on my grandmother's tradition of hiring up-and-coming designers for the wedding attire — you know, give someone new a chance to make their mark in the fashion world. I think it would be nice to extend that same philosophy to the music as well. But otherwise, I'm content to sit back and let the experts do their thing."

Imogen gives Arabella a condescending smile. "I'm afraid there won't be time to hire a designer. You'd need at least a year for that so everything is going to have to be…" She lowers her voice to almost a whisper. "Off the rack."

I have no idea what that means but it must not be good because Arabella stiffens briefly, then swallows and offers an easy smile that I'm not convinced is real. "That's fine. If it's good enough for the citizens of Avonia, it's good enough for me."

Imogen sits down in her chair, then taps her pen on the papers in front of her while she gives Arabella a long stare. "Really? No preference at all about…say…flowers?"

"Other than having the traditional sprig of myrtle, I think we should go with locally- and sustainably-sourced floral arrangements."

"So, I could pick a bunch of daisies growing in the ditch along the highway and you'd be fine with that?"

"I'm sure ditch daisies would be just as lovely as hothouse roses if artistically displayed."

The meeting continues on like this for another twenty minutes with the cameras zeroing in on our faces. I can't help but notice that Arabella is definitely acting odd. The entire time she goes on and on about keeping it simple and modest and how there are so much more important things in a world filled with injustice than what type of card stock to use for invitations — other than ensuring that they are environmentally friendly of course. I sit next to her, thoroughly confused and more than slightly concerned that she's handing everything over to someone we just met, and I can't help worrying that she's going to end up miserable on our wedding day. But for some reason, she's intent on insisting none of it matters to her. At one point, I jot down a little note for her. *Are you sure about this?*

She picks up the pen then quickly scrawls *100%*.

I can't help but get the feeling she's playing to the cameras. The question is, why would she do that?

Finally, the meeting wraps up with Arabella standing and going around the room to shake everyone's hands. As she thanks each person individually on Imogen's team, she says things like, "I think you'll find me one of the calmer brides with whom you'll work," or, "We're going to keep this entire event very simple." To one of them, she actually says, "The last thing you'll find me is a bridezilla. Honestly. No need to worry about that *at all*."

And suddenly, I think I know what's going on.

———

It's late in the evening, and I leave at four in the morning for Bolivia where I'll be filming for nearly two months. I should be home packing, but I'd rather drink in every last second I can with my very Zen fiancée before I go. We're seated at the table in her kitchen—her in nothing but a bathrobe and me in only my jeans—eating flatbread pizza by candlelight, having worked up an appetite in the bedroom earlier.

"I wish I was going with you," she says, slicing a dainty bite off her pizza and popping it into her mouth. After she swallows, she smiles at me. "I'm desperately missing life off the beaten track."

"You are?"

She nods.

"I wish you were coming too. None of these adventures are the same without you there to share them," I say. "Kind of takes the shine off my career, to be honest."

Tilting her head, she says, "If only I weren't so amazing."

I let out a chuckle. "If only…"

Her face grows serious and she says, "At least this will be the last big trip until you're free."

"Thanks to my quick-thinking fiancée."

We eat in a comfortable silence for a few moments, and my mind starts to wander to the wedding planning session. "Belle, I've been thinking about the meeting this morning, and I can't help but wonder if someone perhaps accused you of being a bridezilla?"

Her cheeks turn slightly pink and, instead of answering, she asks, "Whatever makes you say that?"

So, yes, someone did. "Just the number of times you made sure to mention that you were literally going to be the world's most-Zen bride, kind of made me wonder if maybe you had an ax to grind."

She puts her fork and knife down and sighs. "Okay, well, there may have been a news report and maybe some awful bloggers that suggested that I bullied the network and the staff into such a quick wedding, and I just wanted to set the record straight."

She runs her tongue over her teeth before nodding. "I *do* know better than to let things like that get to me, but in this case, I hoped to nip it in the bud before I was given some unfair nickname that I could never shake, like Princess Nasty Bride or…something clever."

Reaching out, I place my palm over her delicate fingers. "I'm sorry that happened," I say "It's not fair, is it? That you get judged while I get off scot-free."

"Well, technically, I *did* bully everyone into the quick date," she admits. "But, I like to think I had noble intentions."

I take a sip of my red wine, then say, "Definitely. Sticking it to Dylan is one of life's higher purposes."

She scowls back but I can see a hint of laughter in her eyes. "To free the man I love from the clutches of evil."

We stare at each other for a second in silence, then we both burst out laughing. When we're through, Arabella gives a tiny, slightly defensive shake of her head. "I'm quite sure payback is one of life's higher pursuits."

"Of course. I bet it says something about that in the Bible, but you would know, being such a devote Christian and all."

"Oh, shut up," she says, her face turning bright pink. "Anyway, I'm *not* going to be an awful, picky, explosive bride, and I really *do* have a healthy perspective on our wedding day."

Leaning back in my chair, I say, "I'm just worried that you're not going to enjoy the wedding if you don't have any say in it at all."

She waves off my words. "None of it really does matter in the end, does it? The important thing is starting our life together finally."

"I suppose, but I think we could strike a balance between ditch daisies and hothouse orchids flown in from Thailand."

She rolls her eyes, then says, "I know it sounds silly, but I just don't want anyone to think I'm one of *those* princesses. You know, the *princessy type.*"

I smile at her. "I don't think anyone could accuse you of that, but I do want to make sure that you *feel* like a princess on our wedding day. All women deserve that—even the non-royal ones."

"As long as you're there, I'll love every second of it."

"I think you just stole my line."

"But it's true. If it wouldn't upset so many people, I would happily run away with you to Scotland to elope like they used to do in Jane Austen books."

I stare at her for a moment, and even though she's got a smile on her face, there's something that doesn't quite match the expression in her eyes.

"Are you sure? Because it's okay for you to have a wedding you'll love."

"Of course, I'm sure. Everything is going to be wonderful. I actually had a look at Imogen's portfolio and I don't think she could do a tacky wedding if she was told she'd get paid double."

"Okay," I say, realizing I'm not going to get anywhere with this. "As long as you don't have any personal touches that you'll be missing."

She shakes her head. "Nothing I can think of." After a pause, she says, "Oh, I thought of a great idea of how to make things up to your family, and of course, I wanted to run it by you before I did anything."

"Sure."

"What if I get everyone to travel to Paradise Bay to meet you when you finish up in Bolivia? We could have a pre-wedding holiday and get to know each other before the big event."

She means because Dylan wants me to stop at home for a few days to film with my family before I come back to Avonia. It'll be a 'get to know the groom in his natural habitat' piece. I try to picture King Winston sitting at the beach bar in his swim trunks but it's really not working. Thank God. "Would your family want to do that?"

"Yes, of course. They'll love it there," she says, but I can tell she's stretching the truth on that one. "It's so relaxing and fun. Not to mention, Dylan will have her crew there live-streaming the whole thing so it'll be great publicity for the resort."

I smile at her and nod. "That is…definitely going to make my family happy."

"That's what I hoped. So, it's a yes, then? I should arrange it?" she asks with a huge grin.

"Yes, definitely," I say, leaning over and giving her a kiss. "It's a perfect idea, really. My family gets more business, and they'll appreciate you for making that happen. Everybody gets to know each other so we can all feel more comfortable at the wedding, and I get to see you a lot sooner."

Arabella lets out a little squeal of delight. "Oh, I'm so excited! Just imagine how much fun James and Flora and Clara are going to have together!"

I chuckle at the idea. "They're going to love each other."

"Agreed." She has her last bite of pizza, then sets her fork and knife down and takes her napkin off her lap. Giving me a wicked grin, she says, "Now that that's settled, I'm going to go slip into something less comfortable. Give me a few minutes, then come find me in the bedroom."

Sleep be damned. "Happily."

She stands, walks over, and gives me a lingering kiss on the lips. I place both hands on her hips and consider undoing the sash on her robe, but she disappears too quickly down the hall.

"I'll be right there." I gather up our dishes, then take them to the counter. When I open the garbage bin to toss one of the crusts in, I see an album stuffed into the garbage. I pull it out and brush off some coffee grounds. *My Dream Wedding by Arabella.*

"Why would this be in the bin?" I mutter to myself, flipping through the pages. A pink unicorn? Patrick Dempsey? "Oh, that's why." I feel a bit guilty having an unauthorized look at Arabella's teenage mind. I know I wouldn't want her seeing what was going on in my head at that age. And yet, I can't stop turning the pages. I simply have to know.

Down the hall, I hear some sexy music floating out of Arabella's bedroom, then she calls, "I'm ready for you!"

My heart pounds in my chest as I realize what I need to do. And I'm going to have to act fast.

Chapter 11

BEING SEXY, TAKE TWO

Arabella

WELL, this is embarrassing. And irritating. And rather cold, quite frankly. I'm lying on top of my bed in a small black negligee waiting for Will, who is taking an *extremely* long time to make it from the kitchen to the bedroom. And I know I said I wasn't going to try to be sexy ever again, but that was *before* the unmentionables I ordered online and had delivered to Nikki's (what would I do without her?) arrived. Once I unpacked them, I decided to give sexiness a second try in the safety of my own home. Wanting to send Will off with a night to remember, I gathered all the candles in my apartment and brought them into my room, made a romantic playlist, and now I'm already on the third song (*Die a Happy Man* by Thomas Rhett) and... no Will.

Getting up, I put my robe back on and go in search of him. Just as I reach the hall, I see him jogging toward me and the sight of his upper body rippling as he runs reduces my irritation by at least three quarters. "Everything all right?"

"Yes, sorry. I spilled some wine on the floor and I was just cleaning it up before it stained."

That's one thing about dating the man who didn't grow up rich — he wasn't raised with the expectation that other people would clean up his messes — a very unattractive trait, indeed.

He gives me a sexy grin. "Now, you said something about getting into something less comfortable. By any chance, is it under the robe?" he asks, raising and lowering his eyebrows.

I nod, then I take both of his hands in mine and walk backwards, leading him into my bedroom.

"Wow, candles and music. Miss Langdon, are you trying to seduce me?"

Letting go of his hands, I undo the sash of my robe, then give it a small tug and let it fall to the floor. "Whatever gave you that idea?"

He devours me with his eyes and shakes his head. "I am one lucky, lucky man."

———

An hour later, we lay with our limbs tangled up in a most comforting way. Even though physically I am utterly happy — and I must say I'm certain he is as well — this is the part I hate because I usually end up crying. I know it sounds stupid, but when you love someone so much that it feels like they are your very reason for existing, it kills you when they have to leave. Especially when they have to go away over and over again. Not to mention the fact that you'll spend the next however many weeks holding your breath until you're back together again because you know that whatever he's doing, it's death-defying.

I listen as Will's breathing grows steady, hating that I need to make sure he doesn't fall asleep because he still has to go home and pack. I trace his gorgeous face with my fingertips, then give him a kiss on the lips. "Hey, sailor, as fun as this has been, I think it's time for you to head home."

He opens his eyes and grins at me. "Maybe we can see each other again sometime?"

"I'd be open to that." I manage to keep a straight face for all of half a second, then the two of us share a laugh followed by some very urgent, meaningful kisses that bring tears to the backs of my eyes.

Will lets out a deep sigh and presses his forehead against mine, closing his eyes. "My God, I hate this part."

I nod, trying to swallow the lump in my throat. "Last time, right?" I say, running my finger over his slightly stubbly jawline, wanting to drink in the sight and feel of him because it is going to have to last me for at least a month.

Will smiles at me and nods. "Last time. After this, it'll all be on *our* terms. Our timeline, our locations, and best of all, when I'm back in town, we won't have to sneak out of each other's beds in the middle of the night."

"I cannot wait to wake up with you every morning," I say.

"It's going to be amazing," he says.

I nod, ordering the tears to stay put but they ignore me.

Will's smile fades as he reaches up and wipes the moisture off the tops of my cheeks with his thumb.

"Sorry," I whisper. "I promised myself I wasn't going to be a baby this time."

"Don't be. I feel exactly the same way. Only I'm a man, so we don't have any tears."

I chuckle, and he gives me a hard kiss on the lips. "One month. We can do this, Belle. We're both going to be so busy the entire time, it's going to fly by."

"I suppose that's true. I have to figure out what I'm going to wear, and I need to wrap up that fundraising campaign, and I'm sure there will be dozens of wedding-related decisions to make, and dress shopping and a bridal shower..."

"See? You're not even going to miss me."

"Oh, yes, I bloody well will."

The clock in my living room chimes two o'clock and I sigh. A few minutes later, we perform our well-worn ritual of snogging each other as though it'll never happen again. Each time, I end up breathless and terrified. "Why couldn't I have fallen in love with a nice dentist?"

"Because you're far too wild at heart for that," Will says, opening the door.

We give each other one last kiss.

"Stay safe," I whisper.

"Always."

And then he's gone, leaving me to wander back through my empty apartment to my empty bed for a quick cry, followed by a short, fitful sleep.

Chapter 12

LIKE A HAMSTER ON A ROYAL WEDDING WHEEL

Will

Bolivia – Two Weeks Later

"Welcome to Salar de Uyuni, the largest salt flat on the planet, here in beautiful Bolivia. You may recognize it from films such as *Star Wars: The Last Jedi*. This incredibly unique place is going to be our home for the next four days. Over the next four days we'll be traveling by 4 x 4 and camping out to discover all that this incredible area has to offer, here at the crest of the Andes Mountains. Salar de Uyuni is over 10,000 square kilometres in area and it sits at an elevation of over 3500 m above sea level, so even though there's nothing to climb out here, there is the danger of altitude sickness. So if you're making a trip here, be sure to bring plenty of water, altitude sickness medication, and Advil. Another must is sunscreen, and don't forget to apply it inside your nostrils, because you'll be living on the world's largest mirror and the reflection gets everywhere! It gets hot during the day here in April and quite chilly at night so you better bring clothing you can layer. And don't forget a swimsuit and towel, because they've got beautiful hot springs that we'll check out later.

"I've got my guide, Juan Carlos, with me, and he is going to take us off the beaten path and give us a chance to explore this incredible area."

"Cut!" Enid says into the microphone. "That was great, Will. Take ten while we set up the next shot."

I give her a nod, then hurry into the tent where Gregory is waiting for me, his face covered in zinc. Also waiting for me is another film crew who is here to capture all my 'off air' wedding preparation moments. So I'm now being filmed basically every waking moment, which is…not irritating at all. But it'll all be worth it in eight weeks and six days.

I guzzle down half a liter of water, then Gregory and I continue on with our etiquette lessons.

"Now, when you fold your napkin in half, is the crease facing you or facing away from you?"

"Facing me?" I ask.

Gregory shakes his head.

"Damn — the crease is *closest* to me. Closest. That's how I'll remember, it—cc… The crease is close. Okay, next."

"Very good, sir. True or false: when eating, the knife stays in your right hand and the fork in your left."

I close my eyes and pretend to eat. "True — fork left, knife right."

"Excellent. When you're done eating, how do you lay your silverware?"

"Diagonally?" I ask.

"Brilliant." He fans his face with the paper for a moment and I feel horrible about dragging him here just to teach me etiquette lessons.

"Are you feeling all right, Gregory?" I ask.

"Quite fine, sir," he says with a firm nod, even though the parts of his face that are not covered with zinc look flushed. "I just need a day or two to adjust to my new surroundings."

"You're a good man, Gregory. Thank you for doing this for me," I say.

"It's nothing, sir. I'm merely doing my job," he says, clearly uncomfortable with the compliment. "Now, can you remember the eight words to avoid at all costs?"

Damn. I can't remember them because they make no sense whatsoever. "Pardon?"

"I said, can you remember the eight words to avoid at all costs?"

"Yes, I heard you. I was guessing that one of them is the word pardon."

He chuckles a little, then says, "Quite right. One down, seven to go."

"Toilet?"

He nods, so I continue. "Couch?"

"Very good."

"Cologne?"

"Close, sir — perfume, but I would avoid the word cologne as well."

"Good tip, thanks." I tap my finger on my knee for a second, trying to remember the rest of the words, but draw a blank. "That's all I've got. Sorry."

"The remaining words are: portion, patio, posh, dad, and living room."

Trixie walks into the tent and says, "Enid's ready for you now."

I stand and give her a nod, then reach into the cooler and grab out a bottle of water and hand it to Gregory. "Try to finish the entire thing before lunch. It will really help."

When I get outside, I see a can of Red Bull sitting nearby on the flats. Enid points at an 'X' on the ground in the distance. "Okay, Will, we're going to set up some fun perspective shots, the first one for the makers of Red Bull. We're going to make it look like you're jumping out of the can."

I nod and walk over, even though inside my brain is screaming 'SELL OUT!' at me. Thank God I won't be stuck doing this for the next several years…

———

We finally finish filming for the day after getting some footage of the incredible night sky and the campfire. Even the wedding prep film crew has called it a night, which is what I've been waiting for, because what I'm about to do is not something I need the world to see. In order to be ready for the reception, I promised myself I would practice ballroom dancing for at least twenty minutes every day. I consider leaving the camp area so as not to embarrass myself, but then I realize I'd have to walk pretty damn far since there's really nowhere to hide out here on the world's biggest mirror.

At least I can go over to the other side of the trucks. That might afford me some privacy. I get up and start walking over, with Reynard, my shadow, in tow. Bloody hell. "You know, you probably don't need to follow me out here. We'll be able to see any danger for miles."

"Sorry, sir, I have my orders," he answers in an apologetic tone.

I give him a nod and stifle the grunt inside me. Once I'm around to the other side of the vehicles, I turn on my phone to watch the tutorial video I downloaded before we came. I watch it for a moment, then I position my arms as though holding Arabella and give it a whirl, quickly losing the beat.

"If I may, Mr. Banks," Reynard says. "I'm rather skilled at ballroom dancing and would be more than happy to help you."

I pause the video and turn to him. "Really?"

"My mother was an Avonian national ballroom champion and, as a young lad, I used to help her practice."

I narrow my eyes for a moment, considering his offer. The last thing I want is to take any help from anyone on my security team. That would mean I'll start *needing* them, and what kind of a man needs other men to protect him?

"Listen, Will," Reynard says, using my given name for the first time. "I know you don't want us around, and as a man, I understand. But the thing is, once you're a part of the family, it doesn't matter how fit or agile or capable or masculine you are, not against someone with a gun. Each addition to the family adds liability and requires careful protection, not just for their own sake, but for that of the whole. Keeping you safe allows us to keep Princess Arabella and Princess Flora and Prince James safe as well."

"Yes, I've been given the speech already, thank you," I quip.

"Well, then, maybe we can approach this from another angle. I got into this line of work because I like helping people," he says. "But, until I was assigned to your team, I have to say I had pretty much the world's most boring job, and I find myself feeling extremely grateful to be able to go on so many incredible adventures because of you. And other than a few things I need to be prepared for and check on during our travels, I'm basically getting paid to travel the world, which, as wonderful as it is, makes me feel rather guilty. So if I can do some small thing to make your life better, it would be a great service to me because I'll be able to fulfill my purpose in life — which is to help. And if said help comes in the form of teaching you how to waltz properly, nothing would please me more."

Well, how the hell do you say no to that? I let out a sigh, feeling like a complete brat for how I've been acting. "Thank you, Reynard," I say, rubbing the back of my neck. "This whole thing has been extremely uncomfortable for me. I have never had anyone watching over me, even as a child, really. We were pretty much left to our own devices — which I loved, to be honest. Well, for the most part." Why am I rambling? "Anyway, you're right, being assigned an entire group of men to look after your safety does feel somewhat... well..."

"Emasculating?" Reynard asks.

My head snaps back and I say, "Whoa. Let's not go there. But maybe some other word that means something similar."

The two of us chuckle, then Reynard says, "Well, should you wish to waltz with me, I promise to let you lead. Oh, and I will never knead your buttocks."

I let out a loud laugh, surprised that he's actually funny. "All right, let's do this. For the sake of my future wife," I add, for no apparent reason.

———

Royal News —The Official Website for All Things Avonian Royal

Forum Thread: Royal Source Says Will Banks Training is Disaster *(567 Currently Viewing, 5742 Total Views, 62 Comments)*

. . .

Will Banks, future husband of Princess Arabella, is currently undergoing extensive training in royal etiquette in order to bring him up to snuff for moving around in high-class circles. According to a source close to the royal family, his progress has been dreadfully slow (embarrassing, even), and it is doubtful that he shall ever conduct himself with the expected decorum.

Cindy (Serene Highness): Are we shocked? Nay, I say we are not.

Felix (Courtier): Who actually expected the Knight of the No Shirt to EVER develop the graces of the upper class? Not me. They might as well put a gorilla in a morning suit and have him dine with the king.

Stephen (Heir Presumptive): I predict disaster.

Chapter 13

BEGGING, CRYING, AND SECRET WEDDING DRESS SHOPPING TRIPS

Arabella

EMAIL FROM: *Arabella*
  To: *Gran, Dad, Arthur, Tessa*
  Subject: *Pre-wedding Getaway*

Hi All,

I'm writing because I need to ask you something and I really am desperate for you to carefully consider your answer before you give one. As you're aware, some members of Will's family were hoping to have the wedding on Santa Valentina Island. Obviously, that won't be happening, but I'd like to suggest a compromise of sorts (and I'm sure you can guess what it is based on the subject line).

I'm proposing we spend a week at the Paradise Bay Resort together. It would be the first time in our lives that we'd all be on a real holiday together, and I promise you'll love it there. It's the world's most beautiful and relaxing place. Just the perfect way to unwind before we face the stress of the wedding.

Now, before you say no, picture yourselves laying on a catamaran soaking in the sun (except Father, I know how you hate boats—you picture yourself poolside with a nice cold drink in hand watching Flora and James splash around in the water).

Also, I've accidentally insulted Will's entire family and am badly in need of a way to make it up to them.

So, all that to say, please, please, please, please, please…

Love you all forever,

Arabella

Email from Arthur
  To: Arabella
  cc: Dad, Tessa, Gran
  Subject: RE: Pre-wedding Getaway

Little A,

Seriously? Do you really think we can drop everything and just take off to some hot, sticky tropical island?

Big A

Email from Gran
  To: Arabella c.c. King Winston, Arthur, Tessa
  Subject: RE: RE: Pre-wedding Getaway

What Big A (who's being a big A, if you ask me) means is, "Of course we can make that happen and we'd be delighted to attend."

Gran

P.S. Should I bring my doctor manfriend or would that be like bringing sand to the beach?

Email from Dad
  To: Arabella
  cc: Gran, Arthur, Tessa
  Subject: RE: RE: RE: Pre-wedding Getaway

. . .

Mother, please. You're eighty-nine, for God's sake. Act like it.

And, yes, Arabella, have Mrs. Chapman contact Phillip with the dates. It's been far too long since I've been anywhere, and the idea of going with the whole family is a welcome one.

Dad

Email from Gran
  To: Arabella
  cc: King Winston, Arthur, Tessa
  Subject: RE: RE: RE: RE: Pre-wedding Getaway

I am acting my age—people so close to death have to drink in every last drop of life. So, suck it, sonny boy. I'm going to get my Caribbean freak on.

Mom

Email from Tessa
  To: Arabella
  cc: King Winston, Arthur, Gran
  Subject: RE: RE: RE: RE: RE: Pre-wedding Getaway

Yes! A tropical vacay is just what we all need—especially Big A. We'll be there, Arabella! ALL of us.

T

P.S. We should squeeze in some swimsuit shopping as soon as I lose the baby weight again.

———

Text from me to Will: *Guess what?! My family's on board for the trip! We'll see you in Paradise Bay!!!*

. . .

The last week has been an absolute blur, which is honestly my prefer-ence when it comes to times when Will has to be away. My brain has been swirling with decisions and meetings with Imogen's team and the family advisors. Spoiler alert: the royal staff doesn't exactly love having unknown event planners trying to take over all the decisions. A wedding 'war room' has been set up in the mid-size ballroom, and let me say, there have been more than a few battles fought already. The teams are here, if not twenty-four hours a day, at least eighteen, which means the kitchen staff have been staying late to feed them. Between our lawyers, my family's advisors, the network and their lawyers, the film crew, and the event planners, the entire thing amounts to a very tense, chaotic environment, and every time I do have to go down to make decisions (which seems to be at least eight times a day) I am a tightly-wound spring by the time I walk out the door.

This is all made far more difficult by what I'm now guessing may have been an ill-advised idea to pretend I'm the world's most calm and carefree bride because instead of saying, "Oh, yes, I love that!" to any of the choices, I say things like, "I don't know, which one is less expen-sive?" or, "Is one more environmentally conscious than the other?"

I'm so coy that in the end, I don't even know if *anyone* knows what we've decided, and I'll be shocked if I walked down the aisle and it's *not* an absolutely horrific mishmash of clashing styles and elements.

So today, I am absolutely thrilled to be taking a day away from the palace and spending it at Forever More Bridal. I managed to arrange it so Dylan doesn't know what we're doing today. The 'official' dress shopping day will be here at the end of the week—complete with Imogen's team and the ANN camera crew to 'capture the moment and share it with the world.' Tessa and Nikki have agreed to come back for the fake shoot, but Gran (who refuses to 'play it up for the cameras') gave me a hard no. But at least she's here for the real one, where I can act like a regular bride and actually share my opinion. Then, we hide it away, along with a few other of the most flattering choices, to model for the cameras. It's all so dishonest and stupid that it makes me hate myself just the tiniest bit, but desperate times call for…secret wedding dress shopping trips.

Anyway, the owner of the shop, Jasmine Lee, closed down the

shop for us so Gran, Tessa, Nikki, and I will be spending a glorious few hours trying on dresses, sipping champagne, and nibbling on hors d'oeuvres. I just finished putting my hair up in a very simple bun to keep it out of the way and giving myself only a light dusting of makeup so as not to get any on any of the dresses. I grab my phone and send a quick text to Will to tell him I'm off to buy a wedding gown and that I love him (just in case he ends up in a spot with Wi-Fi). Then I set off.

Forever More Bridal is the quintessential wedding shop for the women in Valcourt who have a lot of money but are either too sensible (or don't quite have the budget) to commission a dress from a designer. It's an extremely posh store with thick white carpeting, soft blue walls, and lighting meant to flatter even the palest of complexions. I've heard rumors the mirrors take more than one size off your frame as well, which I'm sure helps them close the sale.

The limo pulls up in front of the two-storey brick building, and I smile to myself. It's going to be an absolutely lovely day, with three of my favourite people, away from all of the chaos and tension. Just us and— somewhere in between these walls—the perfect dress. Nikki, Tessa, Gran, and I all pile out of the limo and are immediately ushered inside by Jasmine, who locks the door behind us and greets us all with air kisses and limp handshakes. "Princess Arabella, it is an absolute honour to be dressing you for your big day. I have hand-selected two dozen gowns that I think would suit you perfectly, but if you prefer to start by browsing, we can certainly look at my selections later. Take your time, relax, and enjoy every minute of what is often described as one of the most magical bridal moments."

I happened to glance at Nikki and Tessa when Jasmine said the word 'browsing' and saw their eyes light up, so obviously, in the name of fun, that's what we're going to do. "Why don't we take a few minutes to look around at your beautiful selection and then we'll get to trying things on?"

"Very good, Your Highness," she says with a deep curtsy that seems like a bit much if you ask me. "I shall leave you to it and come back with some champagne in a few minutes."

Nikki waits until Jasmine is out of earshot, then says, "I hope you know this is *not* how store owners act for us regular folk."

I give her the half grin, not knowing exactly what to say to that.

Gran hooks her arm through mine and says, "Let's go find your dream dress—and don't give me that crap about how it doesn't matter to you in the least because I know it does."

"What is that supposed to mean?" I ask, narrowing my eyes at her tiny frame.

Tessa answers for her. "Only that we're not buying the whole 'I'm the least precious bride on the planet' thing you've got going on."

"Well put, my dear," Gran says to Tessa. "It's almost like you've always been a Langdon."

I unhook my arm from Gran and plant it on my hip, but before I can say anything, Gran holds up one finger. "And don't even start. We've *all* seen the dream wedding album."

"Well, that is just…" I trail off, too irritated to come up with a good retort. "You know what? I'm not going to let that bother me," I say, giving them a firm nod and turning from them. I walk over to the nearest rack of dresses and start flipping through them angrily, muttering, "People change, you know. They absolutely change. They mature and their ideas and values shift… I mean, who is exactly like they were when they were a teenager, anyway?"

I turn around and glare at Gran for a second. "I distinctly remember *you* saying you wanted to be *a nun* when you were fifteen and you didn't exactly turn out to be a virgin bride of Jesus, now did you?"

All three of them look slightly shocked, both Nikki and Tessa are holding their lips between their teeth, clearly trying not to laugh while Gran gives me an icy stare with her cool blue eyes. "For someone who's claiming none of this matters, it's surprisingly important to have everyone believe how very much you don't care."

Jasmine reappears with a tray of four flutes, each one a third-full of champagne. She presents the tray to them with a flourish and a slight bow. Suddenly not in the mood to browse, I take one of the flutes off the tray and down it, then say, "You know what? Let's start with the selections you've made for me."

She smiles, clearly pleased, then leads us in the direction of the fitting rooms. Gran, Nikki, and Tessa all take seats on the French provincial sofa set while I walk up the two steps, past the mirrored platform and into the first fitting room I see. Sliding the cream-coloured curtain across, I see two dresses hanging with their fronts to the wall, having been unbuttoned and readied for me. One is a very simple sheath dress. The other is a lace-covered, long-sleeved dress with a large poufy skirt that reminds me very much of Kate's. I quickly undress, then pull the simple gown off the hanger and step into it, pulling it up and sliding my arms into it.

Just as I finish, Jasmine asks, "Are you ready to be buttoned in?"

Good Lord, how is her timing *that good*? Does she have a camera in here?

A few moments later, I step out of the dressing room and walk out onto the platform, giving the ladies a 'Well? What do you think?' look.

They all tilt their heads, none of them smiling, which clearly means it's a no. I turn from them and look at myself in the mirror, seeing that I agree. "It's very sensible," I say.

"Yes, you could grace the cover of Sensible Bride Magazine in that," Gran says wryly.

Jasmine stands behind me and makes a few adjustments, then steps back and stares at me for a moment and shakes her head. "This is not the one."

"It's quite lovely," I say. I mean, I don't look *bad* in it. And it really does have a simplicity that makes me appear to be a no-nonsense bride.

"No, when we find the one, I'll see it in your eyes. Now, how about the other one in the dressing room? Do you care to try that on?"

I shake my head. "I'm looking for something a little simpler than that. Perhaps somewhere in between this and that one."

She gives me a single nod then says, "Say no more, I'll have it replaced with two new ones."

————

Okay, so maybe this isn't the dream morning I thought it would be.

I've tried on at least fifteen dresses now, none of which have had that special spark that Jasmine is looking for, and quite frankly, they haven't exactly brought a tear to my eye, either. It's quite stuffy in here and, at the moment, I'm sitting in the dressing room in my underwear, fanning my underarms with my hands while I wait for something else to be brought to me. Tessa and Nikki abandoned Jasmine's selections three dresses ago, not-so-subtly stating that they may have better luck finding something since they know me so well.

"Knock, knock," Tessa says. "Are you decent?"

"Not exactly," I say.

"Well, I'm coming in anyway. I've seen you in a bikini. Besides, we're basically sisters." She slides into the fitting room, holding up an absolutely gorgeous gown. It has an off-the-shoulder neckline and the bodice is covered in a delicate lace that meets the smooth satin ball-gown-style skirt at a point just below the hip. The sheer long sleeves flare out just the tiniest bit at the cuffs. It's exactly like Sleeping Beauty's blue dress, except in a lovely warm white.

Tessa grins at me, her eyes dancing with excitement. "This is the one, isn't it? It's what Sleeping Beauty would have worn," she whispers.

Completely abandoning sensibility, I reach for it, touching the cool satin with my fingertips and gasping.

"I knew it," she says. "Deep down, you still want the fairy-tale."

"I do not," I say indignantly. "This is just a very beautiful dress, that's all."

Raising one eyebrow, Tessa says, "You're so full of shit. Now, put this on so we can ooh and ahh over you, you can order it, and we can go have lunch."

She hangs it on the empty hook then disappears, leaving me and — let's face it — my dream dress so we can be alone together.

I pull it on, thrilled to see that it's basically my size. Just a few minor alterations and it should fit perfectly. Tucking my bra straps into the wide-open collar, I slide the curtain aside and turn so Jasmine can do up the buttons. She says nothing this time, and steps aside as I lift the front of the skirt and walk toward the mirror, my heart pounding and my head lifted high. And I know this is very silly and I should be above all of this, but *my God*, this is a beautiful dress. It must look as good as I hoped because even Gran has raised a hand to her mouth to cover a gasp.

I turn and take in the first sight of myself in it, and I. Am. *In love.* I look myself up and down for a moment, realizing that, for the first time in my life, I actually *look* like a princess. And I *feel* like a princess. And I actually *want* to be one. Jasmine appears behind me with a veil in her hands. "I've been waiting for the right dress to present this to you. Would you like to try it?"

I nod, feeling tears well up in my eyes. How stupid. To get emotional over an article of clothing, of all things. But somehow standing here with a stranger putting a veil on makes me miss the mum I never knew. I can't help but to wish she were here, dabbing at her eyes with a tissue and telling me how beautiful I am and how proud she is of me. It's always the biggest moments in life that you miss sharing with your mother. Well, and the little ones too, I suppose. I let out a shaky breath and glance at Gran in the mirror. She stands and hurries up the steps to me, squeezing my shoulder. "I wish she were here too." Her eyes fill with tears. "It's really not fair that you had to miss out on all that love."

I reach down and give her a tight hug, and she hugs me back, and, for once, she doesn't have a biting comment on the tip of her tongue or any advice. Only comfort.

When I finally let go, I say, "Sorry, I didn't think that was going to happen."

"Don't be. It's a great loss that you had to suffer. And we're such a small family to begin with, it makes it even harder. It makes me wish your grandfather and I had had more than just the one child. At least then you could have maybe had an auntie to help fill the void."

I nod. "Or if my parents could've had more children. And if…" I shrug and don't finish the sentence because there's no point in wishing for something that didn't happen, or rather, wishing something that *did* happen, hadn't.

Gran pats me on the hand. "But we'll add your young man and his people to the mix and maybe some children to fill the palace halls with laughter."

I nod and smile at the thought, trying to brush away my heartbreak.

Jasmine steps forward. "So, are we decided then?"

Turning back to the mirror again, I sigh. "There's really nothing practical or sensible about it." I chew on my lip for a moment, wishing I didn't love it so much. "I don't know, is it too...young for me?"

Protests erupt from all three of my companions, none of whom are particularly nice about it. Tessa and Nikki make their way up onto the platform, and Nikki fans out the train for me, while Tessa plucks a silk bouquet out of the holder on the wall and hands it to me. "Let yourself have this one thing," she says. "The rest of the day can be utterly eco-responsible and as dull as dishwater. But just let yourself have this."

I nod, a sense of excitement for my wedding day hitting me for the very first time.

Chapter 14

SLEEPY FIANCÉES, LYING, AND DEATH-DEFYING BIKE TRIPS

Will

EMAIL FROM DYLAN SINCLAIR
   To: Will Banks, Princess Arabella
   Subject: Your Amazing News!!!

Dearest William and Princess Arabella,

   I am delighted to hear that the entire royal family is planning to meet at Paradise Bay for a pre-wedding holiday! I of course will respect your need for some alone time, but we'll need to film a few segments with everyone together.

   I am so excited about it, I can barely sleep. Like, literally, I have not slept in three days.

   Will, stay safe in Bolivia, and a wonderful week to you, Princess Arabella.
   Ever yours,
   Dylan

"Hello, darling," Arabella says, looking beautiful as she waves at me on the tiny screen. The sight of her causes an ache in my chest and I find myself wishing to climb into the mobile phone so I can be where she is. (Which, at the moment, appears to be in her sitting room, whereas I am on a cliff in the Cordillera Mountain Range.)

"How are you?" she asks. "You look as though you got some sun."

"A bit, yes, I'm fine. Really, really missing you so so *so* much, but otherwise everything's been running smoothly."

She narrows her eyes and moves closer to the screen, then says, "Are you sure? You look tired."

"Absolutely fine," I lie.

The truth is, the last three weeks have been eighteen-hour days for me between filming, royal etiquette protocol lessons, and waltzing with my bodyguard — not that I'm going to tell her any of that because she'll feel terrible about it, and the last thing I want to do is to make her feel bad. "How are you? You must be exhausted having had to manage all the wedding stuff on your own."

"Oh, no. I'm doing really well," she says with a firm nod. "Things are coming along for the wedding. I've barely had to do anything actually. Imogen's team is absolutely on top of everything, and I think we're set to have a very nice day."

"Really? What a relief," I say, rubbing the back of my neck. "I've been worried about you and imagining there must be so much pressure on you to make a million decisions a day."

"No need to worry about me. The key is to just keep it all in perspective, not get too fussed about anything, and then it all turns out." She smiles confidently, but I have a feeling there's more to the story than what she's letting on. But since we've only got a few precious minutes before I have to start filming for the day, we have to move from topic to topic at breakneck speed. "Did you see the email from Dylan?"

Her smile fades. "Yes, and I can't help but wonder what she's going to try to pull."

"Hopefully nothing. I'm guessing maybe she'll think our families won't get along, which would make for amazing television."

Arabella nods. "Well, she's wrong. I have a very good feeling that my family and yours will be great friends within half an hour of meeting. I just need to have a little talk with Gran about being on her best behavior and we should be fine. And my father, too, I suppose. He can be a bit...standoffish. Well, and Arthur can be rather critical, so there's that."

"But other than that, it'll be wonderful, right?" I ask with a chuckle.

Arabella winces and gives me a worried smile. "Exactly. But seriously, it'll be fine. It's the perfect spot for everyone to be able to relax and get to know each other before the wedding."

"Very true. If you can't relax there, you can't relax at all," I say, quoting the brochure. "So, what's the next week of your life like?"

"Gran is hosting a bridal tea for me — an intimate affair of four hundred of my closest friends."

"That sounds...really nice," I say, oozing sarcasm.

Arabella laughs, then says, "At least I've managed to insist that in lieu of gifts, I would like donations to the People for Animals Fund, the Equal Everywhere Campaign, or the Save the Bonobos Foundation. That'll save me from having to open hundreds of over-the-top shower gifts that we couldn't possibly use in an entire lifetime."

"Good thinking. I can't imagine what we'd do with thousands of tea towels."

Nodding, she says, "Yes. It's bad enough that all of the wedding gifts have started to arrive from around the world. We're up to twenty-six silver tea sets already."

"Whoa," I say. "Twenty-six? What are we going to do with all of them?"

She shrugs. "Usually, in cases like this, we gift them to the staff. They're sworn to secrecy. Anyway, how's Bolivia?"

"Great," I say. "Things have been going smoothly."

She yawns, reminding me that it's late in the evening for her. "You're tired. I should let you go to bed."

She shakes her head. "Not just yet. Tell me what you're doing today."

I glance over the cliff on which I'm standing and say, "Just a little scenic mountain biking thing. Should be pretty easy." Okay, so I may be underselling it a little, but only so she won't worry.

"That sounds absolutely delightful. Oh, if only I were there, I would totally do that with you. How long is the ride?"

"Just over sixty km, but it's mainly downhill."

"Sixty?! Maybe it's better I'm not there," she says.

"You could totally handle it," I say with a firm nod. But she'd hate it with every fibre of her being because this is one of the most terrifying rides on the planet.

"Well, I'm just glad you're not doing anything dangerous for once. I'll sleep easier."

"Hey, you know me, Belle—even when I'm doing something dangerous, I'm totally safe."

"Liar," she says with a small grin. She yawns again and then apologizes. "I suppose I should get some sleep. I have to be up early."

"Okay, sweetheart, I love you. Have a good week. We'll be heading into the rain forest for a few days so I won't have reception, but I'll be in touch as soon as we get back to town. I love you."

"I love you too. Stay safe."

"Always."

"Okay, Will, we're ready for your intro," Enid says as soon as I hang up the phone.

I nod, take a deep breath, and smile into the camera. "Today on *The Wild World*, I'll be making a treacherous five-hour biking trek on a road so dangerous, it's been dubbed The Death Road. Yungas Road, known around the world as the most dangerous road on the planet, is a 69 km switchback built by Paraguayan prisoners during the 1930s to connect Bolivia's capital, La Paz, to the town of Coroico, at the edge of the Amazon rainforest. Between dense fog, landslides, and steep cliffs that drop over 600 m, the road used to claim nearly 300 drivers here every year until 1994. Since that time the road has been widened, but even at that, one wrong slip and it's game over. There are no guard rails, most of it is gravel, and if it rains, the road becomes extremely slick and visibility is basically zero." Smiling, I give two thumbs up to the camera. "But I've had a big breakfast and I've updated my will, so I'm all set for another incredible adventure. Let's go!"

Chapter 15

NASTY NASTY NIGEL

Arabella

EMAIL FROM IMOGEN ARBUCKLE
   To: Princess Arabella, Dylan Sinclair, Phillip Crawford
   Subject: Wedding Costs

Hello All,

The big day is fast-approaching and the wedding plans are going as smoothly as possible given the tight timeframe. We've run into a hiccup with the budget however, which is that we're already at the top end of what ANN has agreed to pay. All services include a rush fee of up to 30% which has created an issue. I need to know who will be picking up the extra costs. There is a $2.4 million overage to account for. Please let me know as soon as you sort this out so I can continue to finalize the details.

Best,
Imogen Arbuckle
Event Planner, Intuitive Wedding Magic, Inc.

Email from Phillip Crawford
    To: Dylan Sinclair, Imogen Arbuckle, Princess Arabella
    Subject: RE: Wedding Costs

Ms. Arbuckle,
    As the palace has already publicly announced that the wedding fees will be paid by ANN, we need to cut costs to make that statement true. Alternatively, ANN can pick up the overage themselves. I trust your team will manage to make this happen.
    Regards,
    Phillip Crawford, Senior Advisor to His Majesty King Winston of Avonia

———

Email from Dylan Sinclair
    To: Phillip Crawford, Imogen Arbuckle, Princess Arabella
    Subject: RE: RE: Wedding Costs

Mr. Crawford et al.,
    We at ANN have a signed contract that stipulates the amount the network is willing to put forward for this event (a very generous $10 million). We are unable (and unwilling) to go above that amount, especially given that the reason for the cost increase is solely due to the wishes of the bride and groom. They can eat the tab on this.
    Regards,
    Dylan Sinclair
    VP Programming, Avonian Nature Network

———

Email from Princess Arabella
    To: Phillip Crawford, Imogen Arbuckle, Dylan Sinclair
    Subject: RE: RE: RE: Wedding Costs

. . .

Hello,

Chiming in here before we wind up in an all-out war. I have enough to cover the overage in my Bainbridge Trust. I shall have Mrs. Chapman withdraw the amount and send it to your team immediately.

Best,

Arabella

I stare at the email for a minute before I press send, utterly pissed that I am now shelling money out of my own pocket for an enormous wedding I don't actually want. And yes, I get that most people pay for their own weddings, I do. But you have to consider that a) I don't want it, b) it's 2.4 million dollars for something I don't want, and c) it's not like I'm allowed to earn money, so I have to be careful not to spend my trust fund all on one day.

Fuck it. Send.

———

"So, when will this air?" I ask Dylan as the sound tech fastens the microphone to my blouse.

We are about to film the pre-wedding special giving ANN viewers an exclusive inside look at life at the palace. The first bit of filming we're doing is in my office, followed by a quick stop at the solarium before making our way to my apartment for a voyeuristic look at my private life. No matter, it'll all be worth it in a few weeks. Unless I'm a disaster, which is definitely possible. Truth be told, everything's been going so well with the wedding plans so far that I'm a little nervous about this. I'm not great in interviews at the best of times, and there's a weirdly superstitious part of me (that I won't ever admit to) that believes that when things go too well for too long, something dreadful is about to happen. I'm just praying it doesn't happen on national television. Taking a deep breath, I tell myself to relax. Exude confidence, warmth, and grace, no matter what. That shouldn't be too much to ask, should it?

"I'm giving this a primetime slot this Sunday," she says with a wide smile. "It's *the best* time slot there is. And with the marketing push already started, we're expecting 50 million viewers that night. And at least that when Will's special airs." She balls up her fist and pulls her arm back in a sort of victory pump thing that athletes tend to do.

"50 million?" I ask, blinking repeatedly as my stomach is flooded by a swarm of butterflies. I *detest* giving on-screen interviews, even small ones when I know only about one hundred thousand people will be watching. But 50 million? That's too many millions.

There's always the chance of a slip of the tongue, of giving TMI, of being too emotional. (That last one forever plagues me since I tend to wear my heart on the *outside* of my clothing.) The pressure on me to be graceful, warm, calm, and confident is…well, it's massive, really. And I never quite manage it. I always find it difficult to contain my emotions when I'm upset or irritated or overly emotional about whatever the topic is. Like the time I teared up on camera over the plight of the introverts in the Avonian Introverts Society when a reporter asked me what I thought it must be like to go through life being so very shy.

And now the stakes are much, much higher than they've ever been because I've spent the last year garnering a level of respectability I've never previously enjoyed. People take me seriously now, which I quite like, and the shit part is that it can all be yanked away with one wrong word today. I take a deep breath and tell myself I'll be fine. *Just stick to the topic at hand. Be bold and detached.* "Can we be sure to mention my foundations?"

"Absolutely."

"When can we get started?" I ask. *Oooh, good one. Very 'in charge.'*

Dylan glances at her watch. "As soon as our host gets here. He's running a few minutes late," she says with a nod before turning and sweeping across the room to bark orders at the camera crew.

I stand and walk over to the window, staring out at the meadow in the distance, wishing I could be out there alone instead of in here.

The door to my office opens, and one of the world's nastiest human beings walks in — Nigel Wood, Avonia's top fashion critic and cohost of ABN's Entertainment Weekly. That's who they picked for the host? Well, this is just perfect. I stiffen reflexively and force a bright smile as he crosses the room to me.

"Princess Arabella," he says, giving me the world's phoniest air kisses. "Delightful to see you again."

"Same to you, Mr. Wood." I offer him a gracious nod while, on the inside, I'm imagining kneeing him in what I'm assuming is a rather minuscule set of jewels for all of the nasty things he's said about Tessa over the years.

"It is going to be an absolute pleasure to watch someone of your style and grace walk up the aisle. You will be setting the tone for brides around the United Kingdom for years to come. Step aside Kate, because there's a new fashion queen in town." He laughs at what I'm sure is a well-rehearsed compliment before being ushered away by the makeup artist.

Okay, Arabella, just smile and get through this. And whatever you do, don't slap him, no matter how much your hand itches.

———

"Greetings, all, I'm Nigel Wood, Avonia's premier fashion critic turned royal reporter as we prepare for *the wedding event* of the decade — Her Royal Highness Princess Arabella, Duchess of Bainbridge, and William Banks, arguably the world's most daring eligible bachelor."

The camera pans out from the close-up of Nigel to include me in the shot. I've been carefully posed at my desk where I am meant to look like I'm very busy working, even though it would take a complete idiot to believe that I am unaware of the fact that a camera crew and reporter are a few feet away from me.

"And here she is, the lovely princess herself, hard at work, no doubt on one of her many charitable causes."

On cue, I set my pen down and smile at Nigel. "Welcome, Mr. Wood."

"Nigel, please," he says with a simpering smile. "Tell us about your beautiful office."

"Of course. I'm very fortunate to have the office that used to belong to Queen Elenora, although when she used it, it was a private sitting room. It's been painstakingly converted into a very practical workspace for me, complete with this antique desk that belonged to my great-grandfather, King Phillip."

"I love the mix of contemporary meets traditional. Would you say that that's your style?"

"I suppose you could say that. My biggest concern with decorating this room was to repurpose items from around the palace and present them in such a way that would create a serene environment that was conducive to productivity. As you know, royals of this century, and the last, are most certainly of the working variety, wanting to both lead and serve the people of our kingdom. I needed a space that would allow me to keep my duties at the forefront of my mind at all times."

The director signals to me and points to the sitting area.

Standing, I gesture to the chairs on the far side of the room. "Shall we have a seat and some tea?" I ask as though I just thought of it. Honestly, I kind of hate myself at this moment. As I cross the room, I remind myself of who I'm doing this for and everything we'll gain in the long run. The thought of having Will all to myself very soon keeps the smile plastered to my face.

Once we're seated, Nigel takes a sip of his tea, then sets it down and gives me a very grave look. "Your Highness, tell me everything. What has the pressure been like as we lead up to the big day? Surely it must be overwhelming at times."

"Not at all," I say with a slight shake of my head. "The people at the network, the wedding planning team led by Imogen Arbuckle, as well as my family's staff, have made the entire thing an absolute breeze. Decisions were made swiftly and without drama, because, at the end of the day, we all want the same thing — a wonderful celebration of our marriage and an event for all the people of Avonia and the Commonwealth countries to enjoy."

He tilts his head and purses his lips at me. "Come on, there must've been some little point of tension or something that didn't quite go the way you hoped."

"Not really," I say with an easy smile. "As surprising as that sounds, things have fallen into place quite beautifully, but even if they hadn't, I believe a healthy perspective on events such as these is necessary in order to truly enjoy them."

"Yes, people have been calling you Princess Zen and there have been reports that you're absolutely unflappable."

Unflappable? Huh, maybe Nigel isn't so bad after all. "Well, I don't know about that, but I suppose that now that I'm thirty, I'm hopefully bringing a new sense of wisdom that I perhaps wouldn't have had at twenty-one. The wedding is really all about me and Will and our families joining together in a lifelong commitment of love, companionship, and family. The day itself is so much less important than each day to follow, and when you set forth with that understanding, even if there are a few mishaps, they simply won't trip you up in the same way."

"That's remarkably mature of you," he says. "And as someone who has been on the wrong side of thirty for quite some time, I can assure you that many people would still fall prey to the pressure, regardless of age."

"Well, I'm very fortunate to have my charitable work to keep me grounded in reality. For example, today, before you got here, I was working on an upcoming fundraiser for the Save the Bonobos Foundation. We're going to hold a silent auction in the late fall and we're hoping to raise a million dollars to purchase and protect a larger piece of the Congo for them."

"Brilliant," he says, even though the entire time I've been talking, he's been looking at his notes. "Now, are you going to give us any hints about the dress?"

I smile coyly. "Only that I absolutely love it and I hope the people will as well."

"Oh, come on, not even one little hint?"

"It's white," I say, then the two of us chuckle.

"Long-sleeved? Short-sleeved? No sleeves?" he asks.

He is a dog with a bone. "You'll just have to wait and find out with everyone else," I say, shaking a finger at him. "Nice try, though."

Nigel looks at the camera. "We are catching Princess Arabella on the day after the traditional bridal tea hosted by her grandmother,

Princess Dowager Florence." Turning back to me, he says, "And how was that?"

"Quite special. Instead of gifts, I requested that those in attendance make donations to a few of the charities that are dear to Will and me."

His face drops, just like I'm sure those of the guests did when they got the invitation and it said, 'In lieu of gifts, donations for the following organizations would be welcome…' "So what did you do if you weren't busy opening gifts?"

"The bridal tea is always such a lovely moment of sisterhood and sharing of marriage advice and hearing stories of those who have made this journey before me. It was a chance to catch up with many of my friends and acquaintances I haven't always managed to stay in touch with on a regular basis." I am lying through my pearly whites right now. The tea was dreadfully dull, I didn't know most of the guests, and most of them were generally quite irritated that they weren't able to one-up each other with increasingly lavish gifts we don't need. It took me the better part of three hours to walk around the room and address each person individually before the entire thing wrapped up and I was able to spend an hour standing at the door bidding them all a good evening.

"That's beautiful. Sisterhood," he says, sighing and nodding. Tilting his head, he gives me what I imagine is his best attempt at a sympathetic look (although to me, it looks like he's holding in a toot). "You lost your mum when you were only three months old. Tell me, Your Highness, is it as hard as one would think to be without a mother at such a momentous time in a woman's life? Is there a mum-sized hole in your life that simply cannot be filled?"

Oh for… "Of course I wish my mother were here. Always. But I'm so fortunate to have my gran, who stepped in to fill that void. I'm also very close to my father, my brother, and to Princess Tessa, who truly is like a sister to me."

"But still…" he says, leaning forward. "You must think about what lullabies she would have sung to you as a child and what kind of advice she would give you now as you prepare to become a wife, and perhaps a mother?"

Bastard. I swallow the lump in my throat and nod. *Don't tear up, you ninny.* "Certainly those thoughts come to mind at times, but again, I find focusing on what I do have is infinitely better than wasting time feeling sorry for myself about things I can't change."

"If she were here now, what do you think she would say?"

I give him a wry smile. "I imagine she'd tell you to stop trying to turn this interview into a melodrama."

Nigel looks taken aback, then says, "Touché."

He reaches down and has a sip of water, then sets the glass down, hopefully ready to move on. "I understand Mr. Banks has been away for several weeks now. You'll probably recall seeing footage of Lady Diana Spencer crying when she had to bid farewell to Prince Charles when he left for six weeks in Australia before their wedding. Your situation reminds me so much of that. Did you cry when he left?"

Ignoring the question, I pivot. "It's always difficult when the person you love has to go away for lengthy periods of time, and we're so very fond of each other."

"I take that as a yes," he says triumphantly.

"Take it however you like."

"Have you spoken to him recently?"

"Yes, we speak every chance we get."

"But I've heard that you aren't able to speak often because his filming locations are so remote that there isn't even phone reception for the most part. Do you lie awake worrying? And if so, do you resent him for making you lie awake at night just so he can go off on another adventure?"

I scoff and roll my eyes, completely abandoning proper decorum. "Not a bit. Having experienced that life with Will out in the jungle, albeit for a short period of time, I do have an understanding of what he's going through out there, and knowing how much he loves it makes it much easier for me to be happy for him while I anticipate his return." *Hmm, I wonder if I could have a career in politics if I hadn't been a princess?*

"Do you think his frequent travelling could negatively impact your relationship over the long haul?"

Shaking my head, I say, "No, I do not. One of the things I love about him is his commitment to and passion for his work. Besides, I'm hardly sitting at home all day bored and pining. I'm also very busy with fulfilling and important work as well, such as my ambassadorship with the Equal Everywhere Campaign. Our goal this year is to…" I drone on about it while Nigel shuffles his papers, then realize all of this is going to be cut, isn't it?

Yes, yes it is.

When I stop, Nigel re-engages. "As you know I'll be meeting Will at his home in Paradise Bay on Santa Valentina Island to offer our viewers an exclusive look at the latest royal groom's childhood home and to get to know his family. Give me the inside scoop, if you will, Your Highness. What can I expect?"

"Expect to absolutely love it there. Paradise Bay is aptly named. It's a terrifically gorgeous part of the Caribbean and there are many untouched natural areas to enjoy. And William's family is most hospitable and incredibly fun."

"Are you looking forward to joining the Banks clan, then?"

"I am. It would be impossible not to feel comfortable with them — they're just such good people."

"Lovely," he says, looking utterly bored. "And will you be having a hen's party?"

"No," I say with what I know is a rather condescending head shake. "That's for much younger women than me."

"So, you're not doing any sort of celebrating with your girl-friends?" Nigel asks, looking skeptical. "Say, maybe a trip to Ibiza like you took with Princess Tessa a few years back?"

My cheeks warm up as my mind flashes back to her, Nikki, and me in a jail cell. "No, nothing like that. They want to take me for a quiet dinner, which suits me perfectly."

"Any idea where you'll be dining?"

"I think they said something about French food but I want them to surprise me."

"Well, *bon appétit!*"

"Thank you."

And go to hell.

———

Totally Zen Princess Bride? This Wild Girl's Not Buying it
Will's Wild Fangirls Blog Post 294

Hello fellow fangirls,

Anyone else find it weird how quickly Princess Arabella and Will Banks are going to tie the knot? Like seriously, in three months? Could it be so Will won't realize what his life is going to be like and he won't run away before Princess Arabella can drag him down the aisle (like she dragged him through the jungle)?

And what's this talk about her being such a relaxed, easy-going bride? Yeah, because that's what royals are known for — being breezy. I caught the trailer for the 'Pre-Wedding Special' on ANN when I was watching reruns of The Wild World, and honestly, it's got to be the biggest pile of crap this side of a Texan cattle ranch. They're trying to sell us this super-calm bride who only thinks of others, when really we all know who she really is—a fame-hungry wannabe who latched on to Will's star just as it was going supernova.

She doesn't love him. She loves the currency he brings to the table as far as making her and her awful family more palatable to the regular people. So I'm starting an online movement, #freewill, to see if we can somehow get him to change his mind before it's too late.

Will, if you read this, please come to your senses and dump her on her royal tush. She's not the right girl for you. She just isn't. And I'm terrified that you won't know this until long after the wedding when she finally takes off her nicey nice mask and you see who she really is…

Peace Out Bitches,
The Future Mrs. Will Banks (AKA Hannah Goble)

COMMENTS:

WillGirl25: You said what everyone's thinking. But maybe it's already too late. Maybe they've accidentally spawned already and another royal mouth for the nation to feed is on the way.

Reply FutureMrsBanks: I think I'd die if that were true. Like, literally die.

RealHouseWivesRock: Bahahaha! 'Biggest pile of crap this side of a Texan cattle ranch.'

Reply FutureMrsBanks: Thanks, I thought that one was clever myself.

RoyalFan1: Sod off, Hannah the Hater. Seriously. How dare you criticize one of the sweetest, most real people on the planet?! Princess Arabella is FAR TOO GOOD for that shirtless moron. As far as I'm concerned, you can have him.

Chapter 16

TROPICAL BREEZE, FUNNY FOUR-YEAR-OLDS, AND IRRITATING SISTERS

Will

I'M HOME. I am finally home. A smile crosses my lips as I stare out the small window of the jet at the palm trees whizzing by as we taxi down the runway. I'll have twelve amazing days here at home to relax in the sun, surf the waves with my brother, Harrison, eat whatever incredible meals my sister, Emma, prepares, and play with my adorable niece, Clara. The ANN jet is going to drop a small group of us, including Gregory and my security staff, here before continuing on to Avonia for post-production on our Bolivia trip.

In a few days, the crew in charge of the pre-wedding special will arrive, but for now, I'm going to lay by the pool, bury my toes in the white sand, and sip beers while I watch gentle waves of turquoise water lap against the shore. I glance up and see that the seatbelt sign is still on, so I ready my thumb to unbuckle the second this plane stops. Tosh and Mac are already in full party mode, and Gregory is fast asleep, having spent the first four hours of our flight tutoring me.

Come on, come on, come on. Stop the plane already. I can run the rest of the way.

We finally come to a halt and I unbuckle and stand, ignoring the fact that the sign is still lit. The flight attendant gives me a look that says I shouldn't be up, and I return it with an 'I know, I'm sorry but I can't help myself' face. After a quick goodbye to the folks who aren't lucky enough to stay here with me in the greatest place on earth, I follow my security team out the door and down the steps into the tropical air that smells like home. It's late in the afternoon and the sun is starting to sink in the sky. The trade winds always pick up a little at this time of day, bringing with them the incredible scent of flowers and the sea. I glance back at Gregory, who looks uncomfortably warm in his suit and say, "I hope you packed some shorts."

He shakes his head. "No, sir, I'm on duty."

"Am I sort of your boss?" I ask, since honestly, I'm not really that sure how this works.

"Of course, sir."

"In that case, stop calling me sir. It's Will. And I insist that we get you some shorts and T-shirts. And also, that you take a few days off."

He opens his mouth to object but is interrupted by the sound of my sister Emma screaming as she runs out onto the tarmac. She's nothing if not subtle.

Damn, I hope she doesn't notice the enormous me on the jet. I'll never hear the end of it.

"WILLLL! You're home!!" she shouts, throwing her arms around me with a hearty slap on my back. After we hug, I ruffle her hair for good measure and she slaps my hand away good-naturedly. "Idiot."

"Is that how you greet your brother after he's been gone for so long?"

Her lips quirk up into a tiny grin and she says, "Welcome back. Some people missed you. Not me, of course, but I think Harrison, and obviously Rosy since you're her favourite."

"Obviously," I say. "But you're not excited at all. I could tell by the way you ran and screamed just now."

"Okay, I may have gotten a little enthusiastic, but only because my baby brother was rolling up in a jet with a giant image of his face plastered to the side of it," she says with a wicked grin.

Clearing my throat, I say, "I was kind of hoping you wouldn't notice that."

"Umm…how could I miss it?" she asks, staring up at it. "You're like…obnoxiously large. Like I could fit in one of your nostrils. And that smile is just…well, I don't even know how to describe it."

I roll my eyes at her, then ask, "Is it too much to hope you didn't take a bunch of photos and that, if you did, you won't be sending them to everyone we know?"

She sucks in some air between her teeth and says, "Yeah, too late for that I'm afraid. It's already happened, and the responses are already blowing up my phone."

"Huh, suddenly I've completely forgotten why I was in such a rush to get home."

———

It's late in the evening and I'm at Libby and Harrison's. I've just read Clara one of her bedtime stories and kissed her good night, then left her with Libby to finish the job of getting their four-year-old off to dreamland. I spent the entire evening desperately trying to get little Clara to remember I'm her favourite uncle (not Pierce, thank you very much). Apparently, I was a little too obvious because at one point, she gave me a slightly disgusted look and said, "Uncle Will, I need some space. You're very clingy." Luckily, my entire family heard it and will never let me live it down. So there's that…

But, setting biting preschooler comments aside, for the first time in months, I am in a place where I can let down my guard and not worry about anything. It's good to be home. However, that'll all change tomorrow, because I'm going to spend the day with the wedding film crew being interviewed for the pre-wedding special. They've brought in one of Avonia's nastiest human beings, fashion critic Nigel Wood, to do an in-depth look at 'Who Exactly is William Banks?' And tomorrow night, my in-laws are going to be arriving on their jet (actually two jets because the reigning monarch and the heir can never travel together). While I'm absolutely thrilled that Arabella is coming, I'm more than a little worried about the blending of our two families—especially because almost all of it will be caught on film. But that's

Future Will's problem. For now, I'm going to enjoy the moment here at home with my family.

I walk out to the back deck where Harrison, Emma, and her husband, Pierce, are visiting. Rosy and her husband, Darnell, were here for dinner, but they begged off an hour ago since Rosy can only stand to be outside for very short periods of time on account of hating all things nature. Grabbing a beer out of the cooler that sits next to the table, I crack it open and take a seat at the patio table.

Harrison smiles at me. "Did she make you read *Don't Let the Pigeon Drive the Bus?*"

I chuckle and nod. "She has good taste. That book is hilarious."

"It's not quite as amusing the two-hundredth time you've read it."

I chuckle a little. "Man, she has grown so much. And the talking… she's like a miniature adult. "

"More like a tiny nasty comedian doing crowd work all day," Harrison says.

"When she told Libby to 'chill sister' after she spilled her peas on the floor?" I laugh. "Where does she come up with this stuff?"

"From Emma," both Pierce and Harrison say at the same time.

Emma gasps, looking highly offended before nodding and saying, "Yeah, okay, so she definitely has a lot of her auntie in her."

We settle into a relaxed conversation and I feel utterly content, listening to the sound of the waves approaching and retreating against the nearby beach. I listen as Pierce talks about the book he's releasing this year—another fantasy novel—and watch as Emma adds all the braggy details that Pierce is leaving out (like how there's a bidding war happening between three networks already who want to adapt it onto screen). Libby comes out, looking sleepy after getting Clara to bed, and seats herself next to Harrison, who takes her hand and gives it a kiss.

I want what they've got. And I know this is what Arabella and I have when we're able to be alone. But the truth is, these types of easy moments are going to be few and far between, aren't they? And that's a thought I wish I could stop from popping into my head.

Chapter 17

UNCOOPERATIVE ROYALS AND THE WOMEN
WHO LOVE THEM (SORT OF...)

Arabella

"Okay, so I just want to go over a few things before the camera crew gets here to film our trip to the airport," I tell my family.

We're standing in the Grande Hall as the staff rush around with our luggage and the twins run in big circles with their arms out wide like airplanes. "First, thank you all so much for agreeing to come with me. I'm honestly so touched that you could all take the time to go on a little adventure whilst helping Will and I in our quest to free him."

Arthur snorts. "You make it sound like he's a prisoner of war or something."

I glare at him until he holds his hands up in surrender and says, "Got it. Angry bride."

"I am *not* an angry bride," I grind out. "I'm a woman dealing with a delicate situation who's doing what she must for love."

Arthur opens his mouth, but Tessa puts her hand on his arm. "Let's let Arabella continue, shall we?"

"Thank you," I say to her. "Now, Will's family is likely to be nervous about meeting you all. Apparently, someone sent them a stack of royal etiquette handbooks which hasn't helped matters."

There's some general tsking and I hear someone mutter Mrs. Chapman's name. I know it makes me a coward and an awful person not to tell them the truth, but technically, she did arrange to have them mailed, so…

So, I'm a coward and an awful person. "Anyway, let's do our best to be really warm and friendly to them. They're such good people, honestly. Salt of the earth. They don't want anything from us. Just to see Will happy. So, best foot forward please everyone, and Gran, *no* hitting on any of the resort guests, staff, and/or Will's friends, okay?"

Gran glares at me. "Perhaps I'll just stay home…"

I let my shoulders drop. "Fine, you can hit on other resort guests if you want, but that's it."

"Who put you in charge?" she asks.

"I did. Now, let's get going. We've got a long day ahead." With that, I spin on my heel and stride toward the door, ignoring the fact that Arthur is trying to get my dad to take me on his plane and my dad is flatly refusing.

So, this is what I've become. A wedding pariah. One step shy of bridezilla. But I suppose desperate times call for desperate measures, right?

142

Chapter 18

THE KNIGHTING OF SIR CRIES-A-LOT

Will

"WELCOME TO PARADISE BAY. I'm your host, Nigel Wood — fashion critic and co-host of ABN's Entertainment Weekly. As the entire kingdom is swept up in wedding fever, I have made a trip to Santa Valentina Island to spend some time getting to know Avonia's latest royal groom, Will Banks. Most of you know him from his show *The Wild World*, which also spent one season entitled *Princess in the Wild*, which is, incidentally, the season in which he and Princess Arabella fell in love off-screen. For those of you who haven't seen that exhilarating and deliciously romantic season, tune in to ANN Monday through Wednesday from seven till nine p.m. as a lead up to the big day, Thursday, June third. As a huge fan of the show myself, I cannot recommend it enough."

I stand on the spot marked off for me in the shade of a palm tree, next to one of the pools at the resort, and wait for my introduction, not particularly excited about having to spend the entire day with Nigel Wood when perfect waves are rolling up to shore and my surf-board is waiting. To be honest, I'm a bit nervous. Well, maybe more than a bit actually. This is what you could call a high-stakes interview, because it's my best chance to show the world I'm a good match for Arabella, and to prove I can fit into her world. And I'm bound and determined to lose that whole Knight of the No Shirt moniker.

Gregory spent the better part of two hours this morning prepping me, leaving my brain in a total swirl of words and phrases to use (and to avoid) so I can sound posh (which incidentally is one of the words to avoid if you want to sound posh). But I've done all I can to maneuver this interview into something that makes me look as good as possible. I've arranged to sail Nigel out to the Island of Eden for a sneak peek at the luxury island getaway where Arabella and I will spend a few days after the wedding. This has the added bonus of me showing off my sailing skills (always a manly thing to do) while showcasing one of the best things about the resort—Eden. So maybe they can call me Sir Skillful Sailor or Sir Manly—that would work too.

My phone buzzes in the pocket of my shorts, and I discreetly pull it out only to see a text from Arabella. *Good luck today, darling. And whatever you do, don't let that nasty man make you cry.*

Ha! As if that could ever happen. There is no way a man like him is going to manage to draw tears from someone like me. No sense in focussing on something that isn't going to happen. I slide my phone back into my pocket just as Nigel is saying, "So let's meet our groom, shall we?"

The camera pans out as Nigel walks over to me and we exchange hellos and shake hands, even though we've spent the better part of an hour together already this morning, then Nigel gives me a little nod and starts with his questions. "So, William, what was it like growing up in literal paradise?"

"Well, I think you just described it yourself. For a person like me, who loves the outdoors and surfing, sailing, snorkeling, and playing sports, I couldn't have asked for a better place to grow up."

"You weren't always the outdoorsman, were you? You did admit to Princess Arabella when you were out in the jungle that the first time you spent the night outside, you couldn't sleep and you had a big cry."

I give him an easy smile and nod. "Mind you, I was seven at the time."

Nigel chuckles, then says, "Why don't we start with the big tour of your old stomping grounds?"

"I'd love to," I answer.

"We're going to hop into a golf cart and Will is going to show us around the resort he calls home."

The tour takes over an hour, with me driving along the wide paved path of the grounds, trying to showcase anything I think will help convince people to book a stay. We start out on the southeast side of the resort and work our way around to the west where the staff housing is, eventually stopping in front of the tiny one-bedroom ground floor apartment that I sometimes call home.

Getting out of the golf cart, we walk to the front door. "So, this is where I stay when I'm not off filming or in Valcourt with Arabella."

We walk directly into the small living room, and it suddenly occurs to me how sparse and empty the place looks. Other than the older style couch and media centre that was added when the resort was renovated, there's only my surfboard to show that someone actually lives here.

"Well, this is rather sad, isn't it?" Nigel asks, looking around the room.

"To be honest, it's more of a place to store my things because I'm not here very often, and when I am, you won't find me inside unless I'm sleeping. Otherwise, I'm either helping out around the resort or off surfing or doing other fun things."

"Has Princess Arabella ever been in here?" he asks, his nose wrinkling up.

"Yes, she was here briefly before we took off on a yacht trip for a couple of months around the South Pacific."

"And did she find it particularly depressing?"

I pause, allowing the biting comment on the tip of my tongue to dissolve. "I don't think so. I believe she said something about how practical it was for me to live a minimalist lifestyle, given my travel schedule."

"Really? It must be true love then because I would've thought she'd have ended up running for the hills."

"Well, she didn't so I guess she's not as shallow as other people might be," I say, maintaining eye contact while I tell him he's shallow. "Anyway, I think we should get out of here and go see a particularly special part of the Paradise Bay Resort where Princess Arabella and I will be spending a few days of our honeymoon — the Island of Eden. I've prepared a special surprise for your viewers. We will be taking my family's yacht and sailing our way to Eden. So let's get going." So I can become Captain Manly Guy.

Tosh shuts off the camera and lowers it from his shoulder while Nigel gives me an impressed nod. "You're good. You have a unique ability to steer the conversation away from where you don't want it to go."

"Oh, was I doing that?" I ask innocently. "Just trying to move things along and keep the pace up for the audience."

Nigel gives me a smile I can only describe as smarmy. "You're not going to win, you know."

"Aren't we on the same team?" I ask Nigel, hardening my gaze and setting my jaw.

"Of course," he says, but we both know neither of us mean it.

———

"And here we are, on the Banks' family yacht, the Waltzing Matilda. She's an impressive ninety-foot schooner built back in the 1920s that the family briefly lost due to financial problems before Princess Arabella bought it back for them. Tell us about that," Nigel says. "Was it a moment of shame for your family?"

Bastard. "No. My brother sold her to save the resort after we'd been hit particularly hard by Hurricane Irma. I had been planning to buy it back with the winnings from *Princess in the Wild*, but we were approximately an hour late getting to the finish line. The opportunity was about to pass by when Arabella stepped in and bought her back for us. A very generous and kind thing to do."

"Be honest, that must have been rather emasculating for you," he says, feigning sympathy while taking a direct shot at my sense of pride. "I know you received a lot of public criticism for that."

"Well, perhaps for a more old-fashioned sort of person. But I like to think of myself as a forward-thinking man," I tell him. "Besides, Arabella felt responsible for us not crossing the finish line in time and she wanted to find a way to make it up to me."

"Do you still blame her for what happened out there?"

Oh for…I shake a finger at him and say, "I see what you're trying to do, Nigel, and it is not going to work."

Nigel tilts his head and gives me an extremely condescending look that makes me want to toss him overboard. "The only thing I'm trying to do is allow the viewers to really get to know you, but the fact that you're avoiding the question may lead some to believe that you do, in fact, blame her."

My jaw tightens even though I'm trying like hell to look casual. "Well, they would be wrong. As the experienced party out in that jungle, the responsibility for our safety *and* our ability to move through the jungle quickly enough was squarely on my shoulders."

Scratching his neck, Nigel says, "But she ate the berries that made her sick which slowed you down."

Through gritted teeth, I say, "And it was my job to stay with her so that she wouldn't come to harm, and I failed to do that."

"So your failure resulted in you being gifted this gorgeous yacht. How fortunate for you."

Fucker. He's got me there, doesn't he?

———

It's late in the afternoon. We've been to Eden and back, and now Nigel and I are sitting at a small round table at the beach bar (which has been closed during the interview). So far, I've managed to avoid making an arse of myself, but instead of feeling relieved, I feel a heightened sense of anxiety, as though I'm going to fuck it all up at the end like a cop who winds up getting shot an hour before he retires.

"So, Will. Let's set the stage. You're a six-year-old boy in Valcourt. It's almost December, and, like all small children, you're getting excited about Father Christmas coming to visit. Your dad, a podiatrist, and your mum, a homemaker, hire a sitter one night so they can go to your dad's office Christmas party. You kiss them goodnight at the door, probably giddy that the sitter will let you eat an extra piece of cake before bed, but you had no idea it would be the last time you'd ever see your mum and dad alive. Talk about that."

I blink a few times, doing my best not to regress back to that night. Not in front of this tosser. "Well, as you can probably imagine, it was quite an awful shock for my brother, sister, and me."

"Of course it was. Orphaned so suddenly when a drunk driver killed both your parents. The life you'd always known ripped from you in a split second. How did you survive that?"

Dammit, he's better at this than I thought he'd be. My nose tickles with emotion. "With the help of my brother and sister, and of course our uncle who immediately came to Valcourt to get us."

Nigel nods his head with a meaningful look on his face. "How do you think that tragedy shaped who you are now?"

Moving to safer territory… "Well, for one, we moved halfway across the world and spent the rest of our childhood here on the island. Obviously, living with an outdoorsman like Uncle Oscar certainly impacted who I would become."

"And tell me about him. He sounds like a larger-than-life sort of man—resort owner, world traveler, sailor. He was obviously the biggest influence in your life and then you lost him just as suddenly when you were only sixteen years old to a heart attack. That must've been far more than a young teenager should have had to handle. Do you think you've fully processed this loss?"

"Umm…sure, yes."

"You must've felt lost at sea. First, your parents, then losing the driving force behind who you were becoming and the only adult to care for you in the world."

Irritation scratches at my throat and spreads through my body, and it's all I can do not to tell him to sod off. "Lucky for us, we had a rather large support network here at the resort. Several of the long-time staff members had already stepped up to help Uncle Oscar raise us. In particular, one woman, Rosy Brown, who in every way has become like a mother to us. She certainly picked up where our own dear mother had left off as far as providing that nurturing and helping us along our way."

Is that a lump in my throat? Bloody hell, I think it is. I clear my throat and sit back in the chair, trying to maintain a relaxed posture.

"And tell me about your brother. I've heard he is somewhat of a surf legend here on the island, and in doing my homework on your family, it sounds as though he has also been a father figure to you."

Okay, no problem. I can talk about this. Just talk but don't really think about what you're saying. But also, don't say anything stupid in the process. "Absolutely. Harrison is five years older than me and he took on a lot of responsibility for my sister and I when we moved here. He made sure we kept up our grades and went to bed on time. I owe so much to him. When I think about how young he was to take all that on, it blows my mind that he was able to do it so well."

"Would you say Harrison is your hero?" Nigel asks, his face filled with compassion.

I nod, at first, wanting to agree just to honour Harrison, but then, I'm overcome with a swell of emotion. *Son of a bitch. Are those tears?* My nose fills and I sniffle, then immediately realize how horrifying that noise is going to be for my future in-laws. Clearing my throat again, I shake a finger at Nigel. "You're not going to make me cry."

He shakes his head, his face reflecting complete sincerity. "I just want the viewers to get to know the *real you*. The man behind the death-defying stunts, the one who has known so much heartache at such a tender age. But let's get back to your big brother, Harrison, and how he sacrificed for you and your sister..."

Shit. I can't exactly brush this off and look like I appreciate all Harrison's done for us—which I do. But now that he's taken me so far down this path, I am an emotional wreck. I nod, tears filling my eyes. "Absolutely, he has. When Uncle Oscar passed away, Harrison took over management of this entire resort. He was only twenty-one at the time. If anybody should be famous, it should be him," I say, stopping to wipe my eyes. "He scraped together the money to send my sister to culinary school in New York and he also took the lion's share of the responsibility here so I could pursue my dreams."

"And you once said you could never repay him. What does that feel like? Knowing you can never pay your hero back for all he's done for you?"

Bloody hell. I'm now full-on crying. "Can we take a break please?"

"Of course," Nigel says, smiling like the cat who ate the canary.

———

The Knight of the No Shirt Has Now Been Dubbed Sir Cries-a-Lot.
Daily Mail Opinion Column by Hazel Nettlebottom

Wedding fever has hit Avonia hard with the upcoming nuptials of Princess Arabella and Avonia's favourite wild man, Will Banks. In the run-up to the big event, the happy couple have agreed to an exclusive behind-the-scenes look at their lives, including pre-wedding interviews. Footage released today from ANN shows Will breaking down into tears while discussing the loss of his parents and his uncle who adopted Will and his siblings.

Instead of finding compassion, sadly, in our world of toxic masculinity, poor Will has been dubbed Sir Cries-a-Lot, an extremely unflattering moniker that this writer is worried he'll have to wear for some time to come. #sircriesalot has been trending on Twitter since the first commercial aired, showing Will crying whilst sitting at a beach bar. In response, another group has started another hashtag: #freewill, used by people declaring that if Will marries into the royal family, he's going to trap himself in a cyclone of hateful criticism for the rest of his days.

What I find insane is that, even though we're in the second decade of the 21st-century, it's still considered unacceptable for men to express any emotion other than anger. I, for one, found it refreshing to see him open up like that. After all, wouldn't it in fact be less healthy had he no feelings about the matter whatsoever?

As silly as the #freewill movement might sound, this entire situation should perhaps serve as a warning for Will about what he's truly getting into in marrying into the royal family—a life of attacks and criticism for everything he does. There will always be those who are jealous of such a daring, handsome, incredible man, who are going to delight in each of his failures (not that crying should be considered a failure). On the other end, his swath of fans who demand he be ultra-masculine at all times are also up in arms over the fact that he's human. They, too, should be ashamed of themselves, but they will never have the good sense to understand how much harm their expectations cause.

Here's wishing for a future where a man will be praised for being brave enough to be vulnerable. In the meantime, let's all try to be a little kinder. The world could use it.

COMMENTS:

Kingslayer99: If you lie down with dogs, you wake up with fleas. He's getting exactly what he deserves.

Will4Ever86: Who asked you, Kingslayer? NO ONE, so shut up. We need to stand by Will. #freewill

SweetandSavoryMan: I agree with Kingslayer. These people don't deserve our pity. Did this Will Banks guy have a tough childhood? Yeah, sort of, I guess, but he also grew up rich (come on – his family owns a resort in the Caribbean?) and has done well for himself. So many folks have it much worse so let's not praise a man for feeling sorry for himself and trying to get the world to join him in his pity party.

4x4Dude: I'm going to call him Sir Cries-a-Lot. Don't know who thought of it, but it's going to stick if I can help it. After all the things he said about Bear Grylls? He can suck it.

Chapter 19

THE GREETING PARTY BLUES...

Will

WELL, that happened in record speed. I only finished filming the special three hours ago, and clips of me bawling have already gone viral. I'm pacing in front of the Paradise Bay Resort lobby while I wait for my fiancée and future in-laws to show up. According to Reynard (who got word from Arabella's bodyguard, Bellford), they'll be here in eight minutes. Reynard is standing in the shade nearby, the pre-wedding film crew is setting up the cameras, and I'm fidgeting like a grade school boy who's had to wee for the last hour.

The horrible truth is I'll never fit in with Arabella's people.

NEVER.

ANN has made sure of it with all these bloody shirtless videos of me and by plastering my face across a plane, for God's sake. And now, I *cried* on television?

Showing emotion is not exactly acceptable among royals. It even says it right in the handbook, "Thou shall not display any emotion that will cause others discomfort." Okay, I'm paraphrasing, but still... This is BAD. I was already a punchline for the upper crust of Avonia (and likely beyond), but now I'm not sure I can come back from it. I can't even imagine what the trolls on those royal forums are saying, but rest assured, there are a lot of grown men laughing their arses off in their mothers' basements today.

When I think about what this'll do to Arabella, my stomach does flips. She had to fight *far* too hard for anyone to take her seriously, and I'm pretty sure I'm going to totally kill it for her (if I haven't already).

The truth is, if this hasn't done it, something else will. It's just a matter of time. I'll just do or say the wrong thing and it'll get blown up in the media as some horrible scandal and…I could ruin her life. The closer we get to the big day, the *less positive* I am that I'm going to manage to make it through the next forty or fifty years without embarrassing her beyond all possibility of turning back.

I turn to Reynard and ask, "What are the chances they'll never hear about this ridiculous Sir Cries-a-Lot business?"

He hesitates and I say, "Zero percent, right?"

Nodding, he says, "I'd say that's likely."

"You know I'm not a wimp, right Reynard?"

"Of course, sir."

Sir.

Sir Cries-a-Lot. Grrrr… "Sir Cries-a-Lot. Psh! How about Sir Until Today Has Only Cried Once as an Adult?" I say, referring to the night I spent wedged into a narrow ravine in the Congo believing I was going to die there. But I only cried when I made a goodbye video for my family, and who wouldn't? You'd have to be made of stone. Sigh, I add, "Or Sir Never Cries Despite Many Tragedies."

"Much better, Will," he says with a comforting nod. "Definitely more on-the-mark, if not a tad wordy."

"Well, we'd have to finesse it…" I say, then stop in my tracks and look up at the blue sky. "We'd have to finesse it? I'm going a little bonkers here."

"Totally natural under the circumstances," he says.

Notice he doesn't deny it? Hmm…

"I know it shouldn't matter *at all*, but let's face it—it does," I tell him, leaning in and lowering my voice. "Not because the world now knows I have normal human emotions, but because it's just one more reason for the family to dislike me. That giant asshat Nigel Wood didn't even manage to make Arabella tear up—and she's widely known as the softest one in the bunch. So, what the hell does that make me?"

He opens his mouth, but I shake my head. "Please don't answer that."

"Anyone to think less of you is not worth knowing."

"Yeah, good point," I say, nodding.

"He's right, Cuddle Bear," Rosy, who clearly has been listening, says as she approaches from the lobby. "Don't give all those jealous haters a second thought."

She reaches up and pinches my cheek.

"So, you saw it already too?"

"No, but the FedEx guy did," she says casually.

Well, that's just great.

"So, where are the fancy schmancies?" she asks. "I thought they'd be here by now."

I give her a look. "Rosy, can you at least try to welcome them?"

She shrugs. "I'll try but it'll be hard. I do not like what they're doing to my Cuddle Bear. They are stressing you out. And that handbook on how to behave? Come on!" she says, her voice getting louder with each word. "You know what's rude? Telling people how to behave!"

I glance over to the camera crew, terrified that they're already filming this, but, thankfully, they're still setting up. "I promise you they're not like that when you get to know them," I tell her.

"Who's not like what?" Emma asks, rushing over in her chef's uniform. She is only able to make a brief appearance before she has to get back to the restaurant.

"The royals aren't hoity-toity," Rosy tells her.

They both look at each other and scoff.

"Who's hoity-toity?" Harrison asks as he, Libby, and Clara come down the steps toward us. Clara's dressed in an adorable sundress and her curly, wild hair is up in a ponytail that makes it look like she's got a mop growing out of her head.

"What is a hoity-toity?" Clara asks.

"An uppity rich person who thinks they're better than us regular folks," Rosy tells her.

Oh God! They have to teach her a new word *now*? At this moment?! "Nobody is hoity-toity!" I say, then I gesture urgently for the family to huddle up. Lowering my voice, I say, "The cameras are about to turn on so we need to be careful about what we say."

Emma taps the side of her nose. "Showtime. Got it."

"Also, whatever you do, don't look directly at them," I say.

"Who? Your future in-laws?" Emma asks.

"The cameras," I say, rolling my eyes.

Clara turns to the film crew and starts to do a four-year-old version of an untrained tap dance, complete with jazz hands while the rest of us look on. I smile down at her, suddenly realizing that with three kids involved, the pressure will be off Arabella and me big time. Kids are natural performers, and they'll keep everyone so busy, we won't have time to get to hate each other.

Jake, the wedding crew director, gives me the signal that they're starting to roll. Clara decides she's had enough of dancing and wants her dad to pick her up. With nothing to entertain us, we all stand awkwardly facing the long road that leads to the highway.

Emma clears her throat. "Lovely weather we're having, yes?"

"Oh, yes," Harrison says. "Not too hot."

There's a long, uncomfortable pause, then Rosy adds, "Did anyone catch *Survivor* last night?"

"No," I tell her. Libby and Harrison shake their heads to the negative as well.

"Was it a good episode then?" Libby asks.

Shaking her head, Rosy says, "I didn't see it either."

"Right," I say.

Oh, kill me now...

My phone buzzes and I pull it out to see a text from Arabella:

We're almost at the resort, sweetie! I cannot wait to jump into your arms. Xoxo

P.S. Please don't obsess over your most-appropriate emotional display. We're behind you all the way. I personally find it rather endearing. Your obvious love for your family is one of the things that caused me to fall for you in the first place, so you needn't be ashamed.

Urgh...

Chapter 20

NERVOUS BURPS, COMMONERS, AND HOITY-TOITIES...

Arabella

"Dad, just try to look relaxed," I tell him, gripping his shoulder and gently shaking it to see if I can get him to loosen up.

He slumps a little in the seat, looking like someone has taped his chin to his chest. "How's this?"

"Terrible," I say. "How do you not know how to be casual?"

"How do *you* not know the answer to that?" Gran asks. "I should have gone with Arthur and Tessa."

"If you'll recall, they did offer, but you told them you'd rather eat glass than ride with the two totally wound-up kiddies screeching like banshees," I tell her.

"I know what I said, and I stand by it," Gran snaps. "What I really should have done is got my own car. Or maybe a moped," she says, as an old woman on a bright turquoise Vespa passes us. "That looks like a riot."

I watch as the woman goes by looking like she doesn't have a care in the world. I'm suddenly chartreuse with envy. Oh, to be that free. Then it occurs to me that I'm the one turning this into the tension-filled insanity that it's become, and I really don't have to. I put my hand on Gran's and say, "I'm sorry. I'm just so desperate for everything to go well between our two families."

"We know," Gran says. "You've only been talking about it since we left the palace. Clam up already. You're making everyone nervous."

Clam up? Well, that was rude. I turn to look out the windows at the palm trees zipping by. I so wish the film crews weren't meeting us here. This trip is a total risk, and to be honest, since I suggested it, I've been second-guessing the entire thing. I mean, what if instead of bringing our families closer together, we end up in some big awful brawl?

Oh God. There's the sign for Paradise Bay. A loud burp escapes from my dad. He covers his mouth and says, "Excuse me."

"Now, look what you've done!" Gran tells me. "You've given him the nervous burps."

The nervous burps is a rather unfortunate family trait that luckily Arthur and I haven't inherited. It almost never happens, but once my father starts, he can't stop. In fact, they get louder and longer until whatever is stressing him out goes away, which could be hours…or in this case, possibly days if we get off on the wrong foot. Guilt floods my chest and I pat my father's knee. "Dad, pay no attention to all my fussing. I shouldn't have been so hard on you. Everything will be fine, I'm sure."

Maybe.

It better be or I'll kill someone.

Stop that, Arabella! Perspective!

We pull up in front of the large, open-air lobby and see Will and his entire family standing off to the side under the shade of the enormous portico. My heart pounds wildly and my palms go sweaty as I silently pray to all that is holy that this goes well.

When we step out into the hot, fragrant air, I draw in a deep breath and hurry over to Will, trying not to look too desperate in front of the cameras, but also totally feeling desperate to wrap my arms around him.

Grinning, he pulls me in for a long hug—oh, wow, that's what I needed—and we give each other a kiss that's somewhere between church-appropriate and soldier returning from war.

Someone clears their throat and I realize it's Arthur, who is standing stiffly, waiting for introductions. Will and I pull apart from each other quickly and a chain of hellos and awkward bows and clumsy curtsies (especially from poor, very obviously pregnant Libby) begins while I say, "Oh, no, you don't have to...that's okay...let's be informal about all of this..."

Too late. It's all done. We stand and stare at each other for a moment, then my dad lets out a loud burp. I quickly start talking in an overly loud voice to cover up for him. "Flora and James, this is Clara! She's Will's niece and she's around the same age as you."

Flora, who looks totally exhausted, hangs off Tessa's hip and gives Clara a disinterested nod. James, who's clearly got ants in his pants zips up to her and pokes her on the nose with one finger, and says, "You're a ginger."

Oh, no, no, no. Let's play nicely, children. I'm counting on you.

Clara gives a confused look up at Libby, who doesn't seem to know what to say. Arthur swoops in, crouching down and saying, "That means he loves the beautiful red colour of your hair. And so do I. My name is Arthur, by the way. I'm Arabella's big brother."

Oh, thank goodness. Arthur can save this, I'm sure. He's wonderful with children (although not as good as their super hot manny, Xavier, who they decided to leave at home). Arthur turns to his son, who is shaking his head and saying, "But I don't love her hair, Father."

Arthur gives him *the look* and says, "Please introduce yourself properly, James."

"My name is James Edward Ruben Winston Langdon. I'm a prince so you must call me Prince James or, if you like, you may call me sir."

Tessa gasps loudly while Arthur takes James by the hand, muttering, "Excuse me." The pair disappear around the corner where Arthur gives him a good talking-to. I know because I can hear every word, and likely so can the cameras. I am guessing right about now that Arthur is really regretting telling Xavier that he could have the week off, that he and Tessa can certainly manage their little angels for a week. Xavier might be getting a raise…

BURP!

I smile down at Clara and say, "Hello Clara, what a beautiful dress you have on."

She grins up at me shyly and nods. Turning to Flora, I say, "Come say hi to Clara. I'm sure you two will be fast friends."

"No thank you, Auntie. I'm not in the mood for public engagements," she says in a haughty tone.

Gran stifles a laugh, obviously finding it amusing to see the next generation of parents being humiliated by their children. Rosy, who seems to think that Gran approves of my niece and nephew's snooty behaviour, glares at Gran and crosses her arms. The rest of Will's family looks on with a mixture of concern and disapproval while I offer an awkward laugh. "I'm so sorry, Clara. I'm afraid James and Flora are rather tired after a long day of travel, but I'm certain tomorrow they'll be much more fun."

She shrugs. "That's okay. They're…" Turning to Harrison, she says, "Dad, what's that word you said? Hotty tatty?"

"I honestly don't know what she's talking about," he tells us, turning bright pink.

"Before they got here. You said a word I don't know and Rosy told me it meant a rich rude person. Remember?"

Covering her mouth with one hand, he says, "Nope, I didn't say anything of the sort. Kids and their wild imaginations."

My father lets out another loud burp, holding his hand over his mouth.

Clara snaps her little fingers and says, "Hoity-toity! That was it."

Oh good lord, now my entire family is shifting uncomfortably in their spots.

Emma, who is dressed in her uniform, says, "Well, I'm afraid I have to get back to the restaurant, but I'm really excited to get to know you all during your stay. Lovely to meet you." She gives Will a 'glad it's you and not me' look, then hurries off, leaving the rest of us with nothing to say.

Arthur and James come back, and Arthur gives James a little

nudge when he gets close to Clara. "I apologize for what I said to you about your hair. Also, you can just call me James."

Tessa and Arthur both visibly relax, then James adds, "It's not really okay for a commoner, but my dad said you get a pass because my auntie is marrying your commoner uncle."

Worst. Idea. Ever.

Royal News – The Official Website for All Things Avonian Royal

Forum Thread: Not So Welcoming Welcome for Our Royals in Paradise Bay *(12 Currently Viewing, 2365 Total Views, 680 Comments)*

For the first time in history, the entire royal family has gone on holiday together to a foreign country. (They do, of course, travel to their lovely North Castle for Christmas and other holidays from time to time.) An ANN film crew caught up with them as they arrived at the Paradise Bay Resort, sparking a huge scandal as Will Banks' family scorned them openly and insulted them by calling them hoity-toity. Looks like we were right all along and a marriage between a commoner such as Will Banks will only spell disaster for Avonia's royals, just as it did in England.

Cindy (Serene Highness): Who couldn't see that coming a mile away? Anyone who's seen Tarzan knows it doesn't end well when a wildling tries to fit into a civilized world.

Felix (Courtier): I'd like to say anyone who thought this union was a good way to bridge the ties between the upper crust and the 'normal folk' is an idiot. Full stop.

Stephen (Heir Presumptive): I must say, Prince James conducted himself in a most disappointing way. I know he's only five and I don't blame him for speaking the truth, but this goes to prove that hiring that brainless 'manny' instead of a proper governess is coming back to haunt Prince Arthur and Princess Tessa.

Felix (Courtier): You've proven my point for me, Stephen. Prince Arthur married a commoner, and we can see the results of her raising the next heirs — they will be classless like their mother.

Kitty (Aristocrat): I, for one, cannot wait for the wedding, especially if those gorgeous Banks brothers were to don kilts. Is that possible? I think I would die to see Will Banks in a kilt (and to see what's underneath it...)

Chapter 21

ONE BIG HAPPY FAMILY

Will

"TODAY IS BOUND to be better, right?" Arabella asks me as we walk along the wide, paved path toward the ocean, our arms loaded with life jackets. It's early in the morning, and we're going to get things set up on the *Waltzing Matilda* for a Langdon-Banks family sail. The film crew is meeting us at the dock and will be accompanying us on a quick tour around the bay, then we're dropping them off so we can have a proper day on the water for everyone to relax. Well, as relaxed as this group can be around each other, which remains to be seen. Rosy and Darnell aren't coming today on account of the itinerary being outdoors, so I'm hoping that cuts some of the weirdness a bit.

Speaking of weirdness, we'll not only have a full security team on board with us, but we'll also have two boats flanking Matilda, both loaded with armed guards, so that ought to give my family pause for thought. Although I'm used to it (sort of, not really), I have a feeling they're going to find it super uncomfortable. Not that I can tell Arabella any of this. So, I keep that all in and just say, "Yeah, today is definitely going to be better. Great, even. The kids were just tired yesterday,"

Of course, I'm completely ignoring the fact that the grown-ups weren't exactly on their best behaviour either. After our initial meeting, the royals all went to get settled in their rooms, but not before Rosy and the Princess Dowager took a few swipes at each other. Also, Libby, who thought she was being nice, told King Winston not to worry about the burping because she, too, was burping up a storm now that she is in her third trimester. She probably should have stopped there, but she didn't. Instead, she kept going, telling him that once the baby comes, she'll go back to being burp-free. Then she glanced at his sizable gut and turned bright pink. Then her nose started to bleed because Libby's a stress-bleeder. And not a delicate one either (if there is such a thing). The spray coming from her nose is instant and shockingly fast. Sadly, she was holding Clara at the time, who started to screech at the top of her lungs, which frightened James and Flora, who also began screaming. This caused the Princess Dowager to clap her hands over her ears and holler at everyone to 'SHUT UP!' and Pierce, who has a surprisingly weak stomach for a man who writes horrific fight scenes in his novels, began to gag repeatedly.

There's a long pause and I wonder if Arabella is also replaying the scene from yesterday's meeting in her mind. Finally, she says, "Once we get out on the water, I'm sure everyone will relax and get to know each other. It'll be wonderful."

"Definitely. By the end of the day, we'll be one big happy family," I say, knowing that the chances of this are slim-to-none.

We round the corner of the path, and the old schooner comes into sight, causing me to let out a wistful sigh. "Remember when it was just the two of us on *Matilda* for a month?"

Arabella nods and looks up at me with longing. "I wish we were just setting off again to take the exact same route."

"Or, better yet, get on and keep sailing forever," I tell her.

"Oh yes, we could just get married on a beach somewhere in a private ceremony."

I groan. "Okay, we better stop this or I'm going to toss these life jackets, throw you over my shoulder, and hightail it out of here with you."

Arabella chuckles, then sighs. "Is it me, or has this all been much harder than you thought it would be?"

"Well, I kind of had a feeling it would be tough, to be honest," I tell her. "But I have a very good feeling things'll get easier. We just have to get through the next few weeks."

"Right, yeah," she answers, looking distracted. "It'll be fine."

"Yes, it really will," I say, stopping on the path and turning to her. "The key is for you and I to stick together no matter what happens."

"Right. Exactly," she says with a firm nod. "We stick together like glue."

I lean down and give her a kiss. "Like glue."

An hour later, we set off with me at the wheel and a light Caribbean breeze filling the sails. The sun shines down on us while Harrison and Tessa slather the children with sunscreen, both with extremely phony smiles in front of the camera. Emma's standing next to Pierce and Arthur, who are casually chatting about whatever rich dudes chat about—I'm assuming stock options and...polo. The Princess Dowager, who apparently managed to get a poker game going in her suite last night, was up until dawn, and is fast asleep on a lounge chair that is bolted to the deck.

King Winston, who's dressed in a white button up shirt, chinos, and an oversized sunhat that looks slightly feminine, is sitting on the chaise next to hers, his hands balled into fists on his lap. He lets out a loud burp, then sighs.

I lean toward Arabella, who is standing next to me, and lower my voice. "Is your father okay? He looks a little nervous."

"He hates boats," Arabella says with a shrug. "Something about almost drowning off the coast of Spain when he was in the navy."

"What?" I ask, my jaw dropping. "Then why are we taking him sailing?"

"He's got to get over it. It's been, like, forty years since that happened," she says, sounding a lot less compassionate than I'm used to. "And it's not like he did drown. He only *almost* drowned."

I stare at her, a little scared of what I'm hearing. She must be able to read my mind because she adds, "In our family, we suck it up and keep going."

"Okkaaayyy," I say.

"What?" Arabella asks.

"I just feel bad for your father, that's all. The point of today is for everyone to relax and have fun, and yet…" I look back at him and Arabella's gaze follows mine.

He's now gripping the bench with white knuckles. "That's it," I tell her. "I'm going to go see if I can help him. You mingle with my family so it looks like we all get along."

I call to Harrison, who has finished lathering his so-pale-she's-almost-see-through daughter with sunblock, and ask him to take over at the wheel. Then I make my way over to my future father-in-law and sit on a deck chair near him. He gives me a quick nod and lets out a small burp. "Sorry, it's a disgusting affliction."

"Don't worry about it," I tell him. Lowering my voice, I add, "I had no idea you were afraid of boats."

His head snaps back and he says, "I'm not afraid of them! I just hate the bloody things."

Shit. I should not have said that. And the cameraman definitely caught that, based on the fact that he's zooming in on us. I plaster a smile on and say, "No, right, I didn't mean afraid. I meant *uncomfortable* on account of your navy incident."

The Princess Dowager opens one eye and says, "Don't bring that up, you ninny. Not while we're *on* a boat."

Arabella, who seems to be finished talking with Libby already, rushes over to us with a wide grin and panic in her eyes. Without moving her lips, she manages to say, "Gran, don't call my fiancé a ninny. He's only trying to help."

Wow, now that's a talent I didn't know she had.

"Well, he could stand to learn a thing or two about what proper help would look like," Princess Florence says, shooting me a sharp glare.

"Oh, hey, everyone!" Harrison calls. "A dolphin!"

He points to the far side of the yacht, causing our fellow passengers to abandon what they're doing to go see, except Princess Florence, who starts to snore lightly, having somehow managed to go

166

right back to sleep. King Winston doesn't move either, and instead lets out a small burp.

I want to get up to join the fun, but I also don't want to seem insensitive. "Do you like dolphins?" I ask him.

When he doesn't answer, I mutter, "Probably not on account of the whole 'needing to be around the ocean' thing."

After a moment, he says, "Listen, William, I appreciate the effort. Very kind of you. But certain things are best left alone, this situation being one of them. The frequency with which I am forced to go out on the sea isn't so great that I need to do a deep dive into my psyche about it."

I nod and offer him a small smile even though it sort of feels like he's a headmaster who's just given me a whack with a ruler. "All right, Your Majesty. If you need anything, please let me know."

"I shall," he answers as I get up.

I walk over to the group, praying this will be the moment that will turn everything around. Dolphins are always the best for creating a sense of excitement and fun. I stroll past the camera crew and hear Clara telling our guests everything she knows about dolphins. "They are not fish, they are mammals."

"It's a fish," James says.

"Nope, I already told you," Clara says, sounding agitated. "They are mammals like us. The mummy dolphins feed the babies milk, just like human mummies do."

"It's a FISH!" James yells. "It lives in the ocean, dumb bum!"

"James!" Tessa says. "No name calling!"

James, of course, doesn't hear Tessa because Clara has decided *she'll* be the one to deal with the great transgression of being called a dumb bum. She shoves James in the chest with both hands—*hard*—knocking him onto his bottom.

"That's it!" both Tessa and Libby announce, each of them grabbing their own child and moving toward opposite sides of the yacht. As they go, I can hear words like 'timeout' and 'early bedtime' being thrown about.

The cameraman starts to follow Tessa and James, but Arthur steps in front of him. "Any footage with my children is subject to my approval."

The guy opens his mouth, but before he can ask, Arthur says, "No. I won't approve any of that."

"Oh dear," Arabella says with a light chuckle. "Here I thought the kids would get on so well."

"It's to be expected, really," Arthur says. Thank God, an olive branch. "Clara's been an only child and has had all the attention, so when two other kids show up on the scene, it's got to be rather off-putting."

Emma sets her jaw. "Oh really? Is that the problem? Because I thought the issue might be coming more from the twins adjusting to a different time zone."

Before things can go any further, I shout, "Is that a great white?!"

That worked. Now everyone is staring over at the nothing I'm pointing to. "I don't see anything," Arabella says.

Seriously, Belle? Do you not know what I'm trying to do here?

Harrison, who obviously doesn't need word getting out that there might be great whites in the bay, speaks up in his most authoritative tone. "Will is only kidding. There are no sharks in these waters."

"No sharks? In the ocean?" Arthur asks, sounding highly skeptical.

"He means great whites," Emma tells him. "Of course there are sharks, but little ones, like reef sharks. Nothing dangerous."

"Exactly," Harrison adds. "We've never had a shark attack here in Paradise Bay. Not one. It's completely safe."

"Really?" Arthur asks. "Not one? In the entire history of the island?"

Harrison narrows his eyes. "Nope. Not one."

Oh, please stop, you pair of dumb bums.

"I find that hard to believe," Arthur tells him.

"Well, it's true," Emma answers with a scowl.

"What's stopping them from entering the bay? Some magical forcefield?" he scoffs.

Arabella makes a Pffft! sound. "Magic forcefield. Oh Arthur, you're so funny." She turns to the rest of us with a tight smile. "My brother's sense of humour is an acquired taste, I'm afraid. Always with the jokes!" She gives him an urgent look, then adds. "Stop teasing, Arthur! People will think you're serious."

Tessa and James come back at the same time as Clara and Libby. Both children have quivering bottom lips as they face each other. Clara gives James a nod, and says, "I'm very sorry I pushed you."

"Good, Clara," Libby says. "Hands are for helping, not hurting, right?"

Off to the side, I hear the Princess Dowager snort out a laugh. Apparently, she is awake after all. And I'm not the only one who heard that snort because Libby has now crossed her arms over her belly and is glaring at the old woman.

Tessa nudges James on the shoulder. "And what do you have to say for yourself, young man?"

"I shouldn't have called you a dumb bum. That was very wrong of me."

"Thank you," Tessa tells James. "And thank you, Clara, for your lovely apology. Hands *are* for helping."

There's a tense moment where everyone stands waiting for someone to say something and I see Tessa and Libby exchange glances that are somehow both conciliatory *and* disapproving at the same time. Wow. How do they do that? Women are seriously a real mystery to me.

Clara, clearly not satisfied with James' apology, leans toward him. "You're 'posed to say you're sorry too."

"I did," he snaps.

"No, you didn't," Clara tells him, with one tiny hand balled up into a fist. "You said you shouldn't have called me a dumb bum, but you didn't say you were sorry."

. She's not wrong, but I really do wish she'd let it go because this is awkward A.F. and the film crew looks far too delighted. Arabella glances around, looking utterly panicked. "Who wants some booze?"

Princess Florence raises one hand in the air. "Me! And whatever you're making, I want a double."

Chapter 22

LET'S GET READY TO RUMMMBBBLLLLE!

Arabella

"Okay, so clearly this isn't going the way we hoped," I whisper to Will as the two of us quickly make Moscow mules for the adults. I'm busy slicing limes whilst he's pouring generous amounts of vodka into several tumblers lined up on the counter in the galley. We have to be as quiet as possible because the director is sitting at the table with the recording equipment, watching everything the two cameras are picking up at all times. He's got a headset on and is occasionally giving directions to the crew out on deck, but, knowing our luck, they've mic'd up the kitchen too.

"Clearly," Will whispers back. "We have got to get the film crew off the yacht a.s.a.p."

"Precisely, but we also need to give them some really great footage to use so they'll scrap the fighting bits," I tell him as I squeeze some fresh lime into the glasses then drop a slice in each one for garnish.

He gives me a look that says he's pretty sure they're using the fighting stuff too and I offer him a conciliatory nod. "We tried having everyone together for the cameras. Now I think it's time to separate. Perhaps we could each interview our own family members on film.

Easy questions—what was I like as a child, what sort of person did you think I'd marry, etc."

"Brilliant," Will answers. "That's why I love you, Belle. You're not just a total smoke show, you're also part genius."

"What do you mean, part?" I ask.

"Nothing, you're smart. Very smart," he whispers, sounding panicky. "I only meant because part of you is really hot and part of you is...you know what? I should probably stop now, shouldn't I?"

"I'd say so."

We load up a tray with the drinks, then I dig around in the freezer for some ice cream sandwiches for the kids and we head back outside. After a bit of cajoling, we manage to put our plan into action, hosting the impromptu interviews at the stern of the yacht where there's a small table for four. Will starts to interview Emma and Pierce while I rush around playing cocktail waitress and making sure everyone's drinks are topped up (with Libby getting a non-boozy one, of course).

Things seem to be going well for a few minutes, and even the kids are having fun together, now that they've filled up on ice cream. As luck would have it, all three of them are huge fans of some cartoon called *Jake and the Neverland Pirates*, so they're now rushing about yelling about doubloons. I hurry back into the cabin to make more drinks and, to my delight, Libby comes with me to help. See? We *can* be one big family unit.

Libby and I set to work and I hear the director say, "Zoom in on Prince Arthur and Tessa, but don't get too close. I don't want them to notice." He fiddles with some settings and all of a sudden, I can hear Arthur's voice. And so can Libby.

"...pushy brat. Will's sister, the chef, tried to blame it on our kids lacking sleep. Well, it certainly wasn't one of my children shoving anyone."

Oh God! NO!!! Stop, please!!!!

"Don't say that," Tessa says. "Clara's just having trouble control-ling her temper. She's probably not used to being around other chil-dren, but she'll figure it out when the baby comes, I can tell you that much. That'll be a rude awakening for her."

"True," Arthur answers. "Good luck with that. And no sharks in these waters? Give me a break, buddy. It's the ocean. There are bloody well sharks."

"He's just trying to protect his business," Tessa tells him.

Gran, who is now wide awake and ready to party, is heard next. "Yes, well, what can you expect? All brawn, no brains in that family." She pauses, then adds. "Is this the yacht we bought them?"

"Uh-huh," Arthur answers.

"I can't believe it would be worth what Arabella paid for it. It's more rickety than I am."

Libby scoffs and I stammer, not knowing what to say to fix this. "I am....I'm...that is..."

She holds up one hand and storms out, presumably going in search of Harrison. The director sounds positively gleeful as he says, "Make sure you follow the big pregnant one. It's about to go down."

I stand at the tiny sink and take a deep breath, trying to figure out how to salvage this and ordering myself not to cry. Arthur and Gran's words slap around inside my head, physically hurting my grey matter. Sucking back my entire mule in one go, I slam the glass down and hurry outside.

But it's too late. Libby is now telling Harrison everything she overheard and now the yacht is making a sharp turn. Shit. I rush over to Will, who is chuckling away with Emma and Pierce. I stand behind the cameraman and wave urgently at him while mouthing, "Code Red! Code Red!"

He squints his eyes at me, then says, "Can you excuse me for a second?" He slides out of the booth and hurries over to me. I grab his hand and take him around the corner, but the crew follows us, of course. I'm just about to tell him what happened, but he's now getting the full picture because Harrison and Arthur are in a full-on argument. Harrison's voice is raised as he stands behind the wheel. "...our hospitality, but clearly it's not up to your standards, so you might as well get back on your fancy jet and go home!"

"Listen, we're very sorry," Tessa says, clearly trying to calm things down. "It was definitely taken out of context."

"Oh, yeah?" Libby asks, sticking her huge pregnant belly out and using it (quite effectively, I might add) to intimidate Tessa. "Which part was 'out of context?'" Air quotes, of course. "The bit where you said my daughter's in for a rude awakening when the baby comes or when your nasty grandmother said my husband and his family are all brawn and no brains?!"

Tessa opens her mouth, then closes it. Libby gives her a 'yeah, that's right, shut your mouth' nod, then turns to Gran, who is currently looking up at the sky innocently. "I heard you and I won't forget it."

"All right now," Arthur says. "Gran is eighty-nine years old, and she has a heart condition, so I'll thank you to go easy on her."

"Oh, like as easy as she went on us?" Libby asks.

"Okay, fair point," Arthur says.

"YES, IT MOST CERTAINLY IS!" Libby shouts. "And you know what? Dolphins are mammals, so who's the dumb bum now? Not my kid!!!"

Oh fuck.

All three of the kids have stopped playing and are watching the scene unfold.

My dad has finally left his lounge chair and hurries over to put his diplomacy skills to use. "Libby, my dear, allow me to apologize on behalf of my family. Our behaviour has been—"

Ignoring him, Libby continues. "I sure hope your daughter was born first because I'm not sure your son has the brain power to rule a kingdom."

"No, you didn't," my father says, his voice rising to a boom. "That's enough, madame! We will not allow insults to be hurled at the children!"

Libby swivels on him, knocking him back with her belly, and my dad loses his balance, circling his arms wildly as he tries to propel himself forward, but it's no use. He lets out a high-pitched yelp as he tips overboard, headfirst.

And that's when things really start to get ugly.

Chapter 23

HUMPTY DUMPTY HAD A GREAT FALL...

Will

Breaking News from the ABN News Center with Giles Bigly

"GOOD EVENING, I'm Giles Bigly with the ABN news desk. We interrupt your regularly scheduled program to bring you a breaking story from Santa Valentina Island, where it has been a near-tragic day at sea for our beloved monarch, King Winston. I've got ANN producer, Miranda MacEwan, joining us live via the telephone. Miranda, you were on the yacht at the time of the incident, is that true?"

Footage of King Winston bobbing up and down in the ocean begins as Miranda begins to talk. "Yes, Giles. We were filming a pre-wedding special on what was meant to be a relaxing morning sail aboard the Waltzing Matilda, Will Banks' famed yacht—a gift from Princess Arabella actually."

"My goodness," Giles says. "Miranda, I'm going to interrupt you for a second because I'm seeing this footage for the first time. Can you please explain to the viewers what exactly is happening in this clip?"

"Certainly. Here we see Will, as well as the king's head of security, jumping into the water to save King Winston. Now, the next gentleman to jump in is Will's security guard, presumably to save Will perhaps, although, as you can see, he's not exactly a strong swimmer, so his attempt at bravery resulted in Will's brother, Harrison, jumping in to save him. On the far right of the screen, you can see two speedboats coming onto the scene with two more teams of security officers while Will holds King Winston up under his armpits."

The camera zooms in on Will and the king, who is thrashing about wildly with his ladies hat, hanging off his neck by a string, slapping Will in the face. With a grave tone, Giles begins to speak again. "This does look extremely dangerous indeed. You can see here that King Winston is clearly in some type of distress."

"Yes," Miranda says. "But I want to assure your viewers that the king is fine and did not suffer any physical injuries during his fall."

"Really? No injuries. Miraculous," Giles says. "What exactly happened to cause his fall?"

"Well, this is the shocking bit, Giles," Miranda says. "A heated argument broke out on the boat over whether or not dolphins are fish or mammals."

After a pause, Giles says, "Um…are you certain?"

"Quite. I can't get into further detail as we need to run some things past the network's legal team, but I can say we've got it all on film."

"But surely everyone knows they're mammals," Giles says, his face appearing on the screen again next to the words "KING ALMOST DROWNS IN YACHT MISHAP."

"Apparently, not everyone," Miranda answers.

"But who was arguing on the side of fish?" Giles asks.

"I can't say."

"Wow. And how exactly did King Winston wind up going overboard?"

"That's the odd bit. Mr. Banks' sister-in-law, a one Ms. Libby Banks, knocked him over with her pregnant belly."

Giles stammers. "Are you…sure about that?"

"I watched it happen," Miranda says authoritatively. "She's got a huge pregnant belly, to be honest. Apparently, there's only one baby in there, but that's got to be one enormous child."

"That is…well…I don't even know what to say. In all my years as a newsman, I've never heard of a woman using her baby bump as a weapon. Did she mean to do it?"

"Oh, yes. She was quite furious," Miranda says, quickly adding, "But, I really can't say anything more. In fact, I probably shouldn't have said that much."

"Wow, shocking. Absolutely shocking." Giles shakes his head, then says, "I guess we'll have to wait until the story unfolds further. In the meantime, God save the king."

———

Well, that couldn't have gone much worse. My family is now in an all-out war with Arabella's, and I'm certain things are broken beyond repair. I only heard the rest of what happened on the yacht second-hand from Emma. I was on one of the rescue boats with Reynard for the trip back to the resort, but from what she told me, there was a significant amount of yelling, many tears, and lots of snot. All the transgressions of the last twenty hours came out, including, but not limited to: a) my family being judgemental, as proved by their use of the phrase hoity-toity, b) her family being told in no uncertain terms that they definitely *are* hoity-toity due to their use of the word commoner, c) lots of back and forth over who's smarter than whom, and d) my family being accused of being horrible liars, trying to lure unsuspecting tourists to their death by great white shark.

Oh, and in the irony to end all ironies, apparently the three kids started to like each other so much that they all bawled and clung to each other when it was time to get off the yacht (which was the cause of the aforementioned snot). And it's all on film, which is just terrific.

While I'm not sorry I missed it, the reason I was in the rescue boat and not at the helm of the yacht with Arabella was because my future father-in-law broke my nose by bashing it with the back of his head while he was panicking. This meant Harrison had to climb back aboard to sail to shore while I waited for the bleeding to stop, which it didn't. So I had to go to the hospital to have my nose reset. It was either that or live with it being sideways for the rest of my life.

The speedboats arrive much quicker than the yacht, so I didn't even get a chance to see Arabella before I was whisked off in an ambulance along with my father-in-law, who burped and shook the entire way into San Filipe. He's fine by the way. The waters are too warm to get hypothermia, and I managed to get to him within a few seconds of him falling in, so, other than a mouthful of water, he's got nothing to complain about. Well, except for being taken out yachting in the first place, and I suppose being knocked overboard. He and I didn't say a word the entire ride, but, needless to say, it was awkward.

It took four hours for me to have my turn with the doctor who reset my nose (not fun). Apparently, King Winston was released after an hour when the full team of doctors who attended to him gave him the all-clear. And now I'm on my way back to the resort, with Emma at the wheel of one of the resort's jeeps. She's been surprisingly quiet since she picked me up. Not one sarcastic comment. Not even a tiny joke about the super suave nose splint I have to wear for the next five days.

Finally, after we ride in silence all the way through the streets of San Filipe and make it onto the highway, she glances at me. "You okay?"

"I'm fine," I say, my voice sounding like I have the worst cold of my life. "This is nothing."

"No, I meant about the big dust up."

I blow out a puff of air and shake my head. "Why couldn't everyone just be nice to each other? Seriously? Would it have been so hard to just let things slide? It's not like we're going to have to spend much time together in the future."

Emma nods. "Yeah, that was rough. It was like we all just brought out the worst in each other. And that shit Arthur said about Clara— not cool. I don't care who you are, you don't talk about my niece that way."

I close my eyes and lean my head back against the seat. "I figured it might be a little uncomfortable, but I had no idea it would turn into this."

"For what it's worth, Libby feels awful about knocking the king overboard with her baby bump. She said she forgot how big she is."

I wave off the comment. "I know she didn't do it on purpose. But how the hell do we move on from here?"

"Oh, I can't see that happening," Emma says, rounding the curve on the road so the ocean comes back into view. "There's no salvaging it, I'm afraid. Especially because the royals are probably gone by now."

My eyes fly open and I sit up. "Are you serious?"

Emma nods. "I heard Arthur telling his bodyguard to have someone prepare the jets." She puts on an uppity accent as she says that last bit and my heart sinks to the floor.

A sense of panic overtakes me. My stupid phone was lost at sea and Arabella didn't meet me at the hospital, which I thought she would. And now I'm worried that I know why. "Was Arabella going with them?"

"I'm really not sure."

We make the left turn into the long driveway that leads to Paradise Bay and I start to bounce my legs, worried that she's already gone. I barely wait for Emma to come to a full-stop before climbing out, thanking her, and running into the lobby to see if the family has checked out.

Rosy is at the desk. She gasps when she sees me and comes rushing out to me with her arms out. "Cuddle Bear! What did that awful man do to your beautiful nose?"

"It's fine, Rosy," I say quietly, wishing she wouldn't make a public scene. I've had enough of those for a lifetime. "It wasn't his fault anyway. A lot of people panic when they think they're drowning."

I take her hand and walk off to the side, then lower my voice. "Are they still here?"

She nods, looking unhappy about it. "Apparently their pilots got day drunk so they have to wait until tomorrow to go home where they belong."

"Rosy," I say, "I know things got off to a bit of a rough start, but…"

"A bit?"

"Really rough, okay?"

She raises one eyebrow and purses her lips.

"Horrible. A horrible start, but please, for my sake, can you just try to make nice with them when you see them next?" I stare into her dark brown eyes with a pleading expression. "Please? For my future wife and me?"

"You sure you want to go through with this whole thing?" she asks. "They're pretty much the worst people I've ever met in my life. And I used to work at a prison."

Rolling my eyes, I say, "Yes, I'm sure. Now, I have to go find Arabella."

"Okay, if that's what you want…"

"It is."

"Then go find her," she says, turning and walking back toward the front desk. "But, you know, there are lots of lovely island girls right here who would make you very happy."

I spin on my heel and leave without bothering to argue with her. I've got bigger fish to fry than worrying what Rosy thinks right now. Now to find the love of my life and make sure she's okay.

As I hurry along the path to the building her family is staying in, I tell myself to calm down. She and I are a team and we're going to stick together no matter what.

I hope.

Chapter 24

BRIDEZILLA IS IN THE HOUSE!!!!!

Arabella

I FINALLY FEEL like I've calmed down enough to speak to my family about what happened today. In an effort not to go all insane bitch bride on them, I have spent the last couple of hours soaking in the tub, listening to calming meditations. And when I finally felt serene enough to conduct myself with a sense of grace, I made the short trip down the hall to Arthur and Tessa's suite. Although, now that I'm here, my rage is bubbling up in my chest again. There are two adjoining rooms (one on either side) where my father and Gran are staying, and, I know from Tessa's texts, they're all here waiting to 'make it up to me.' As if they can.

I hold my hand up to knock, then put it back down by my side. Bellford, who is standing slightly behind me, speaks up in a gentle voice. "If I may, Miss, perhaps you should sleep on it before you confront your family."

He means because I've polished off all three of the tiny bottles of gin in my bar fridge, which is more than enough to get me tipsy. I consider his words, but then reach up and knock. "I'm too angry to sleep," I mutter.

Arthur opens the door, his face filled with remorse. "Hello, Airy Fairy," he says. Airy Fairy is his childhood nickname for me. He only uses it now when I've either suffered some great loss (like being dumped) or when he's fucked up royally (like today).

Lifting my chin, I give him a look that matches my mood—very dark grey—then walk past him into the suite. I find my father sitting on a sofa with Gran, and Tessa in an armchair with wet hair and a robe on. She winces when I glance at her, and I can't say I have any desire to let her off the hook. She can bloody well dangle there along-side my brother for all I care. Arthur takes a seat on the arm of Tessa's chair and they all wait for me to speak.

I open my mouth, take a deep breath, then start talking. "I'm not going to yell, so don't worry. You all know what you've done, and you most certainly deserve the tongue-lashing of a lifetime—except you, Dad. In fact, you don't have to be here if you don't want to."

"Brilliant," he says, getting up. "I'm actually quite tired." He hustles in the direction of the connecting door to his room, calling over his shoulder, "Good night, all."

Then, with a quiet click, he's gone, leaving Gran, Arthur, and Tessa shifting uncomfortably while I narrow my eyes at them. "The three of you should be ashamed of yourselves," I say. "Especially you, Arthur, you horse's ass. How dare you treat Will's family with such… such…disdain?!" Oh, I'm raising my voice and I promised myself I wouldn't. I spread my palms and press down on the air in front of me as a way to tell my brain to calm down. Screaming will get me nowhere. "It's one thing for you to insult me, but it's an entirely different thing when you go after my future husband's family. Calling a four-year-old child a pushy brat?!" I ask Arthur.

"You heard that bit?" he asks, looking confused.

"So did Libby. We were in the galley getting you drinks when you two decided to have a chat about her awful child. We watched the entire conversation on the closed-circuit telly."

Arthur's shoulders droop and he says, "I don't suppose it'll help if I tell you I've never felt worse about anything in my life."

I tap my chin for a few seconds as though considering his offer, then bark, "Nope! Not really. Your remorse doesn't actually help me at all because I've got the rest of my life to spend with a man whose family very likely hates you. For good reason." I lean toward him, and even though I'm a good six feet away, he leans back. "And now, they're going to have to come to Valcourt in a couple of weeks for the big stupid wedding I don't want where they'll all feel like we think we're too good for them. Won't that be fun for them?"

"Oh, Arabella," Tessa says, her voice cracking. "I am so, *so* sorry, sweetie. I never should have said anything about Clara."

"No, you shouldn't have. She's a little child."

"True. Very true. Although I was understandably upset that she shoved James to the ground. That was uncalled for. Also, all I said was that bit about her being an only child. Arthur's the one who said the really awful things."

Arthur gives her a look. "So much for standing by your man."

Keeping her eyes trained on me as though I'm a lioness about to pounce, she says, "Hey, in this situation, it's every woman for herself."

Gran decides now is a good time to pipe up. "Really, Arthur, were you planning to hide behind your wife's petticoat? Grow a pair."

Spinning on her, I say, "And YOU! *All brawn, no brains* in that family?! Really?!"

"Well, I…" Gran starts, then shuts her mouth.

"And calling Matilda a rickety yacht? And suggesting that *we* bought it for them?" I ask. Okay, now I am yelling. Well, so be it. They've earned it. Besides, serenity is overrated. "Do you have *any idea* how humiliating that is for their family? I only bought the boat for Will because I lost it for him in the first place by being an idiot! And now you've made it sound like our family pooled together for it like some sort of charitable donation. Are you insane?!"

"I most certainly am not," Gran says. "And I'd advise you to watch your tongue. I'm still your grandmother."

"Then act like it for once!"

"Listen, they're not exactly innocent either," Arthur says. "Calling us names behind our backs, and that little Clara had no reason to get violent. It was merely a disagreement."

Tessa rolls her eyes and I scoff. "Okay, so they may have said something about us being hoity-toity, but it's true! Who is more hoity-toity than a *royal family*? No one! That's who. No. One. Plus, I had just sent them books about how to act appropriately around us, which, in hindsight was a very bad idea. But then…you three…"

"Fine, okay, we screwed up," Arthur says. "But they did too. What do you want us to do about it?"

"Nothing."

"Nothing?" he says, raising one eyebrow.

"That's right, nothing, because you'll only make a bigger mess of things."

There's a knock at the door and Bellford answers, then lets Will and Reynard through. Will looks awful with two dark purple bands around his eyes and a splint on his nose. "Oh, darling," I say, rushing to him. "Is it quite painful?"

"I'm fine. I just feel silly," he says. He glances at my family without greeting them, then lowers his voice. "Listen, can we talk?"

I nod, taking his hand and leading him over to my awful family. "Yes, of course, but I believe some people have something to say to you first."

"I am very, very sorry," Arthur says. "I was way out of line and I've insulted your family in a most unforgiveable way."

Will gives him a slight nod. "Yeah, you really have."

Tess and Gran also offer apologies which Will seems slightly more ready to accept. "It's okay," he tells them.

"It most certainly is not!" I say to him. "These…*people*…have ruined everything! They've made your family feel horribly uncomfortable and they've completely disregarded our relationship in the process." Turning back to the three unwise men (well, one man and two unwise ladies), I shake my head. "This is supposed to be *the best time of my life*—getting ready to marry my soulmate and best friend. My wedding day is quickly approaching, and you've killed it like a bunch of traveling psycho wedding killers!" I mime stabbing like that psycho guy in that Alfred Hitchcock movie.

Oh, I'm on a roll now and this train is not stopping. "I do everything for this family. EVERYTHING! I take on all the shit charities without a word of complaint."

"That's not true," Arthur says. "We all take on some pretty shit charities."

"Oh really, Arthur? Have you ever spent the day with the Nonagenarian Mall Walkers??! Huh? Ever had *that pleasure?*"

"No, but—"

"Then zip it!" I say, pointing at him. "And you two messed up your wedding so badly that now Will and I have to suffer through the entire formal shitshow! And I had to shell out two and a half million dollars for a wedding we don't even want! Yeah! How's that for shitty?"

"Wait. What?" Will asks, turning to me.

Oh shit. That's not how I wanted Will to find out. "Yeah, we're way over ANN's budget and because the family announced they're not paying for it, I had to make up the difference."

"Were you ever going to mention it to me?" he asks, looking understandably angry.

"Yes, of course, but to be honest, with everything going on, I kind of forgot about it."

"You forgot you spent two and a half million dollars?" he asks.

"Yes," I murmur. "But it's fine because I'm incredibly loaded—I should say, we're loaded, once the wedding happens, obviously."

"We won't be if you spend that kind of cash on a wedding…"

Arthur has the nerve to say, "He's got you there."

I turn on my brother and shout, "Shut up! It's none of your business."

"Then maybe don't have the discussion in my suite," Arthur quips.

And that's the moment I finally snap.

"You know what? Forget it!" I holler, not even really thinking about what I'm saying. "The wedding's off! Screw all of you and screw the people of Avonia with their unending *wedding lust*! I'm *done*. Done, done, done, done. If you can't act with a proper sense of decorum, I'm out!" I nod at Will, then say, "We're going full Megxit!"

His head snaps back while the others gasp.

And honestly, I'm not entirely sure what I'm saying at the moment, but I am loving the fact that they're all terrified. "That's right. FULL. MEGXIT. We're eloping. Let's go, Will! Scotland is waiting!"

Will just stares at me. "I'm not sure that now is the right moment to make this type of decision."

"Are you serious?" I hiss at him.

"You're upset and this is just a really huge thing you're talking about. And it's not the type of thing to decide when you're angry," he says in his regular calm voice that is irritating the shit out of me right now.

"Are you actually saying you want to live the big stupid royal life? With these...awful wedding spoilers?" I've finally cracked. I'm a completely bonkers wild bridezilla now, aren't I?

Yes, yes, I am.

It's like I'm having an out-of-body experience brought on by all the stress. I'm more like an observer to the insane woman screeching than actually being the one who's responsible for all the noises coming out of her mouth. "Well, I'm out! In case you missed it, I'm DONE. Now, are you with me or are you with *them*?" I ask, dragging the word 'them' out for several seconds.

"Obviously, I'm with you, but——"

"Good choice," I say, cutting him off. "We pack now and leave as soon as one of the pilots is sober."

"Belle, it's my wedding too, right?" he asks gently.

"Yeah," I say sounding horribly sarcastic.

"And if we do what you're suggesting, it means I won't be getting out of my ANN contract."

"That's fine!" I tell him. "I'd much rather have you working for Dylan for the rest of our lives than have to deal with my idiot brother for another minute!"

"Well, I wouldn't," he says simply.

"Oh really? You want the big stupid royal wedding with the million people we don't know sitting in the stupid old cold stone church without any sense of whimsy whatsoever? And these awful people right in the front row?!" I ask, pointing at my brother. "Then marry someone else because I sure as shit don't want them there!"

Will sighs and says, "Belle, it's been a really bad day for all of us, okay? Me included." He points to his nose. "But we're not going to solve anything tonight so why don't we just calm down and sort this out tom—"

Arthur, Tessa, and Gran all make quiet 'ooohhhhhh' sounds.

"Calm down?" I ask in a deadly-quiet voice. "Did you just tell me to calm down?"

He nods. "Yeah, I did, because, quite frankly, you're not acting like the patient, wonderful woman I fell in love with."

"Really?!" I ask. "Well, I apologize if I don't fit your perfect definition of who you thought you were getting, but when I get pushed into the corner, I come out fighting!" I roar at him for good measure, then add, "Like a tiger."

Tessa stands and walks over to me, then puts her hands on my shoulders. "Arabella, sweetie, I love you. We all love you and we get it. You've been under an incredible amount of strain with the film crew following you everywhere and the wedding plans and…us behaving like children. I went totally nuts myself before our wedding. That's what weddings do to brides—especially royal ones. Awful, beastly things. But please, we're all very sorry and we'll do *anything* to make it up to you. And if you want to be furiously mad with us, that's understandable, but don't take it out on Will."

"I'm not!" I say, shaking loose from her hold.

"Yeah, you kind of are," Will says.

I stare at him for a second, then shake my head. "You're supposed to be on my side."

"I am. I have been the entire time. I just don't want to hop on a plane to Scotland in a few hours," he says. "I mean, why Scotland?"

"Because it's Jane Austen!" I shout.

Holding up his hands, Will says, "Okay, I'm going back to my place to get some much-needed sleep. I suggest you do the same."

With that, he strides out, not bothering to shut the door.

I stand in the middle of the room feeling utterly stupid and alone. Part of me wants to run to him and apologize, but I'm still too angry. I glare at my brother, and say, "Thanks a lot for ruining my life. I hope you're very amused."

Then I turn and leave, but instead of going to find Will, I go back to my room to find another drink.

Chapter 25

BUCKETS OF BEER, MOONLIT TALKS ON THE BEACH, AND BAD IDEAS...

Will

INSTEAD OF GOING to my cottage, I head for the beach bar, say a quick hello to Lolita, one of the bartenders (and one who thankfully can pick up on my body language that I really prefer not to talk about my nose). I grab a bucket, fill it with ice, and pop three bottles of beer into it. Then I make my way down to the beach where it's dark and quiet this time of night. Sitting on the sand, I crack open my first beer and listen to the waves roll in. I need to be alone so I can figure out what to do from here. Reynard, who followed me down here, of course, is standing back near the cement steps that lead back up to the resort.

The truth is, I'm exhausted, extremely disappointed, and, even though I won't admit it, my nose hurts like hell. After weeks of eighteen-hour days spent either filming or preparing for the wedding, followed by two days being caught in the middle of the Family Feud, Royal Edition, I'm wiped. I don't want this stupid wedding any more than Arabella does, and to be honest, I'm really worried that this is just a microcosm of a life neither of us wants. And now, she's shelling out more money than I've ever earned for one lousy day? What a freaking mess.

I suck back half my beer in one go, letting the cold liquid slide down my throat without even tasting it, then I set it down and sigh. There's a small cough next to me and my first thought is to tell whoever it is to sod off, but when I look up, I see Arabella's face. I'm about to ask how she knew where I was, but then I realize, in her family, you can always find out the whereabouts of anyone. You just have to ask your bodyguard to ask theirs.

"Can I sit down?" she asks.

"I don't know. Are you going to yell at me?"

"No."

I gesture with my head that she can sit, then have another sip of beer.

I offer one to her, but she shakes her head. "I've already had a few drinks this evening." She pauses and lets out a long sigh. "How's your nose?"

"It's there."

"So, that's a plus, I suppose," she says. "You still have something to hold up your sunglasses."

I let out a half smile but can't manage more than that.

"I need to apologize to you for losing it earlier," Arabella says. "And ordering you to go with me to Scotland to get married. And forgetting to tell you how much the wedding is costing. And I need to apologize on behalf of my terrible family for treating your family like garbage."

"It's okay," I tell her with a shrug. "Don't worry about it."

Her voice is so quiet, I can hardly hear her over the waves. "No, I have to worry about it. We've made a huge mess and I don't know how to clean it up. Not *we* as in you and me, we as in my idiot family and me. The last thing I wanted was for things to go so far off the rails, but whoa, did they ever."

"Yeah, it's been rough."

"I don't know why they couldn't just get along. Would that have been so hard? Seriously? Like, what is the problem? As if this wedding isn't stressful enough…and I just feel so bad for you, having to spend every waking hour trying to learn all the stupid rules…"

"It hasn't been that bad."

"Yes, it has. I know you've barely slept in weeks. Reynard told Bellford how hard you've been working to prepare," she says, her voice cracking a little. "I thought coming here would be a way to make it up to you and to your family, but now…it just couldn't be worse, could it?"

I let out a frustrated chuckle. "Probably not."

"You must be so upset."

I turn to her. "I'm not going to lie to you. This is hard. The whole thing—the etiquette lessons, the dancing, and now this big public fight that is never going to go away, is it?"

She shakes her head. "Probably not."

"It's all just so stupid. Your people hate that you're marrying me and mine hate that I'm getting married at all. The constant online chatter about us, the fact that our families can't stand each other…it's a lot worse than I thought it would be."

"So much worse, right?"

"Yeah." I nod. "But we can't just call off the wedding."

"Why not? I mean, if neither of us wants the enormous production, maybe we should just elope and be done with it." She stares into my eyes. "I don't want to force you into this life. I don't even want it myself. Let's just get out now so we can build the life we want."

"Oh, Belle, that is *so* tempting," I tell her. "And for that reason, I need you not to bring it up again."

"Why not? I'm serious, Will. After today, I definitely want out."

Shaking my head, I say, "*Today* you do, but I know you'd come to regret it in the long run because it'll tear your family apart. You watched the Oprah interview of Harry and Meghan. You saw how that turned out…"

"After how my family behaved, I'm not even sure I care."

"They weren't *that* bad," I tell her. "Okay, maybe Arthur…" I nudge her on the shoulder.

"He can be such a world-class wanker."

"I know, but you love him anyway. He's your big brother," I say.

"Besides, canceling the wedding means I'm stuck riding out my contract, and neither of us wants that. No matter how awful it's going to be, it's going to buy me over two years of my life back. Plus, we get to fulfill your greatest wish…"

"Being your wife?"

"Sticking it to Dylan."

Arabella lets out a laugh, then says, "The truth is, I don't even care about that anymore. All I care about is you, and us having a wonderful life together, which means getting it off to the perfect start—one that's made for you and me. I mean, who wants to start their marriage with some big phony compromise?"

"Neither of us, but there's just so much at stake."

"Sod it," Arabella says, her eyes growing wide. "This is you and me. We decide what our life will be—starting with our wedding. I'm done being pushed around. We'll send an email to tell everyone the wedding is off. Then you and I elope, and when we get back from wherever we go—not Scotland because you clearly don't want to go there for some unknown reason even though it would be totally romantic like a Regency romance novel, but whatever—we'll live by our own rules."

Hope fills my veins and I grin at her. "Really?"

"Really," she says, flipping her legs so she's kneeling and facing me. "Let's climb aboard Matilda at dawn. It'll be so romantic. We can sail off to the Cook Islands again and get married there. Just the two of us. And no one can say a word because they all contributed to the cause."

I listen to her, feeling myself get swept up in the idea of being truly free. I nod at her. No more etiquette lessons. No more dancing with my bodyguard. Just her and I. Suddenly, I see our future so clearly and it's amazing. "Okay."

"Yeah?"

"Yeah, let's do this!" I tell her with a wide grin. "The rest of the world can just sod off. It's you and me now."

Arabella squeals with delight and wraps her arms around my neck, squeezing me tight, then gives me a hard kiss on the mouth that causes me to flinch in pain. "Oh God! Sorry!"

"That's okay," I say, tilting my head a little so we can kiss properly.

After a gentle moment of our lips together, she presses her forehead to mine and whispers, "I've never been so happy in my entire life."

"Me too," I tell her, even though there's a tiny voice in the back of my mind that is saying this is not a good idea.

Chapter 26

SNEAKY MCSNEAKERSTEINS

Arabella

"CAN you believe we got out without anyone seeing us?" I whisper as Will and I hurry down the path toward the pier, each of us with our Bearz backpacks slung over our shoulders. The sun is just starting to come up, bringing a beautiful pink glow to the water as it laps against the shore. Today is the start of a new life. I can feel it in my bones.

Neither of us even bothered to try to sleep. Instead, we stopped at my suite to pack a few things I'll need, then we went to Will's and finished preparing for the trip. Because we can't bring much with us, we'll have to stop for food on one of the other islands, but we have what we need—our passports, credit cards, and each other. We had to climb out of Will's bedroom window to escape the security team, but now that Matilda's in sight, I feel like we made it.

"I feel so alive," I tell him. "Like, really alive for the first time since I jumped out of that helicopter in the Congo."

He grins at me from under his nose splint. Poor lamb. "Just don't start swearing at the top of your lungs. We're not in the clear yet."

I glance behind us and see that we aren't being followed. "Where do you want to get married?" I ask him. "I'm thinking the first place we stop. We find a preacher and a beach and get it done."

"Deal," he says, grabbing my hand and helping me climb the one big step onto the wooden pier where Matilda is docked. "Oh, we should get a couple of rings too."

"Oh, yes. That too," I say, making a mental note of it. "And I wouldn't mind stopping at a shop to get a dress. Not a real wedding dress or anything, just something new and pretty." My heart squeezes a little at the thought of my dream dress back home in Avonia waiting for me. I guess I'll never have the chance to wear it which is…a little sad, really. But, no matter, this is much better.

"Should I get a tuxedo?" Will asks, as he pulls the ladder down and waits for me to climb aboard.

"No, I'm picturing you in a white button-up shirt and some chinos. Bare feet."

When I get to the top, I step to the side and wait for him to climb up to me. Oh, this would be so much sexier if he didn't have that nose splint and the black eyes. But never mind that. It'll add to the story we'll tell our kids someday. Kids. I can hardly believe we're doing this.

Will grabs my hand and leads me to the door of the cabin so we can drop off our bags and prepare the boat to sail off to our destiny. "I wonder if they read our email yet?"

Will yanks the door open and stops short. "I'm pretty sure they did."

"Do you think so?" I ask, bumping into his back.

"Yup," he says, his voice going up two octaves.

And that's when I see them. Harrison, Libby, Arthur, Tessa, Emma, Pierce, Rosy, Gran, and my father all standing inside waiting for us. My shoulders drop. "I guess we weren't as sneaky as I thought," I mutter.

"Guess not," Will says, holding tight to my hand. "You were right. We probably should have waited until we were out on the water to send that email."

I glare at them, anger building in me at the very sight of them. They're here to convince us to go through with the wedding. They're going to expect us to carry on as if nothing happened. Well, I'm not going to do that, thank you very much. I'm thirty, dammit. Women my age chart our own courses. Well, along with their super hot, daring fiancés if they've got 'em.

My father steps forward and gives us a sad smile. "We're not here to stop you."

"Good, because we're not changing our minds. We want out," I say, straightening my back.

"I know, and you have every right to do this. You really do," he says. "In fact, part of me hopes you do go through with it and you make a wonderfully adventurous life together, beholden to no one and nothing."

"But?" I ask.

"But we didn't want you to leave angry at us. We thought maybe we could make things up to you before you go so you can have a beautiful wedding without worrying about us," he says in a quiet voice. "Also, we very much want both of you in our lives and if you choose not to be, we'll miss you terribly."

Oh, well, that's not what I was expecting. I thought he'd go all 'I'm the king and you'll do what I say.' In fact, I wish he had because then I could yell no at him instead of tearing up at his words. I blink quickly and tell myself to woman up.

Arthur clears his throat. "I've contacted the legal team to see what they can do to get you out of the contract with ANN. It may not be possible, and someone will have to pay back all the expenses, but they're going to try to see what they can do."

"Seriously?" I ask him. "Why would you do that?"

"Because we want you to be happy," Arthur says. "Really happy, and if this is what you need to do, we want you to do it."

Harrison nods. "We're all really sorry for what happened. We embarrassed you both and added so much stress to your lives at the exact moment when we should have been here supporting you."

Libby tries to say something, but it comes out in the form of loud sobs. Finally, after a few attempts, she wails, "I'm so pregnant!"

"Oh, sweetie," Tessa says, wrapping an arm around her. "Isn't it just the worst thing ever?"

"Yes!" She sniffles. "I hate it so much. I never would have yelled at any of you if I were in my normal frame of mind. Not-Pregnant Libby is really nice."

"That's true," Emma says. "Super-organized and super-nice."

"I'm sure that's the case," Tessa says, rubbing Libby's arm. "And I don't even have an excuse for what I said. Well, except I've been dieting to get the baby weight off again in time for the wedding so I'm really grouchy."

Libby nods at her. "The pressure of looking good for the cameras is just awful! I've only had it for two days and I'm ready to punch the film crew. I don't know how you do it."

Is this really happening or am I hallucinating from exhaustion?

Oh, it's real. Gran just rolled her eyes. Libby and Tessa are in a full-on hug now, both of them crying and apologizing. Libby says, "I never should have said that about James. I watched a YouTube video of him speaking in French. He's a very bright boy! He could definitely be king when Arthur dies."

"He totally could," Tessa agrees. "He's highly intelligent like all my brothers. One of them is an actual rocket scientist. But, setting that aside, Arthur *never* should have called Clara a pushy brat. I yelled at him for a good hour over it last night. Clara was right to shove James. Girls need to stand up for themselves in this world," Tessa tells her.

"They do," Libby says with a nod. "They really do."

Gran sighs, then cuts in with, "I've already offered my heartfelt apologies to Harrison and Emma about the 'all brawn' comment, but I need to do the same for you, Will. I know you're a smart young man. If you weren't, my granddaughter never would have fallen in love with you."

Will nods. "Thank you, Your Highness. I appreciate that."

"You are rather brawny, though. Kind of makes me wish your grandad were still alive," she says with a wink.

"Gran!" I hiss. Then I glance back and forth between all of them, not knowing what to do with them. They're making it exceedingly hard to stay angry. And staying mad is the only way I'm going to manage not to feel guilty about cutting them out of the wedding. "As nice as it is that you all made up, Will and I are quite determined to elope. Consequences be damned."

"Of course you should. It's your wedding and you should have it however you want it, wherever you want it," Rosy says, walking over and capturing Arabella and me in one of her big, bosomy hugs. "We love you so much. And we're going to be one big happy family. All of us. The royals and the royal pains in the butt." She lets us go and takes Arabella's cheeks in both hands. "You're my Angel Bear."

Pierce stifles a laugh, and Emma gives him a look. "What? Do you want me to tell them what she calls you?"

He shakes his head, then says, "No thank you. I'm not really involved. In fact, I'm not even sure why I was made to get up this early to be here."

"Because, Bootsy Bear, this is an all-hands-on-deck situation," Rosy tells him.

Now Arthur lets out a snort and Pierce glares at him. "That stays on this boat."

"I'm sorry, but there is no way I can *not* tell everyone we know," Arthur tells him.

Pierce shakes his head and chuckles. "Prick."

Harrison pipes in with, "Hey, come on. Don't be slagging my new sister-in-law's brother-in-law."

"So, what? You're suddenly all best friends?" I ask, staring from one to the other.

"Maybe not, but there's definitely potential," Rosy says, walking over to Gran, linking her arm through Gran's. "It turns out, your grandmother and I have something in common."

Gran nods. "We both love looking at young men." She leans in toward me. "Apparently, the FedEx guy who comes here has the best buns in the world. When we're done here, I'm going to her office to wait for him."

I glance up at Will, not sure what to think. Lowering my voice, I say, "Are we buying this?"

He nods, his face spreading into a wide grin. "Everything they've said is so odd, it makes me think it must be genuine.

"So, maybe we don't elope?" I ask.

Will mutters, "Do we have ten million dollars to pay the network back?"

I nod, but then add, "It would be a rather large cut of my inheritance though, to be honest."

"Hmm…and then there's letting Dylan win," he says.

"God, I'd hate that."

"I know you would," he says. Glancing up at his family, he says, "And I know I said I had never thought about my wedding, but that's not true. I have thought about it…a few times actually. And in every version, it includes my family."

"Oh," I say, my face crumpling. "That's so sweet."

Will shrugs. "What can I do? I love the crazy bastards."

I turn to our families. "Has anyone looked at the buzz online about the big fight?"

They all nod and start murmuring about how bad it is. Sighing, I say, "How do we fix it?"

Arthur lifts one hand. "We were brainstorming before you got here, and we may have a plan. It's utterly insane, but we all agree a high degree of insanity is necessary given the situation. Also, Arabella, you're going to love it and since you are the bride…"

Chapter 27

THE PART WHERE THE FAMILIES EMBARRASS THEMSELVES ON LIVE TV TO MAKE THE WORLD FORGET THEIR BIG FIGHT...

Will

"ARE you absolutely certain you want to do this, sir?" I ask King Winston, who is currently dressed in a red sequined pantsuit ala Sisters Sledge. Apparently, *We Are Family* is a big number at the resort show, so they already had the choreography, and the costumes are loose enough for most of us to fit in (although some of us are stretching the seams—I'm looking at you, King Winston).

So, yeah, we've spent the last two days rehearsing and learning all the words while Rosy's niece babysat the kids. Now we've donned the ridiculous red sparkly jumpsuits and are about to humiliate ourselves on live TV in exchange for the film crew leaving first thing tomorrow morning so our families can have a proper holiday together. Oh, and because it'll replace the video of Libby baby-bumping King Winston off the yacht as the new clip that plays every hour until the wedding.

"Not at all," he answers, tossing his sparkly red scarf over his shoulder. "In fact, it's a terrible idea, but I guarantee it'll work. Also, I'm a little drunk so I don't care as much as I probably should."

Reynard and the resort's dance/yoga instructor/choreographer, Hadley Jones, have worked their buns off to help us get this routine down and some of us definitely have struggled more than others with it. King Winston, Pierce, Harrison, and I are all in the back because we suck hard. Libby, Emma, and Tessa are in the middle, with Arabella, Arthur, and Rosy, who have 'natural talent,' in the front. The Princess Dowager is sitting backstage in a black ball gown after using her heart as an excuse to get out of making a fool of herself. I feel like it's a valid reason, but the royals aren't buying it. She's going to come out at the end and wave to the crowd. We're currently waiting behind a big curtain on the outdoor stage for showtime. On the other side, the crowd of hotel guests grows restless, and I feel like I want to vomit.

"I can't believe Arthur made front row," King Winston tells me. "He's not even that good."

"Agreed," Pierce says. "I think he charmed Hadley into the front."

King Winston nods. "That's so Arthur. Prick."

Arabella hurries over to us with a huge grin. "I can't believe we're doing this!"

"Me either," I tell her with a deadpan expression.

"Hey, if doing a musical number was good enough for Princess Diana, it's good enough for us," she says. That's like the fiftieth time she's mentioned that. "Are you all set?"

We all mutter that we are, and she grins excitedly at us. "This is the greatest thing my family has ever done!"

"Better than, say, raising hundreds of millions of dollars in charitable donations for worthy causes?" King Winston says.

"*So* much better." She gives each of us a quick hug, then gives me her pity face. "Your poor nose."

Before I can tell her it's nothing, Hadley calls her name and she says, "Gotta go!"

I roll my eyes at her dad and mutter, "The spotlight's waiting."

He snorts out a laugh. "My children really are obnoxious, aren't they?"

"A little bit," I tell him with a grin.

The emcee starts hollering into the mic. "Are you all ready for a royal surprise?!"

The crowd screams and my stomach flips. There are a lot more people out there than I thought there'd be (not to mention the ones watching from home and all the ones who will see it on their phones and laptops for the next twenty or so years...)

Hadley rushes around, spacing us all out, and whisper-yells, "The whole point is to have fun, okay? If you're having fun, the crowd'll have fun too! Now, go for it!"

With that, she hurries off-stage without making a sound, even though she's in high heels. How do women do that?

"Please give a warm Paradise Bay welcome to the Bankses and the royal family of the Kingdom of Avonia!!!!!!"

The curtains open and the music starts up. Time to make fools of ourselves...

Chapter 28

SECRET BEACH WEDDINGS AND OTHER MAGIC...

Arabella

Royal News – *The Official Website for All Things Avonian Royal*

Forum Thread: It's Finally Happened. The Banks Family Has Turned the Royals Completely Insane. *(328 Currently Viewing, 42659 Total Views, 8992 Comments)*

In a bizarre turn of events, all of Avonia's senior royals performed a dance/lip-sync to the old disco tune We Are Family, by Sisters Sledge. Apparently, this was their pathetic attempt at making the world forget what awful people the Bankses are.

Stephen (Heir Presumptive): The only thing shocking about it is how quickly the Banks family managed to drag the royals down to their level. Next thing, we'll see shirtless photos of King Winston all over the place.

Cindy (Serene Highness): Or better yet, shirtless Prince Arthur...

Felix (Courtier): Yup, we all knew they'd humiliate the family. And now, it's happened.

Kitty (Aristocrat): I loved it. They looked like they were having fun for once.

It's another beautiful morning here on Santa Valentina Island. The sun is hot, the water's warm, and we're now on the fifth day of our families getting along in a row. A miracle, really. Will was able to take his nose splint off last night, so, other than a bit of yellowing under his eyes, he's back to normal.

Today we've been having the best time ever at the beach (with the exception of Rosy, who popped by for a few minutes, but then hustled back inside to get out of the un-air-conditioned air). I'm sitting on a beach towel with Will while the kids play in the water with their dads. Libby and Gran are snoring away on lounge chairs nearby, while Tessa reads a book in the shade.

Will leans over and kisses my bare shoulder. "Who knew things could turn out this well?"

"I did," I tease. "I knew things would turn out the whole time."

"Really?" he asks, giving me a skeptical look.

"Of course," I say with a shrug. "The problem with you is you tend to overreact when things get stressful. You need to learn to relax."

"That's it. I'm throwing you in the ocean," Will says, grabbing me around the waist and lifting me up with him as he stands. I squeal and try to wiggle out of his grip, but it's no use. We're going in.

A few moments later, I hear splashing, then feel the warm water on my dangling feet. And now, we're both in. We swim out for a bit, then I remember about the sharks and I start to tread water, watching for large, dark fins.

"Are you thinking about Jaws?" Will asks me.

"No, of course not," I lie. "Well, maybe…"

"Don't worry. All you have to do is be able to outswim the slowest person in the water," he says, pointing to a large man floating on his back. "Pretty sure you can beat that guy."

I let out a laugh, then say, "You're terrible."

"I know," he answers, reaching out and pulling me to him. "Do you still want to marry me?"

"Sadly, I do," I tell him with a wry grin.

"How about today?"

"What do you mean, today?" I ask.

"I was thinking, now that I've got my really sexy nose splint off, we could maybe have a secret wedding at sunset." He gives me a lingering kiss. "No cameras, crowds, no royal forums or fan girls putting their two cents in…just you, me, and our crazy families. What do you say?"

My heart leaps and I let out a whoop. "I say, yes!"

———

"Okay, so the dress is your something borrowed, your necklace is old," Tessa says. "The flowers are blue, and we just need something new…"

I snap my fingers and say, "The rings are new."

We're in my suite at the hotel getting ready. Libby lent me a gorgeous blush off-the-shoulder dress with a flowy chiffon skirt. I have my hair down in loose curls and light make-up on. Around my neck is Gran's solitaire diamond necklace and on my face is the brightest smile I've ever worn.

We're really doing this.

Libby went to the flower shop and quickly had them make a bouquet for me, one for Tessa, who will be my matron of honour (I asked Gran as well, but she rolled her eyes and said she'd rather eat bugs), as well as two miniature versions for Clara and Flora, who are our flower girls. Harrison and Will picked up simple gold bands for us, along with a pillow for James to carry them on.

In about five minutes, we're all going to get into golf carts and zip down to the beach, where a preacher friend of the Bankses, Will, and his family will be waiting for us. I check the clock for the hundredth time in the last hour, hoping it's time to go. We're about to start our life together our way. No big production. No phonies among us. No people cheering for us to fail. Just the people who love us most. My only regret is that Nikki's not here, but she'll be up at the altar next to Tessa and me at the official wedding.

There's a light knock on the door and Tessa hurries to answer it.

My dad is at the door and his eyes tear up as soon as he sees me. He walks in, shaking his head. "You look absolutely beautiful, my lamb."

I give him a huge hug, trying unsuccessfully not to cry. "Thanks, Dad."

We pull back and he says, "I'm so proud of you, my girl, and I'm absolutely thrilled that you're marrying William. There's not another man on this planet that would make you as happy as he's going to, and, at the end of the day, that's all that really matters."

"It really is."

"Are you ready?"

I grin and nod. "Are you?"

He tilts his head from side to side, then says, "A father is never ready for this moment, but don't worry about me. I'll get through it."

Chuckling, I loop my arm through his. "I'm glad. Let's go."

Chapter 29

THE BEGINNING OF HAPPY

Will

Now this is my kind of wedding. I'm standing under a wooden arch with my bare feet in the sand, in chinos and a button-up shirt. No tie, no tails, no top hat, no tabloid photographers jockeying for the best vantage point. No debilitating nerves about screwing up. Just us. Right here in my home with the people who love us most.

Clara, Flora, and James start toward us from the path down the sand, the girls tossing flower petals as they hurry along in their cute, poufy dresses. James, who's wearing shorts and a Polo shirt, carries the rings, looking bored. Next comes Tessa with a huge smile on her face as she makes her way toward us.

And now, I see her—my beautiful bride, on the arm of her father, who at this moment doesn't resemble a king, but a proud dad. I get a lump in my throat at the sight of them, wishing for a second that my own parents could be here. But somehow, being out here in the fading light, with the first stars appearing in the sky, I can't help but think maybe they are.

I clear my throat and dab at my eyes, and Harrison, who's standing next to me, nudges me on the shoulder. "I know."

And he does.

The waves roll in and out behind me and I can smell the tropical air, and I know I'm going to remember this moment for the rest of my life. This is the happiest I can ever imagine being.

King Winston looks like he's going to cry (and I kind of hope he does because it really couldn't hurt to have another cry baby in the family). Finally, he and Arabella reach me. They turn to each other and hug. He tells her he loves her more than anything and then he takes her hand and places it in mine. "Take care of her, William."

"I will, sir."

And now, Belle and I are staring into each other's eyes and everyone else seems to disappear for a few seconds. She's smiling up at me, just on the verge of tears as we hold hands.

"You are so beautiful," I tell her, leaning in and giving her a kiss.

The preacher, Father Timothy, clears his throat and says, "William, you're jumping the gun a bit."

Everyone chuckles, and Belle and I turn to him so we can finally start our life together. The next few minutes somehow are both slow and a blur at the same time. Each word I speak is the most important one that's ever come out of my mouth. I listen as she vows to love, honour, and cherish me for all the days of our lives. I feel the cool gold as she slides the ring onto my finger. I breathe in the scent of her perfume while I promise to be her partner, champion, and soft place to fall.

And now, Father Timothy gives us the go ahead and we kiss each other like there's no tomorrow. I lift her off the ground and spin us slowly around on the beach while we kiss and laugh and, yes, maybe even let a couple of tears fall.

"I'm going to love you forever," I say.

"And I'm going to love you right back," Arabella tells me.

Later in the evening, as we're sitting next to each other at a dinner that Emma and Pierce host for us, Arabella leans her head on my shoulder and sighs.

"Are you okay?" I ask.

"I have never been happier or more content in my life, but I was just wondering if I'll ever be this happy again."

"This is just the beginning of happy."

Chapter 30

AND NOW FOR THE BIG, FAT, ROYAL WEDDING...

St. Stephen's Church - 2:00 p.m. - June 3rd

Arabella

ANN Royal Wedding Special Event

"Hello, I'm Nigel Wood. Welcome to this ANN Royal Wedding Special. I'm here with special correspondent and VP of Productions at the Avonian Nature Network, Veronica Platt, who will be co-hosting today's festivities."

"That's right, Nigel," Veronica says. "It's a beautiful afternoon here in Valcourt. There's not a single cloud in the sky as we await the arrival of the Duchess of Bainbridge, Princess Arabella. She'll be arriving shortly in a horse-drawn carriage, along with her father, King Winston, for the wedding of the decade to Avonia's most eligible bachelor, Will Banks."

"Indeed, Veronica," Nigel adds. "This truly is a momentous occasion and cause for celebration as two worlds join in holy matrimony—that of commoner and royal. So many people with so many opinions about their union, but today, the only two points of view that really matter are that of the bride and groom."

"We've got a camera crew at the palace, waiting for them to emerge from the gates, and we'll be following them the entire way to the church," Veronica says with a wide smile at the camera. "The entire kingdom is abuzz with the excitement that can only be brought about by a royal wedding. And it's about to happen."

"That's right. Any second now, they'll be appearing."

"They sure will…" Veronica says, her smile frozen on her face.

"Indeed."

———

I slide my wedding band off and give it to Arthur for safekeeping until it's time for James to take it up the 'real' aisle. We're in my apartment at the palace and there's been a flurry of activity all around since four a.m. I'm tired, nervous, and also pretty damn excited because I'm in my Sleeping Beauty dress, which looks even better than I remembered. Eek! I look like a Disney Princess (which is totally an okay thing for a thirty-year-old bride who wants to be taken seriously to want).

Nikki is just finishing my fancy schmancy up-do (as she calls it). She's dyed her hair a very normal dark blonde for today and she and Tessa (who finally gave up on losing the baby weight again and realized she's perfect as-is) are in matching soft lilac gowns.

"You lucky bitch," she says to me, stepping back and shaking her head. "Totally gorgeous, rich as sin, and about to marry one of the hottest men on the planet."

"Well…" I say, referring to the fact that we're already married.

"You know what I meant," she says.

"Yes, and you're right. I'm one lucky bitch." Standing, I say, "Okay, let's do this so we can get on with the party already."

———

The carriage ride feels like a total fairy-tale. I'm with father and Gran, and Tessa, Arthur, Nikki, and the kids are in a Rolls Royce ahead of us. I wave at the people, suddenly happy that we didn't cancel and take this away from them. They look so thrilled.

And now, we're at the steps of the church, and the doors are about to open. I take in a deep breath, preparing myself to enter the cold, stone building and float past the thousand-plus people waiting. You know who else will be waiting? My super-hot husband, William Banks, who yesterday was made a Knight of the Most Noble Order of the Lion and Duke of Bainbridge (so we're matchy matchy now). So, suck it, Hateful Hannah Stalker Face. I'm the current Mrs. Will Banks and that is not going to change. I'm so nice, he's marrying me twice.

Oh, wow, where did that cockiness come from? Good thing I kept that in my head.

The doors swing open and we step inside, then I stop in place and gasp. "Holy mother of pearl!" I whisper. (No swearing allowed. We're in a church after all.)

It's the enchanted forest from my wedding planning album. The entire ceiling is covered with wisteria vines that drip down from the rafters in purple and green tendrils. A long ivory runner serves as the aisle, with beautiful ivory and ivy floral arrangements secured to the side of each pew.

My father leans in and whispers, "Do you love it?"

I nod, tearing up. "How?"

"Your husband."

"Seriously?" How did he know?

"Yes, he spent hours on video calls with the wedding planners to make this happen. He's actually quite the groomzilla, as it turns out."

Covering my mouth with one hand, I let out a laugh. "I can't believe he did all this."

"He really loves you."

He is going to get so lucky later. So, so, lucky. Like, I might even pull out the edible undies. Hmm, okay, I won't. Still too fresh. But really very lucky because, as I walk up the aisle of my fairy-tale wedding that exists inside my real life fairy-tale, I am certain that one thing is true: Will and I are going to spend the rest of our lives surprising each other. It may not always be good, but it'll always be exciting.

I walk past the pews, smiling at members of the Avonian Introverts Society (at the very back, of course), foreign dignitaries from around the globe, my UN Equal Everywhere friends, the Sharpe family (who take up two rows themselves), and Will's co-workers from ANN. My eyes land on Dylan Sinclair, who mouths, 'You look GORGEOUS! LOVE IT! Love the dress!!!' I mouth back 'thank you,' realizing I don't hate her anymore. She's not evil. She's just a really driven woman who will go to any lengths to achieve her dreams. Huh, maybe I'm not angry at her because we're not that different after all. Or maybe it's because I won and, by midnight tonight, Will's contract will be going through a shredder while we drink champagne.

Suck it, Dylan.

Okay, maybe I'm still not her biggest fan.

When we get to the front of the church, my dad does the whole handoff thing again, and this time, we're all so much more lighthearted about it than the first time. The first time was for us. This time is for show.

Will grins down at me, looking devastatingly gorgeous in a dark grey morning suit, white shirt, and a pale blue tie. "What do you think? Are you glad we didn't skip it?"

"So glad." I glance up at the wisteria. "How did you know?"

"I found your album in the garbage, so I took some pictures—not of Patrick Dempsey or the unicorn, but most of the ones I thought you'd still be interested in."

Completely forgetting the entire world is waiting, I lean in and whisper, "Is that why you took so long to come to bed that night?"

He grins. "Worth the wait?"

"*So* worth it."

"Should we get this over with? Because you've kind of got that look that says I'm going to get very lucky later, so I wouldn't mind hurrying this along," he whispers.

"Agreed. Let's do this."

We turn to the priest, who looks slightly exasperated by all our chatter, and just as he's about to begin, Will whispers, "Hey, that's quite the dress. You remind me of Sleeping Beauty…"

Epilogue

MR. & MRS. HAPPY FOREVER

Arabella

One Year Later – Paradise Bay

"OH, HANG ON, MRS. BANKS," Will says. "I need to carry you over the threshold for good luck."

"You did that last time," I tell him, secretly thrilled that he's about to pick me up and carry me inside our beachfront villa.

"And I'm doing it again," he says, opening the front door and lifting me under my knees.

Once we're inside, he kicks the door shut and sets me down in the sun-drenched foyer that's about a five-minute bike ride to his sister Emma's and ten minutes to the resort. It's our winter home where we'll live, well, in the winters actually. The rest of the year, we live in a cottage just outside Valcourt.

(Okay, so some would call it a mansion because of the size and grounds, but it looks like a quaint cottage, so I call it a cottage.) Anyway, living in Avonia most of the year allows me to be close to my family and continue my work with my various foundations. It also allows Will to be near our production company headquarters,

EarthMax Films, dedicated to highlighting the best of nature and human achievement. We sell most of the shows to ANN, but on our own terms, and when we get the adventure bug, we find a new place to explore where we can have fun, test our limits, and highlight various charitable and environmental causes.

"How long until my family arrives for dinner?" Will asks me as he walks me in the general direction of the bedroom.

"About an hour."

"That early?" he asks, looking slightly put out.

"Libby and Harrison need to leave by seven to get baby Will to bed." Baby Will—as much as I love the sound of that, I'm a little jealous there's no niece named Arabella. Although Emma's going to have a baby girl in four months, so I'm hoping…

"What do you say we make use of the next sixty minutes and break in the bedroom?"

"I'd say let's do this." I give him my best smoldering look.

"In that case, we're going to have to make this fast," he says, pulling me to him for a lingering kiss.

"No time to get into my edible knickers?" I ask with a laugh. It's our running joke because I will never wear edible undies again in my life.

"Not today, I'm afraid. Maybe when they leave?" he asks.

I scrunch up my nose and shake my head. "Probably not."

He kisses me again, and when our lips part, he grins. "Did you ever think your life would turn out this way?"

"No," I tell him, shaking my head. "Until I met you, I pretty much thought I had a life of sitting in drawing rooms sipping tea and having the same ten conversations over and over until I died. You?"

He shakes his head, pulling me closer to him. "I thought I'd be alone forever, just swinging from vines and climbing mountains."

"This is better, yes?" I give him a quick kiss before he can answer.

"So much so," he tells me. "But there is something missing…"

"What?" I ask, slightly panicked that he's not as completely wonderfully happy as me.

"A tiny Arabella to love."

I tear up immediately and give him a huge squeezy hug, then whisper, "Or a tiny Will?"

"I think I'd prefer a daughter first, actually."

"Really?" I ask, pulling back.

"Yeah, she can keep her little brother in line."

Chuckling, I say, "How about we just take what we can get?"

"Deal."

"I love you, William Banks, Duke of Bainbridge."

"I love you too, Belle."

"I am so glad I drunk-applied to be your co-host in the Congo."

"Me too. I feel like it worked out really well."

"Should we go have sex now?"

"Yup."

I guess life really begins at thirty-one. Or, well, I suppose it's beginning again every moment of every day because there's always some new adventure right around the corner.

If you say yes.

Text in the City...

Available Now

AN ALL-NEW SERIES WRITTEN BY MELANIE SUMMERS AND USA TODAY BESTSELLING AUTHOR WHITNEY DINEEN!

The **Accidentally in Love Stories** are fast-paced, hilarious and heart-warming, modern romantic comedy books set in the Big Apple. Five couples navigate their way through the highs and lows of falling in love in the age of texting (and all the mix-ups that make the road to happily ever after a rocky one. With casts of quirky, loveable side characters, cringe-worthy moments, and loads of romantic moments that will have readers swooning, this series is an instant hit.

Text Me on Tuesday (An Accidentally in Love Story)

All is fair in love and texting ... One caterer looking for her break in the Big Apple. One stressed-out architect with no time for love. It's hate at first sight, but when a mix-up finds them unknowingly texting each other, an undeniable connection forms and they both start to wonder if romance might be on the menu...

The Text God (An Accidentally in Love Story)

Text and you shall receive ... One starving artist desperate for her big break. One attorney who's forgotten how to enjoy life. When a mix-up has these two texting each other, they just might discover they're the answer to each other's dreams.

217

Text Wars (An Accidentally in Love Story)

*May the Text be with you...*When a super serious astronomer is forced to make a weekly appearance on the morning news with one of New York's biggest astrologers, their disdain for each other has enough thrust to launch a rocket to Mars.

Coming Soon

IT'S ALMOST TIME TO ESCAPE TO PARADISE BAY...

Resting Beach Face
~ A Paradise Bay Romantic Comedy, Book 4 ~

Melanie Summers welcomes you back to Paradise Bay for a ridiculously romantic, laugh-out-loud tale of reluctant homecomings, lost loves, and second chances...

Yoga instructor, Hadley Jones, has loved Chase Williams since high school. Fifteen years later, she still does. And while he hasn't popped the question yet, she knows it's only a matter of time. Little does Hadley know Chase has been busy making wedding plans—just not with her.

Heath Robinson left the Santa Valentina Islands the first chance he got. He's about to be named CFO of a fortune-500 company when he gets a call that has him boarding a plane home. Now, instead of sipping whiskey sours with the big boys, he'll be watching his bed-ridden mother sip from a juice box. His plan is to help her recover from her moped accident as quickly as possible so he can get back to his real life—hopefully before he runs into the girl who crushed his heart, Hadley Jones.

Will Hadley realize that Heath is the real man of her dreams? Will Heath forgive Hadley? Will his mum ever ride a moped again?

Find out in this delightfully funny tale of life coming full circle! *Resting Beach Face* is sure to leave you smiling.

Print Afterword

MANY THANKS FROM MELANIE

I hope you enjoyed Arabella and Will's journey. I hope you laughed out loud, and the story left you feeling good. If so, please leave a review.

Reviews are a true gift to writers. They are the best way for other readers to find our work and for writers to figure out if we're on the right track, so thank you if you are one of those kind folks out there to take time out of your day to leave a review!

If you'd like a fab, fun, FREE novella, please sign up for my newsletter at www.melaniesummers.com.

All the very best to you and yours,
Melanie

About the Author

Melanie Summers lives in Edmonton, Canada, with her husband, three kiddos, and two cuddly dogs. When she's not writing, she loves reading (obviously), snuggling up on the couch with her family for movie night (which would not be complete without lots of popcorn and milkshakes), and long walks in the woods near her house. Melanie also spends a lot more time thinking about doing yoga than actually doing yoga, which is why most of her photos are taken 'from above'. She also loves shutting down restaurants with her girlfriends. Well, not literally shutting them down, like calling the health inspector or something. More like just staying until they turn the lights off.

She's written fourteen novels (and counting), and has won one silver and two bronze medals in the Reader's Favourite Awards.

If you'd like to find out about her upcoming releases, sign up for her newsletter on www.melaniesummersbooks.com.

CPSIA information can be obtained
at www.ICGtesting.com
Printed in the USA
BVHW041200140921
616739BV00015B/152